About the Author

Charles is an Australian who has worked for the past twenty years in a range of different countries as an international lawyer. His inspiration for *Shoot for the Face* is drawn from experiences while living and working in Moscow, Russia. He now lives in Switzerland with his wife and children.

To Danny Richards

Charles Anderson

SHOOT FOR THE FACE

Crime and Punishment
in Moscow Today

AUSTIN MACAULEY PUBLISHERS™
LONDON • CAMBRIDGE • NEW YORK • SHARJAH

A CIP catalogue record for this title is available from the British Library.

ISBN 9781786931344 (Paperback)
ISBN 9781398416109 (ePub e-book)

www.austinmacauley.com

First Published (2020)
Austin Macauley Publishers Ltd
25 Canada Square
Canary Wharf
London
E14 5LQ

Acknowledgements

To my wife Cecile and children Juliette, Oscar, Zoe and Hugo, thanks for being patient with me these past few years while I was writing away. I would like to thank James Anderson for his encouragement throughout the writing process and thorough review of the manuscript. Sincerest thanks as well to Julian and Michelle Anderson for their invaluable contributions. Many thanks as well to Stephen Watson for his excellent cover design.

CHAPTER 1

I T WAS A PERFECT SUMMER'S DAY IN MOSCOW. THERE was barely a cloud in the sky. The sun beat down mercilessly on the giant concrete metropolis, heating it up like a furnace.

From his office on the 48th floor of Falcon Capital's new offices in the enormous, vertiginous glass skyscraper that had recently been opened in the newly developed financial centre, Jason Rogers, (or "JR" to his colleagues) its CEO and principal shareholder, a native of Austin, Texas, could see all the way out to the city's main airport, Sheremetyevo. In the distance, he could see planes landing and lifting off, shipping wealthy Russians and the billionaire oligarchs backwards and forwards from glamorous locations on the Mediterranean, or shopping sprees in Paris or London.

There was so much glass in his office in the firm's new headquarters in the unimaginatively named Moscow City (Moscow's equivalent of London's Canary Wharf) that Rogers occasionally felt slightly queasy when looking out for prolonged periods. The new office was fitted out with state-of-the-art listening and security equipment, a white noise machine and all manner of devices to make it as impenetrable as possible to the prying ears of the local security services and to his many competitors.

For Rogers, a gifted, charismatic communicator who spoke in short, sharp sentences, without ever uttering an "um" or an "ah", the economic paradigm was changing: the decaying, over-regulated, over-unionised and over-taxed economies of Western Europe and the US were about to cede economic and political power to the thriving, dynamic, less regulated economies of the East. That was the mantra that he would repeat, like a broken record to his employees at town halls and whenever he could get the opportunity.

It was hard not to be impressed by Rogers. Tall, imposing, in great physical shape, always immaculately dressed, he had set up Falcon Capital as the first western- style, independent bank in post-communist Russia, in the Wild West 1990s. Russia, at the time, was tearing itself apart – and a handful of canny businessmen fought for assets the government was selling – often for a song. Rogers had survived that turbulent period and made millions, hundreds of millions, possibly billions.

But he was not a man who his colleagues could ever say they knew well. He was taciturn and discreet. He avoided small talk or discussion of any subject that might open the door to his inner emotional being. It was this fortress-like approach to his dealings with the rest of the world that was the secret to his longevity in the world of corporate Russia – where the merest slip could result in an ignominious – perhaps violent – fall from grace.

Down the corridor from Jason Rogers' office sat Carl Fitzmaurice, Falcon Capital's legal counsel. Himself a tall man – broad shoulders, medium-length black hair and razor-sharp intellect, he was the perfect person to handle a difficult creditor or disgruntled employee.

Sipping on his double espresso, Carl glanced through the English language version of *Kommersant*, the Russian business daily. More of the same he thought to himself: rival oligarchs ripping each other off – and the ever-expanding influence of the "siloviki" (government-connected former spies and politicians) who were carving up Russian business like a Christmas turkey, gorging themselves – in a shameless feeding frenzy – on the country's prized assets.

Carl was a popular member of the business. He was gregarious, sociable, able to enjoy life outside the office and the incestuous world of Russian banking. His career had started conventionally enough. Qualifying as a lawyer in a respectable law firm in his hometown Johannesburg, South Africa, he soon found himself in London, at a prestigious City law firm, earning much more money than he ever thought possible for a lawyer of his age, and cutting his teeth in the heady world of mergers and takeovers of Europe's biggest businesses. But as the years went by, he grew tired of the predictability of his job, the endless weekend work and grey London weather.

So, when a call came from a Russian headhunter with an intriguing opportunity at a boutique investment bank in faraway Moscow, Carl knew he just wouldn't be able to say no. Colleagues, friends and family all thought he was mad.

He had not regretted, for one minute, the new adventure. From the instant he joined Falcon Capital, the powers that be had dumped on him the most questionable and troublesome matters affecting the business. He earned a reputation for stubborn and uncompromising behaviour and in the process, the admiration of management.

As he turned back to his computer screen Carl saw arrive an email marked "urgent", from the irascible and volatile Chief of Operations, Klaus Schwartz. A short, burly Austrian in his mid-60s, Schwartz was fond of terrorising employees and just about anyone he exercised any form of influence over. A dinosaur of the Russian business world, he had survived an assassination attempt, been married four times, imprisoned by the Russian authorities, fathered at least eight children with a range of women and lived to tell the story. He had indomitable will and a conviction that he was *invincible.*

The email was typical Schwartz. No text, just a subject in bold and italics … *"Come to my office – big fucking problem with the Kandinskiy loan!!"*

The Kandinskiy loan was the deal Carl had just closed. A US$250 million loan to Ari Petrovich Kandinskiy, one of Russia's best-known real estate developers (mercurial, urbane and utterly untrustworthy). The transaction had been a non-stop two-month spell of all-nighters, cold pizza and epic quantities of coffee and Red Bull to keep going through ill-tempered negotiations with Kandinskiy's advisers.

Carl considered Kandinskiy's men to be nothing better than petty gangsters despite their Savile Row suits and Dunhill cufflinks. When the documentation was signed and the money finally paid out to Kandinskiy's offshore company in Panama, Carl and his colleagues celebrated in spectacular style at White Rabbit, the restaurant for Moscow's glitterati and uber rich. Bottles of Dom Perignon, the finest Bordeaux reds and beautiful hangers on were in abundant supply.

However, that post-signing euphoria was now a distant, blurry memory.

As Carl walked into Schwartz's huge office down the corridor, Schwartz was at his desk in his black pin-striped suit with braces, attention fixed on his computer screen. He gave Carl a stern look.

"This fucking Kandinskiy is an ungrateful fuck," he said in his thick Austrian accent, veins bulging out the side of his neck. "The guy tells us a pack of lies, borrows two-fifty million from us and goes tits up within weeks, I mean what the fuck was he thinking?"

More like what the hell was Falcon Capital management thinking, Carl said under his breath. Everyone with half an eye on what was going on in Moscow had seen the newspaper articles about Kandinskiy's property empire spiralling out of control, unpaid bills to big-name architects and construction companies. It was only a matter of time before someone very big and powerful called in the debt, and Kandinskiy would have to find the money for it.

Kandinskiy realised that he needed to find a "patsy" with deep pockets – a bank desperate to earn quick money on transaction fees and a "couldn't give a fuck" attitude towards the long-term viability of the deal. Falcon Capital ticked all the boxes.

It wasn't, however, the time or place for Carl to point this out. Schwartz had launched into a tirade of expletives directed at Kandinskiy and his representatives.

The Austrian was virtually frothing at the mouth. When he thumped his oak desk, his brightly decorated business shirt burst at the seams so dramatically that one ivory cufflink went flying across the room.

"We have to sort this prick out," Schwartz said gruffly, eventually regaining his composure and grabbing the jettisoned cufflink from across the room.

"The bastard can't get away with this, we have to take action, shut his accounts down, do whatever it bloody takes to get that money back, and make sure we sack the fuckers who authorised this loan. I want the whole lot of them on their asses in the street right now!!"

And he slammed his fist again onto his coffee table, sending his fourth espresso for the morning crashing to the floor, its contents leaving an untidy stain on the beige carpet.

As he left Schwartz's office, the old Austrian's voice ringing in his ears, Carl thought to himself that it was going to be a Herculean challenge to get a penny back from Kandinskiy and his empire.

Lending money to offshore vehicles in Panama was like kissing the company's money "*dosvedaniya*" (goodbye). But for the investment bankers who structured the deals and collected the nice fat bonuses, what happened later just didn't figure in the equation – the classic "you're gone, I'm gone" principle of investment banking.

It just didn't seem though that the brains trust of Falcon Capital had anticipated the deal would explode *quite so fast*.

When Carl returned to his office, he noticed that the temperature there was quite humid – outside, dark clouds had started to form in what, earlier, had been an otherwise perfectly blue sky. He drank what was left of his cold coffee and unlocked his computer. "It's going to be a difficult week," he said to himself as he adjusted his glasses nervously.

CHAPTER 2

AFTER SPENDING THE BETTER PART OF HIS DAY running through every aspect of the loan to Ari Kandinskiy, harassing colleagues for whatever information he could get about Kandinskiy and his opaque business arrangements, Carl realised that it was nearly 8 pm and he had not eaten all day. He was overcome by a profound hunger which he knew he could not ignore any longer. He packed his briefcase with a copy of the bank loan to Kandinskiy and financial accounts for Kandinskiy's real estate business. He quickly scanned the view from the window of his 48th floor office.

The traffic jams that paralyse Moscow were in full force by now, having started early afternoon and progressively got worse. Kuznetsky Prospect, the main artery to western Moscow had been brought to a standstill by a series of VIP motorcades passing through – the President and Prime Minister all heading back from the Kremlin to their palatial residences in Rybolovka to the west of Moscow. Carl had seen that 20 heavily armoured black Mercedes followed by two military helicopters, armed to the teeth, would escort the Russian president to his residence every evening. It was an awesome sight from Carl's office window at Moscow City. He could only imagine how empowering it felt to travel through this gridlocked city, in the Presidential entourage, at 150 km per hour.

Carl eventually gathered his things and got out of the building at 8.15 pm. His driver Valentin, a short, stocky man in his mid-40s, brown wavy hair with a friendly, jovial disposition, was parked in his usual place outside the skyscrapers of Moscow City, which were shimmering in the evening light. Valentin put on a smile for his boss, as he did every evening, no matter his mood.

"*Privet* (hi) Carl, did you kick ass today?" he said, with an embarrassed laugh, doing his best to mimic an American accent.

"Of course, Valentin! Well, truthfully, probably not, but there is always tomorrow," and he slapped Valentin affectionately on the shoulder.

Valentin was an unusually positive, cheerful driver. From the south of Russia, he'd grown up on the Black Sea where winters are relatively mild and summers hot affairs – to be spent by the beach.

Valentin didn't have the gruffness or uncouthness of some of his countrymen from less hospitable parts of Russia. For him, work was scarce – as for so many Russians from the regions. He was forced to move to Moscow with his wife and children, and to rent a tiny one-room apartment where the whole family would sleep together.

He lived from month to month on the salary he earned, scrimping, saving and borrowing when funds ran short. As his only source of income, Carl's safety and well-being was paramount. He saw himself as Carl's fixer, always one phone call away from someone who could help Carl with problems, big and small.

As the enormous, hulking Chevrolet Tahoe revved up and edged out into the already clogged thoroughfare, Moscow's embankment (the "*Naberezhnaya*"), Carl could feel the tension of being in the office slowly starting to ease and his mind turned back to dinner.

In his rudimentary Russian he told Valentin to head towards the French brasserie Jean Jacques in Tsvetnoy Bulvar, the elegant tree-lined boulevard at the end of the Arbat district in central Moscow. Jean Jacques was styled as a French bistro but had its very own distinctive artsy, underground feel. Considered a hangout for Moscow's literati, dissidents and political opposition, it was, most evenings, full of students, writers and Moscow's intellectuals. It had none of the vacuous bling of Moscow's more chic restaurants where women with expensive dresses, Jimmy Choo high heels and inflatable chests would hang out in the hope of meeting a man with money, whether he be banker, lawyer, businessman, gangster or government apparatchik.

As he neared the restaurant a text came from a colleague, Ronnie Allan.

"What's up for dinner?"

"Jean-Jacques – 10 mins," Carl replied.

Ronnie, a former soldier in the British army, was an intense character from northern England. A bit under six feet tall he was slim but muscular, with a narrow face dominated by a broken nose that made him look like an ex-boxer.

Ronnie had worked his way through the ranks of the army until he realised that there wasn't a lot of money in the military game but that there were other, more lucrative opportunities in the world of banking for someone with his logistical capabilities and flair for adventure.

He started on a City career and found his niche in the ever-popular world of "emerging markets". Unlike most bankers in the emerging markets world who'd never set foot in the countries they were meant to be "experts" on, Ronnie was the real deal. He knew the markets he was operating in and had an uncanny ability for making the impossible, possible. Management loved him for that, and he earned eye-watering bonuses.

This particular evening, though, Ronnie was in a black mood. He greeted Carl with a quick handshake and without saying a word sat down next to him at the small table Carl had grabbed next to the bar.

"Today has been utter shite," he eventually blurted out, "an absolute fucking disaster."

News was getting around Moscow of a local banker and an old client of Ronnie's who'd been murdered over the weekend in his palatial home in a posh Moscow suburb, Serebriany Bor.

The police who arrived on the scene, not wanting to have to conduct a thorough investigation and complicate their lives, originally deemed the banker's sudden and unexpected death to be a *suicide*.

The problem for the Moscow cops was that it had to rank as one of the most unusual suicides in history. The victim, a well-known banker in the Russian forestry sector who was known to take risks his colleagues would baulk at, was discovered at the bottom of the family swimming pool, both hands tied behind his back, his face black from the blows that had rained down on him but which were self-inflicted if you believed the police.

"This has caused a massive stink in the market," Ronnie said.

"It's not just the callousness of it," Ronnie went on, "but the fact that someone as important as this guy, working for a government bank, could end being fucked up so badly … the second client of mine who's been murdered in as many months …"

"Any implications for you?" Carl asked, at the same time gesturing to the waitress to bring them two beers.

"Fuck knows mate, I hope not," was all Ronnie could respond.

The restaurant was starting to get busy as local students and Moscow's bohemian brigade started to arrive, many already quite boisterous and rowdy. As the alcohol from the first beer started to course through his veins, Ronnie's mood began to improve, and he started to loosen up. He chatted to Carl about a new client, Ari Bronsky, an Israeli businessman with a reputation about as bad as one could hope for.

Frequently accused of hiring mercenaries in sub-Saharan Africa to intimidate business competitors or anyone trying to get in his way, Bronsky was the sort of client that terrified most investment banks, but not Falcon Capital. He'd approached Falcon Capital for a quick loan to pay off a coterie of ministers in a West African country who controlled access to its prized oil reserves.

With his poisonous reputation and compliance officers in banks worldwide crapping themselves at the mere mention of his name, Bronsky knew that his only option for quick money was from the cowboys at Falcon Capital.

This is where Ronnie was in his element.

"This is going to be a great deal Carl – the fees will be massive – I want you to be personally involved," he said, sitting back on the stool, taking a large swig of cold lager.

"I'm OK with that Ronnie just so long as I don't end up like your last client!" And they laughed a little callously, clinking their beer glasses together to seal the arrangement.

As the night wore on, Ronnie and Carl were in merry spirits thanks to copious quantities of the cheap beer served by the jovial waitresses who worked at a blistering speed to keep their thirsty clients happy.

One of their more colourful colleagues, Benny Goldsmith, a loud, brash New Yorker who offered a view on any subject and almost always knew more than anyone else about the politics and peregrinations of Falcon Capital, wandered into the restaurant. Newspaper in hand, he was wearing his trademark New York Nicks cap.

Carl beckoned him over and Benny proceeded to sit down, taking a swig of Carl's beer. He looked at both men and a wry smile spread over his face.

"Why are you so happy?" Carl asked curiously.

"The Kandinskiy loan Carl! I have never seen Schwartz so pissed," he said, chuckling with delight. "Everyone is saying that it's Schwartz's fuck-up. I almost feel like I should give Kandinskiy a bottle of champagne to say a big fucking thanks."

Goldsmith hated Schwartz, and Schwartz well and truly reciprocated by making everything Goldsmith did in the office a complete misery, undercutting him at every corner and making him look as redundant and ineffective as possible.

Goldsmith was a piece of the furniture at Falcon Capital. He'd started with Jason Rogers in the days when Falcon was just a collection of smart, bright young guys from the West with a few desks and chairs. He was the office wacky soothsayer, with an antenna for gossip that was unsurpassed at Falcon Capital and the network of expats in Moscow. He could sniff out conspiracies like a bloodhound on a hunt.

"It's like everything Schwartz touches, Carl, turns to utter shit! This dude Kandinskiy just played us beautifully, didn't he?"

"Yeah, it's pretty damn hard to argue with that Benny. We're in the shit and we have to figure out a solution," Carl responded, slightly irritated by Benny's persistent negativity.

"Fuck that Carl, it's aaalways time for the blame game, this is Russian investment banking!" And he let out a huge laugh, high-fiving Ronnie who was also enjoying Carl's discomfort.

Ronnie, not wanting to be outdone, dangled out the one piece of information that he knew would strike the fear of God into his colleagues.

He cleared his throat a little and said with something approaching a half smile, "Guys, I hear that the Chechens have just bought up a large chunk of the money owed to Kandinskiy, so technically we're now competing with these lunatics to get our money back!"

Carl slowly put his beer down, and Benny nearly choked on his cigarette.

"Fuck me, are you serious?" Carl could barely whisper.

"Deadly," Ronnie responded. Ronnie loved delivering bad news to colleagues and watching their reaction. Yet, he could never understand why it gave him so pleasure. Not being the introspective type, though, he seldom allowed himself to over-analyse this particular feature of his psyche.

He grabbed a pen from his briefcase and started to plot out on the paper tablecloth – half soaked in beer and wine – the various creditors and gangsters on Kandinskiy's tail.

"You see guys, our Muslim brothers have bought a chunk of the debt from the mayor's wife," and he drew a large circle around a figure of US$250m and a neat scrawl of a mosque with minarets. "The mayor's wife," he continued, "has decided she can't be bothered going through the shit of getting Kandinskiy to pay – the lawyers' fees, the wasted management time and the general aggravation. She's realised it's easier to get fifty cents in the dollar now and the satisfaction of knowing Kandinskiy gets either whacked, terrified out of his wits or all of the above."

Ronnie, loving every bit of the suspense he was creating, continued.

"See Carl you just have to pay these guys, you can't default. They threaten to kill your kids, parents, girlfriend, pet poodle and wait for you to blink, very few people call their bluff ..." Ronnie concluded, dramatically. He then with a flourish placed a giant cross over Falcon Capital and the US$250 million he had scrawled alongside its name.

"Ronnie, this is a goddamn fucking disaster!" Goldsmith coughed, slamming his beer down on their small dining table, attracting the attention of the patrons sitting next to them.

"Indeed Benny," was all Ronnie responded, a wry smile plastered across his face.

By midnight the bar had become packed and rowdy. A mix of students, leftie-looking intellectuals and random loners now occupied every square inch of available space, and a fog of smoke and humidity permeated the unventilated restaurant, along with the smell of vodka and beer.

Goldsmith was starting to receive abusive messages from his Russian wife. Taking his cue, he staggered up the stairs and left the bar with Carl and Ronnie in tow. The three men said drunken good-byes to each other and walked off in separate directions.

The rather disagreeable security guard Igor, well over six feet tall and fists the size of baseball mitts, was doing his best to look menacing (and doing a good job of it), ensuring none of Moscow's "bomzh" (bums) were lucky enough to make it inside.

The bomzh were Moscow's silent heroes, exposed to sub-zero temperatures for months on the gritty streets of that unforgiving city during the long winter months – ever so lucky if they made it through alive. It was not unusual, when the snow would finally thaw in late March/early April, to find bodies of the city's homeless in parks and under bridges, where they had lain hidden for weeks, even months, beneath piles of snow.

After trudging the length of the tree-lined Tverskoy Boulevard, Carl turned into Tverskaya Street to be greeted by the roar of the enormous thoroughfare. Cars sped past at breakneck speed in the direction of the Kremlin. Mercedes, 4x4s, Bentleys, Maybachs – all with chauffeurs, and full of bodyguards – shared the street with ricketty Ladas and Volgas, doing their best to keep up.

Eventually Carl got to his enormous apartment building, imaginatively named "Number 4" in Tverskaya Street. It had been home to apparatchiks of the old Communist regime, star scientists and decorated soldiers.

The concierge, a woman in her late 60s, in every sense the typical Russian "babooshka", beckoned him to speak to her. Reeking of vodka, the old lady adjusted her glasses and said carefully, in Russian, "Two men, they looked like government people, came tonight and asked if you lived in this building. I said you were a good boy, never caused trouble … and then they left."

"OK, thanks Marina Alexandrovich, I appreciate you letting me know, maybe they were just migration agents making sure that I'm living where I'm meant to be living …" and he did his best to give her a reassuring smile.

He liked the fact that the concierge shared the Russian distrust of anyone who worked for the government. And it worried him that he was being spied on.

CHAPTER 3

CARL WOKE WITH A JOLT AT 6 AM, MUCH EARLIER than intended but often the way when he'd had too much to drink. His mouth was dry and his head hurt enough to guarantee it would be impossible to return to sleep.

He'd been dreaming about his family house in Cape Town. He was playing cricket with his brother Tom in the garden. His older brother had as usual won their epic match which had lasted all day in the brutal summer sun – at least that was the way it seemed to him as he drifted out of a deep sleep and into consciousness.

Rather than lying in bed feeling the effects of the previous evening's entertainment, Carl decided to put his early start to good use by getting some exercise. His gym was at the chic Park Hyatt Hotel in Neglinnaya Street. Close to the Bolshoi Theatre it was one of the hotels of choice for visiting executives and wealthy foreigners.

As he trudged slowly along Kamergerskiy Lane with its cobblestones, theatres and all night bars, he was doing his best to ignore a headache that had not been diminished by a cocktail of painkillers. He momentarily flirted with the thought of returning home and recovering over a coffee but thought better of it. The guilt of not going to the gym would gnaw at him all day.

Carl spotted a few street workers clearing broken tiles from the rooftops of the cafes that lined Kamergerskiy Lane. The tiles were shaped like daggers ready to impale unsuspecting pedestrians. One of the men was barking at a compatriot in a dialect Carl didn't recognise. His colleague had got perilously close to the edge of a roof and forgotten to strap himself in. Realising his mistake in time the man who looked frozen by cold slowly moved his hands around the rope which had been thrown to him and was the only thing separating him from a spectacular, bone-crushing fall.

Carl continued his march to the hotel gym. He came across a couple of heavily intoxicated Russian girls in their early 20s, no doubt rich young socialites. The pair were weaving down Kamerger-skiy Lane, likely still high on cocaine, wearing only skimpy dresses covered by enormous fur coats. As they staggered down the narrow laneway he heard them babbling away in Russian, mostly profan-ities (largely beyond the comprehension of Carl. Russian swear words are numerous and much richer and more complex than their equivalents in English). They waved down a taxi and collapsed into the back seat.

As he entered the luxurious Park Hyatt Hotel, Carl was greeted by Raymond, the Ugandan doorman, a powerful looking fellow with impeccable presentation and manners.

"How are you today Carl?" he asked in his deep, baritone voice.

"Pretty tired Raymond, too early for me but you know it's been nearly a week since I last made it to the gym." He smiled, shaking Raymond's enormous hand.

"Don't worry Carl, you're still a young man and have plenty of time to look after your health …" and he let out a huge belly laugh that echoed throughout the entrance to the hotel.

Carl walked through reception and took the glass lift up to the fifth-floor gymnasium. In the atrium below he could see a short, thickset man with large black glasses, sporting a diamond-encrusted watch, in earnest conversation with another man, of medium height, elegantly dressed and flanked on either side by muscle-bound body-guards. The two men were having an animated conversation.

As the lift reached the fifth floor and Carl stepped out, he realised that the thickset man was none other than Ari Kandinskiy.

"What the hell was he doing here?" Carl thought to himself as he entered the hotel's plush changing room. The other man in the meeting below in the hotel lobby exuded a self-confidence and a smugness that made Carl think he must be a government guy with serious connections. Of course, being a smug government apparat-chik didn't mean much in Moscow – they were a dime a dozen.

As Carl started running slowly on a treadmill, he waved to one of the gym's regulars, an older guy of at least 65 who had the physique of a bodybuilder half his age, sinewy and taut, rippling with muscles. He had none of the blubber and fat of half the people who paraded around the gym in designer sportswear.

"Tough old bastard," Carl thought to himself.

The older man waved back at Carl and continued his sprint on the treadmill. Carl kept on with the slow jog, switching through the TV channels in front of him.

He quickly came across a story on Moscow morning TV about Ronnie Allan's unfortunate and recently murdered client. After a shrill, monotone introduction by a thirty-something female newsreader, the story began with footage of the victim's luxurious house in a well-to-do Moscow suburb.

In the background, corpulent policemen joked with each other as they wheeled the body out of the house on a stretcher, clearly not the least disturbed by the city's latest execution. The TV journalist at the scene, a boyish looking man in a cheap suit, announced that the authorities considered this murder was most likely the result of a private disagreement over money or an adulterous relationship.

No chance of a Russian broadcaster making a connection between the murder and organised crime or better still, Russia's siloviki, notoriously tough when it comes to business deals which have gone sour. To do so would have been to acknowledge that beneath the false veneer of respectability, corporate Russia was a lethal place for those who made the slightest misstep or lost their "krysha" (roof or "protection") at an inopportune moment. Carl laughed to himself and continued his slow jog. His legs were starting to warm up and the lethargy which he had felt all morning was starting to dissipate.

Switching back to the studio, the newsreader, wearing a conservative grey suit, and sporting a hairstyle reminiscent of those worn in Soviet Russia, announced in her shrill voice that a Duma deputy, Igor Melnikov, was soon to be appointed the new Minister for Armaments.

"Wow," thought Carl to himself, that's the pasty-looking apparatchik who had been sitting downstairs with Kandinskiy. Footage showed Melnikov with the President, sitting at a large wooden table, the President congratulating his new appointee with a cross between a smile and a grimace.

Kandinskiy, Carl assumed, was clearly in the sights of the powers that be. A future Minister for Armaments was a huge player in Moscow politics – the potential moneyman for billions of dollars in military contracts, a mover and shaker in national politics. Most certainly also a fixer and bagman for the President and his inner circle. His meeting with Kandinskiy signalled that the sharks in the Kremlin wanted their cut of the failing corporate empire of the erstwhile Russian oligarch – that much was certain.

Carl was by now drenched in sweat. He'd reached his maximum speed of nearly 15 kilometres per hour, his legs pounding on the narrow, rubbery treadmill which shook ever so slightly.

After his run, which lasted a little under an hour, Carl took a shower and changed. He put on his smart business suit with Zegna tie and cufflinks and headed out to Neglinnaya Street where his driver Valentin was patiently waiting for him in the giant black 4x4, black coffee ready, one of the perks of having an attentive driver.

"Spacibo (*thanks*) Valentin, you are a mind-reader," he said appreciatively. Crawling slowly into work through heavy traffic, slowed down by the limousines, four-wheel drives, Ladas and traffic control angling for *vzyatka* (bribes in Russian vernacular) he noticed an old Soviet-era ambulance outside the city's most prestigious hotel, the Ritz-Carlton. On second thought it looked more like a body truck than an ambulance Carl thought to himself.

As the Tahoe crawled along Tverskaya Street and got closer to the body truck, Carl spotted the torso of a man who had been run over by the driver of a Russian-made Volga, the female driver standing over the body, shocked by what she had done, being questioned by an obese, unkempt traffic policeman who was nonchalantly scribbling down the driver's account.

As his 4x4 snaked past the victim he noticed a skateboard next to the body and saw two wooden stumps where his legs had once been.

"Jesus Christ", Carl muttered to himself. The dead man was a beggar, Andrey Vosnesenky, who rode through the traffic on a cheap wooden skateboard, one of many who braved Moscow traffic morning, noon and night to beg for loose change that Moscow's drivers would occasionally hurl out their windows in random directions.

Getting run over was an occupational hazard for Andrey and the statistical realities of his profession had finally caught up with him. He'd lost his legs fighting for mother Russia in Chechnya, at the sprightly age of 19.

The incongruousness of the image struck Carl – the opulence of the Ritz-Carlton, the Lamborghinis and Bentleys parked out front, the enormous opulent façade – and the contrast with the young disabled man lying dead after one too many forays into Moscow's deadly traffic.

Eventually the Chevrolet Tahoe crawled into the car park at Falcon Capital in Moscow City. It was a hive of energy at this time of the morning with bankers, lawyers and secretaries rushing in to their offices. As Carl walked into the lobby to grab his lift to the 50th floor, he spotted Jason Rogers entering the building with his bodyguard. A huge, broad-shouldered Russian from Siberia, Viktor, the bodyguard, glowered at anyone who came near Rogers. Thankfully for Carl, Viktor had long since figured out that he posed no existential risk to his boss. Once Rogers had spotted him, he was however temporarily stuck within Rogers' vortex until the lift arrived at its destination.

Rogers was taller and broader than Carl and he used his height and physical energy to full effect whenever he could. He turned around to face Carl, his blue eyes squarely fixed on him, arms folded in an inquisitorial manner. Not one for small talk, Rogers got right down to business.

"Carl where is the strategy for the Kandinskiy loan? I thought you promised Klaus something yesterday?"

"Coming today," Carl responded curtly, he'd learned to be very economic with his answers, not promising too much. He met Rogers' gaze and the two men stared at each other for a few seconds before Rogers diverted his gaze to his watch and told Carl to have it ready later that morning.

"We need to be on our game with these guys Carl, not one backward step. I lose here and I'm done in all the other struggles I'm currently facing." He slapped Carl on the shoulder, nodded to his bodyguard and the two men exited the lift.

After grabbing a quick espresso, Carl started perusing the note which a colleague had prepared for recovering Kandinskiy's assets, a neatly crafted five-page summary identifying the Mediterranean villas, art works, English country estates and bearer certificates that were vulnerable to attack by creditors. It was perfect, just what management would need to see to be made to realise they had their work cut out for them if they wanted to get their hands on the steadily diminishing pool of available assets.

As Carl approached Schwartz's office he could see him sitting at his desk, resplendent in a multi-coloured shirt from the men's store Pink in London. Carl found the effect of the portly Austrian banker stuffed into the colourful shirt rather comical but Schwartz was clearly in anything but a merry mood. Putting his copy of the *FT* down, he glared at Carl as he sat himself down.

"I need your report today," he barked, veins bulging, his eyes looking a little red from what was undoubtedly a boozy dinner the night before.

"It's done Klaus. We've got a list of assets in key jurisdictions and the beginning of a strategy for going after them," and Carl handed Schwartz the report which the older man promptly snatched away from him and placed on his desk.

"OK, fine, I'll read this right away. Before you piss off there's something that I need to discuss with you. As you may have heard this matter is getting very damn complicated very quickly. There are people all over the city angling for a piece of Kandinskiy's empire," and he took a sip from his espresso, before continuing.

"We've heard that one of the key players running the debt recovery for the government is a guy at Moskvy Neft, Igor Cherney, a tough son of a bitch who's going up the ranks very fast. The guy is a complete piranha and has a razor-sharp mind. He has spooked Kandinskiy and his coterie of advisers with a succession of threats – in the process he has them bending over backwards to accommodate him, at the expense of outsiders like us."

"OK," responded Carl, a little curiously. "I assume you and Rogers will be meeting with him to run over things?"

"Actually Carl," Klaus responded, his voice getting lower and his large blue eyes narrowing, "We think you're the right person to meet with him, you know the file and you're good at bullshitting people with facts and figures … The meeting is being scheduled now, I'll let you know where and when." He gave his knuckles a little crack as if to emphasise the non-negotiability of his proposition.

Carl recoiled at the thought of being sent to a meeting with someone as high profile and potentially dangerous as Cherney. But if he blinked then it was his bonus and position as a rising star at Falcon Capital down the toilet. He also knew that Schwartz was right, there was no-one in the company with a better understanding of what sat within Kandinskiy's corporate empire.

Realising he had no say in the matter, Carl responded, "OK, Klaus I get it, I will meet with this guy. I just need as much intel as we have on him, can you arrange that … please?"

"You'll have that in a few hours Carl, I have Roman Lebedev (Falcon Capital's head of security) preparing a dossier for you. He will run you through everything you need to know."

"Don't fuck this up Carl," Schwartz continued, his tone menacing again, "the whole business is delicately poised and if we lose the money we've lent this fucking asshole then we can *all* kiss our bonuses goodbye, and probably our jobs!"

When Schwartz finished his little diatribe, he swivelled around on his chair and turned to his computer, his fat fingers banging on the keyboard.

Taking the cue to leave, Carl got up and walked out of the office. As he left, Schwartz's assistant, Yana, a Russian woman in her 40s who hailed from an industrial town in the Ural Mountains, and had worked with Schwartz for years, gently asked Carl how the meeting went.

"He seems pretty tense Yana, good luck with today."

She let out a hearty laugh and responded, "Carl, he's like that every day!"

Carl wandered into the office of his junior Russian lawyer Vadim Petrovsky. A short, round man with thick black glasses and medium length, oily, brown hair, his crumpled suit long past its use-by date, Vadim was a member of the Russian intelligentsia and the consummate corporate lawyer. He could deftly dissect legal problems like a butcher chopping lamb cutlets. Carl deployed him on his trickiest and most problematic assignments. The Kandinskiy file would be right up his alley.

"I'm exhausted Carl. I can't say anything which you might possibly find useful," Vadim said matter of factly. That was pure Vadim. Blunt, unable to prevaricate or dissemble. It was a character trait that had appealed to Carl from the moment they first met.

"Vadim, thanks for the paper, it's fabulous. I want you to get on the phone to our London lawyers and brief them straight away that we're going after everything Kandinskiy has, starting with the assets you've identified."

"Thanks Carl, yes we have been quite lucky. I know a former employee of Kandinskiy who is … how do I say, 'disgruntled'? Anyway, he has sent through a file of information and some of it is very good."

Vadim ran his hands through his hair and folded his arms. He looked more pensive and introspective than usual.

"What is it Vadim? What's bugging you?" Carl asked.

"You know Carl, I feel very sceptical about this whole exercise. It is going to be very difficult for us to get much, if anything back from Kandinskiy. The people we are up against have links to the FSB, the Kremlin, they are powerful, and they have so much information, we just can't compete …"

His hands trembled ever so slightly from a lack of sleep and too much coffee. The facial tics which he managed to suppress most of the time were now obvious and demonstrated Vadim's sense of anxiety.

"Vadim, that's pretty much the case with everything we fucking do here. Every day in this city, in this market we have our arses to the wall. We're the hundred-pound weakling. If Rogers and Schwartz don't realise this, then they are delusional. But if we can get part of this money back then we've achieved something pretty damn incredible, don't you think?"

"OK, Carl, you know I'll do whatever you ask. I am, as the French would say, 'le bon petit soldat'. I am made for the front line – no questions asked," and he let out a slight chuckle, his eyes blinking rapidly.

CHAPTER 4

I T WAS MID AFTERNOON. DROPLETS OF RAIN STARTED to trickle down the huge glass window of Carl's office overlooking Moscow. Wind battered the 50-storey skyscraper and Carl could feel the building moving ever so slightly from side to side. Huge clouds descended on the city and the building was covered in a wall of rain that would last for several hours.

Carl ruminated over the latest peregrinations with his new and problematic file. He could feel a knot forming in the pit of his stomach at the very thought of being drawn into meetings with the Russian siloviki. He daydreamed about being back in South Africa, driving on the outskirts of Cape Town, bushland and veld stretching as far as the eye could see, not a building in sight.

His daydreaming was brought to an abrupt end by the loud ring of his office phone. It was Schwartz's assistant, Yana.

"Carl," she said purposefully, "your appointment with Roman Lebedev is scheduled for 4 pm, in an hour. Roman is a very punctual person so be sure to be in his office on time," she purred.

"Yes, I know about the yearning for punctuality Yana, I'll be there at four, *spacibo bolshoy*," Carl responded.

Roman Lebedev was the quintessential Russian spy. Intelligent, articulate and urbane, Lebedev had had a highly distinguished career with the KGB in the days of the Soviet Union.

He had honed his trade while working in various Russian embassies in Western Europe. And in that time he'd mastered English, German and bits of other languages. He was the sort of man that western authors wrote spy thrillers about. With his extraordinary intellect and aptitude for strategic thinking, it had looked as though he was headed towards great things, maybe even the top job at KGB headquarters in central Moscow: the Lyubyanka.

That was until his career came crashing down along with the Berlin wall. Like so many Russians at the time he had to recreate himself in the uncertainty of post-Communist Russia.

So, when the opportunity of a cushy private sector job with Falcon Capital came around, he did not think twice – it was the perfect compensation, in the new Russia, for his loss of status as a KGB general and its promise of a very comfortable retirement. He did not want to end up like the country's academics, scientists and doctors – once revered in Soviet society – now scrounging for a living on paltry government wages.

Lebedev, a tall, thin man with a shiny, bald head, was sitting in front of his computer when Carl entered. The first thing that struck Carl about the office was its impeccable neatness, not a paper out of place. The only personal effect was a photo of his wife, a pretty woman in her 50s, no doubt childhood sweethearts. Lebedev, dressed immaculately in a navy blue, checked suit, greeted Carl warmly.

"Come in Carl, it's good to see you. Please sit down. Coffee?"

"No thanks Roman Petrovich," Carl responded, using Lebedev's patronymic out of respect for the older man, "too much coffee already today," and he smiled.

"Of course, Carl, occupational hazard of working in an investment bank," and he gave a little laugh.

"Can you give me your mobile phone please?" Roman asked Carl, calmly and politely. "I can't allow any phones in this office because our friends down the road have hacked them all so effectively," the smile showed his cigarette-stained teeth. Lebedev handed Carl's phone to his assistant. She dropped it into a steel-plated box.

With pleasantries out of the way, Lebedev fixed his dark brown eyes on Carl.

"Carl, I have been following your progress in the firm with a lot of interest. You could say that I greatly appreciate the way you have been managing yourself in this firm. Moscow … Russia, it's not an easy environment.

"There are, how do we say, lots of *complexities* and *complications* that can arise if things are not handled carefully. It is our job to provide you with all the information you need, and to *protect* you."

Carl was listening intently, slightly transfixed by Lebedev. Every word was weighed up and well thought out. There was nothing superfluous in his speech or gestures. The old spy, who communicated with such ease in English that Carl wondered to himself whether he had ever heard a foreigner speak the language so well, emphasised the words which mattered most to him, around which there could be no ambiguity.

His preamble out of the way, Lebedev got down to business.

"Here's three files – one on Kandinskiy himself, quite a bit of information, accessed through our friends in high places, as well as a file on the minister he met with this morning, Comrade Melnikov and one on Igor Cherney who I understand you're meeting tomorrow."

He carefully placed three neatly sorted manila folders in front of Carl.

"Carl, I want you to understand one thing – the information in these is extremely sensitive. I trust you to keep it strictly confidential. People lose their lives if this ever goes public …"

Before Carl had time to respond, Lebedev continued. "We have a little information on Cherney. A 'young gun' lawyer, now a 'repat' as you foreigners like to call them. His family were exiles from this country in the seventies.

"Young Igor realised in the two thousands that his fortune could be made back here in the homeland, given his language skills and his understanding of the … *Russian way of doing things*." Lebedev nodded at Carl, assuming that he understood what was meant.

Lebedev opened his drawer and took out a long, thick cigar. He lit it slowly over a gas lighter that emitted a long blue flame. The old spy blew a perfect smoke ring that wafted slowly and inexorably up to the ceiling of his office.

Still with Carl's undivided attention, Lebedev continued, "Cherney was doing very well, climbing up the corporate ladder, and then like so many people who rise fast in this country *without* the right protection, he had a very unfortunate situation.

"About six years ago he was kidnapped, spent two days in a room covered in black plastic, expecting to be killed any minute. He was subjected to a rough beating, tortured and forced to authorise transfers of all his money to the kidnappers. When he was let free, he was completely broken physically and mentally … But he's a tough 'son of a bitch' as the Americans say and he eventually got back on his feet and re-established himself. The experience, though, has left him very rigid and inflexible. But then that is to be expected of such an experience, isn't it, Carl?"

Lebedev paused momentarily to see if Carl was absorbing all the information he was imparting. Satisfied that Carl seemed to be getting the drift he continued.

"Cherney eventually scored it big with a senior job at Moskvy Neft. That's given him a whole new level of *krysha* and network. He's rising up the ranks there because he's a workaholic and very, very smart. He manages Moskvy Neft's rather gargantuan debt with Kandinskiy and it's very likely he is calling the shots on which creditors get what – at least that's what we hear from my old colleagues who are working for this outfit."

"Thanks, Roman Petrovich, what an interesting guy. I am a little curious about one thing though."

"Yes Carl, what exactly?"

"What happened to the kidnappers, did he ever get even?"

"Hah! The one fact that interests you is the kidnappers!" and Lebedev laughed a little ironically.

"As it happens, yes he did. Moskvy Neft security took care of it, a sign of appreciation for him signing on the dotted line ... the kidnappers returned whatever money they had left and were then disposed of at a cement works in central Moscow. I understand they're now scattered all over Moscow's new western highway," and he blew another perfect smoke ring into the air from his enormous, fat cigar.

CHAPTER 5

BY EARLY EVENING THE STORM THAT HAD BATTERED Moscow had moved eastwards and the drenched city was now bathed in sunshine.

Carl looked out from his office at the skyscrapers going up around him at Moscow City. The light bounced off the windows and the exposed steel beams of the building opposite, where a construction worker was hanging perilously from a rope. Carl wondered how on earth these men from the "Stans" (as the locals called them) had the nerve to risk their lives every day for meagre pay. They came from all over the former Soviet Union, making a bit of money from backbreaking hours and dangerous work and sending every penny they earned back home to feed their wives and kids.

The skyscrapers they were putting up would, when finished, look every inch the classy edifice one sees in New York or London, and make their owners vast fortunes.

The conditions the workers lived in were basic too. They slept in tiny cramped bunk beds in rooms with minimal heating in the freezing winter months and unbearably hot in the short but sweltering Russian summers.

The building workers had no health insurance, holiday pay or anything that the people sitting in air-conditioned offices in the skyscrapers of Moscow City considered very basic entitlements.

If a building worker was a minute late to the site, or injured or sick for a short while, he'd be out of a job right away, and replaced by any one of the millions of men itching for an opportunity to work in this huge metropolis.

Carl's moment of reflection was interrupted by a knock at his door. His office was surrounded by glass so visitors had no need to announce themselves. This visit was from Benny who, as usual, had been circulating, picking up gossip and news and wearing a hole in the carpet.

"Hey Carl, wanna come upstairs for a cigarette?"

"Yeah fuck it, great idea Benny," Carl replied.

"Upstairs" meant the 48th floor. It was reserved exclusively for meeting rooms. In a fit of extravagance Jason Rogers had rented the whole floor. No expense had been spared: rare artworks from Africa and Asia spread themselves over the walls of meeting rooms along with paintings by some of the world's better-known contemporary artists.

Most important, though, for the thirty-something bankers at Falcon Capital, a cigar room had been installed with humidors, Cuban cigars, vast whisky collection and English gentlemen's club décor.

Carl stretched out on an elegant leather Chesterfield and started puffing on a Cohiba robusto he'd helped himself to from the wooden humidor in the entrance of the fumoir.

"Fucking great cigar," he said to Benny who'd pulled out his packet of cigarettes and was furiously smoking away.

"Don't need that stuff Carl, will rot your mouth my friend," he barked, a little hypocritically.

Carl noticed that Goldsmith was even more agitated than usual. His nervousness was contagious.

"I hear that business is much worse than any of us thought," Goldsmith started in a low voice, almost whispering, "a few deals in the pipeline have been cancelled and a new loan that was meant to be coming from the European banks is now likely to be cancelled … it's not looking good," and his eyes darted around anxiously.

"Our bonuses are going to be completely fucked this year if it all goes on like this …" and his voice drifted off.

Goldsmith had a natural inclination to blow things out of proportion and his main preoccupation, as with all investment bankers, was his own economic welfare.

Nevertheless, Carl suspected there was an element of truth to what Benny said. He'd noticed that some of the bankers who faffed around and made a lot of noise about their big new clients and deals had less of a spring in their step.

"Carl, you've probably got the message that the Kandinskiy thing is getting really fucking important now. Schwartz and Rogers have figured that out – they're reaching out to all sorts of people to ensure they don't get screwed on it. They'll be watching you very closely to see how you perform on this," and he nervously put out his cigarette in an enormous Hermes ashtray on the coffee table in front of them.

At that moment there was a knock at the door and the office receptionist, a six-foot brunette from Vladivostok, with high cheekbones and a figure that would be right at home on a Paris catwalk, came in with coffees. Goldsmith must have been on his tenth espresso for the day and was in a state of high animation.

"Olga, you're a darling – when are you going to accept one of my invitations to dinner?" Goldsmith cheekily asked the glamorous receptionist.

"I don't date married men," she shot back with a smile, flashing her immaculate white teeth and a personality that had Goldsmith practically foaming at the mouth.

Carl realised he'd had enough of dealing with an animated and highly strung Goldsmith.

"Benny, I need to get some rest tonight, big day tomorrow. I'm going to grab a bite to eat somewhere and head home ..."

"OK mate, good luck with tomorrow," Benny replied, now distracted by the crimson pink sunset whose light was bouncing off the windows of the buildings of Moscow City, creating an effect worthy of a sound and light show.

Carl went back to his office, collected his bag and the manila files that Lebedev had so efficiently assembled for him. He headed down in the lift to the 1st floor and into the car park, past the senior management's Bentleys and Range Rovers and their army of bodyguards and drivers. He was accosted by Schwartz who himself was heading off for the evening.

"Carl, the meeting with Cherney is now scheduled for 9 am. I'll send you the details. We won't have time for a briefing beforehand. The message from JR is clear – kick ass and don't be a pussy with him!" Schwartz's body language was positively hostile, and Carl felt a strong urge to hit the older man.

"Klaus, understood. I'll be in touch as soon as it's over," he replied, doing his best to keep his temper.

Carl greeted Valentin with a warm handshake and tried to be upbeat. But Valentin could sense his boss's nerves were frayed. As they negotiated the traffic on the mighty Novy Arbat, a vast boulevard bordered by enormous Soviet-era residential skyscrapers and a long line of shops, restaurants and strip clubs, Carl became lost in thought. He stared at the neon lights shining down the long boulevard. In a blur of orange, yellow and red, they lit up cars and pedestrians, and the patrons smoking shisha-pipe on the terraces outside.

It was an utterly psychedelic image that Carl found both compelling and disorienting. Valentin handed Carl a mint from a small packet on the dashboard, just below the Orthodox cross that dangled off the rear-view mirror and smiled.

"*Davai* Valentin, take me to Bosco on Red Square," Carl said to Valentin, deciding that the neon lights of Novy Arbat were a bit too much for now. Located at the edge of the enormous Soviet era department store called "GUM", Bosco was the restaurant of choice for Carl when he wanted to eat alone. Full of Moscow's glitterati, it offered endless people-watching opportunities and yet was discreet, allowing Carl to dine alone in comfort and in complete anonymity.

As he was dropped off, he decided to take a short stroll around Red Square before heading into the restaurant. Vast, impressive, awe-inspiring, bursting with history, the vast "*Krasny Ploschad*" (Red Square) as it was known in Russian felt like the central nervous system of Russia. At one end the sterile and macabre mausoleum of Vladimir Ilyich Lenin. Next to the mausoleum in a straight line the busts of the leaders of the Soviet Union from Stalin to Chernenko. Carl stared at the bust of Stalin. Even in death, commemorated in stone, there was something frightening about him.

A wave of hunger suddenly overcame Carl and thoughts of Soviet despots became secondary. He headed to the restaurant. The place was jammed full of Moscow's beautiful people, Russian prima donnas with inflatable chests and lips, Louis Vuitton handbags and Jimmy Choo high heels, accompanied by men who were Russia's version of the Disney character, Shrek. He was quickly shown to his table by a buxom waitress in impossibly high heels.

The table was perfectly positioned in the corner of the restaurant to take full advantage of the comings and goings of patrons without attracting too much attention to himself. As he sank into the sofa chair he spotted a copy of the English language *Moscow Times* on a small table. It was wafer-thin, one of the only remaining publications in Russia prepared to criticise the government. But there was always some little gem of information in there about what was going on in Moscow –and today's edition was to be no exception.

Carl quickly fell upon an item about Anna Kandinskiy, wife of Ari. Her face was splashed across the social pages towards the back of the paper. Despite her husband's financial problems, it looked as though she was the lucky buyer of a Picasso at a Russian art show sponsored by a prestigious English art auctioneer.

With enormous botox lips and a fake cleavage that had been enhanced a few times, Anna Kandinskiy was every bit the wife of a Russian oligarch. She lived a life of absolute luxury, cruising around Moscow in her soft-top Bentley, travelling the world in her husband's private plane. With his recent financial issues they'd had to downsize a little, offloading properties in Monaco and California. No matter how acute her husband's financial troubles though, Anna Kandinskiy was determined to stay part of Russia's jet set.

Having grown up in a comfortably-off family in Soviet Russia, she had seen her parents go from respected members of society as scientists to people entirely forgotten by the new Russia. They and others like them could not keep up in the transition to a market economy that greatly enriched families connected to political power or those bold enough to blast competitors into obscurity and claim for themselves all the assets of a newly privatised company.

It was the engineers, soldiers, doctors or scientists who slowly descended into obscurity and poverty. They faced the prospect of having to live on the incredibly modest Russian state pension, and would be forever at the mercy of runaway inflation and a fluctuating rouble.

With Ari's bankruptcy looming and creditors swooping over his assets the Kandinskiys went to the wedding registrar's office one cold Moscow weekend and terminated what had otherwise been a very successful and relatively happy union of nearly 20 years. Having transferred properties in France, Russia and the Seychelles to his wife just prior to the divorce, along with a fleet of vintage cars, not to mention the Bentley, Kandinskiy had moved all of those assets out of the range of creditors, all of whom were naturally outraged.

The Kandinskiys were taking a big risk, but one they had no choice but to take. They were never going to return to the normal life lived by 99 per cent of their countrymen; it was either a life of unlimited luxury or concrete boots in Moscow River, and nothing in between.

After Carl had washed down what was left of a delicious serve of veal goulash with a glass of Bordeaux red, he got the bill and started to walk back slowly to his apartment on Tverskaya Ulitsa, only 10 minutes away.

It was still oppressively hot outside – his shirt stuck to his back and he could feel droplets of sweat trickling down his forehead.

In the sweltering heat, Moscovites would stand outside underground stations and near kiosks that sold drinks and cheap cigarettes, with a can of beer in one hand and a Marlboro in the other. They would chat until the early hours of the morning, often until sunrise at 3 am. Then, they'd remember they had jobs or uni classes to get to later that morning and stumble home.

He passed a group of young student types, joking and laughing away, being eyed off by a couple of policemen who clearly didn't appreciate having to work on a sweltering hot July evening in Moscow, and resenting the fact that young well-heeled Moskvichi could enjoy life far more than they could ever hope to.

"What the fuck are you doing here at this time," snarled the older policeman of the two, almost certainly from the regions, a corpulent, gnarled-looking fellow, with a bulbous nose and ruddy complexion.

"None of your business fatty," responded the solitary girl in the group, no older than 18, dressed in ripped jeans and a loose-fitting t-shirt designed to show off her magnificent figure. Everyone in her group laughed, as did the younger policeman of the duo.

The response was too much for the slandered policeman, and everyone in the student party soon realised that. The girl knew she'd made a fatal mistake by showing disrespect to a member, no matter how lowly, of the Russian state. The older policeman, shaking with anger, walked up to the girl and gave her a slap over the face with such brute force that he knocked the girl to the ground and loosened a couple of teeth.

As she hit the ground, she let out a deep groan. She slowly got to her feet, shaking, her mouth full of blood. The old cop was about to line her up again with a kick, but the younger policeman interceded, calming his older colleague down.

"You fucking Moskvich have no respect," the old man yelled, spitting everywhere, "You're nothing but a pathetic pack of hippy losers. You should leave and go to some pathetic liberal country in the west where you can live like the bohemians you are!!"

The younger policeman had to use all his strength to restrain his more senior colleague from inflicting more suffering on the injured student.

The young Moskvich stood there motionless, shaking. They stared at the old cop, paralysed with fear, realising that he could dish out the same punishment to any one of them without any fear of retribution or punishment from the authorities. He was the law and it was for him to administer as he saw fit. They soon left the alley they'd been drinking in and headed home. The injured girl was taken to a nearby hospital in a taxi. She'd never forget her encounter with the policemen, the moment a careless joke cost her a few teeth and taught her the place she occupied in a Russian society that was dominated by men in uniform.

As Carl returned home, he slammed shut the door of his apartment and tossed down his bulging briefcase on to the glass table in his foyer. He wandered slowly to the kitchen and pulled open his fridge door. He swore to himself that the beer he was about to pull out of it would be his last for the evening. Without it though he wouldn't be able to relax. His mind and body knew that.

He was not astonished or surprised by the little scene he had just witnessed but he found it unsettling nonetheless. It was another reminder of the omnipotence of the state and the bullies who ran it. And he knew that his meeting tomorrow might be no exception. The Cherneys of this world were no different from the hooligan cops patrolling central Moscow – at least he feared that would be the case.

As he leafed through the files handed to him earlier in the day by Roman Lebedev, it was obvious to him that Cherney was a mass of contradictions. And in his unpredictability would likely prove a formidable obstacle for Falcon Capital if they played their cards wrong.

From the file it was clear that Cherney, once a respected New York litigation lawyer, had turned into a hard man of Moscow politics. Leafing through the photos on file Carl saw a man who could have fitted right into a New York or London law firm partnership. Immaculate suit, perfect, slicked back hair, Armani glasses, teeth perfectly white and vertical – nothing like his own, Carl thought.

Lebedev's dossier also dealt with Spencer Pearson, Kandinskiy's own right-hand man when it came to legal matters. Pearson was a posh, 55-year-old English barrister turned law firm partner who specialised in getting high net worth clients off the hook and out of trouble, no matter how egregious their crimes.

A colourful, flamboyant character known to go to extraordinary lengths, even if it meant telling the odd fib, lie, or wanton fabrication to a gullible judge when it made the difference between winning and losing. Pearson understood that very few English judges had any idea how Russia and the Far East operated; they had little chance of distinguishing the truth from a pack of lies. He had been able to leverage off that lack of understanding with incredible success, winning unwinnable cases for very grateful foreign clients who showed their gratitude by paying Pearson very handsomely indeed and indulging his increasingly extravagant habits and peccadillos.

Tired from reading, his eyes closing, Carl sensed that he was about to doze off. Before doing so he took a look out his window at the traffic as it crawled up Tverskaya Street towards the brilliantly lit Mayor's building, a grand, opulent structure that was a power-base in Moscow second only to the Kremlin.

And Carl remembered the new apartment in secluded Patriarshiy Ponds that he was moving to – far away from ten lanes of exhaust fumes here in Tverskaya.

CHAPTER 6

CARL WOKE UP WITH A START AND DRENCHED IN sweat. He must have had another bad dream. It was a lot easier to control his conscious state than his unconscious one. Too tired to go to the gym and probably out of time anyway, he made himself a coffee and started to get ready for his 9 am meeting.

As he finished his coffee and shower, Valentin knocked on the door and without saying a word handed him a copy of *Vedomosti*, the Russian business daily. Emblazoned across the front page was an article on the shooting of a former head of the Russian central bank.

God they're dropping like flies Carl thought.

"*Spacibo* Val," said Carl.

"This city is going back to the nineties," replied Valentin, a look of resignation on his face.

The spate of killings pointed to a growing instability in Moscow and the country generally. The President had been able to quell much of the rampant criminality and assassinations that character-ised the dark years of the 90s but it seemed that old habits died hard and that certain forces within Russian society were slowly resorting to their old ways.

Time was getting on, and not wanting to be late for his meeting Carl told Valentin to have the car ready for their departure.

As they weaved their way through the backstreets of Moscow to get to Igor Cherney's offices in Barrikadnaya, on the Garden Ring close to Moscow Zoo, Carl scoured the newspapers for a reaction to the central banker's murder.

Most reports were guarded, treating it almost as an anticipated occurrence rather than the shocking murder of an otherwise respected and capable banker who was considered above the fray and untainted by the corruption scandals that had plagued his predecessors.

Maybe he'd refused to play by the rules Carl thought – refusing a bribe can be almost as dangerous as taking one. In the new Russia, dominated by the President and his entourage, it was never open to the media to suggest that events were beyond his control, that there was anything to be worried about. It was self-censorship in its purest form, no need for the State to intervene, society at so many levels was docile, compliant.

Entering the building where Igor Cherney's offices were housed, Carl was struck by the opulence and luxuriousness of the place. The furniture and light fittings must have cost a fortune he thought. Enormous TV screens on every wall extolled the virtues of the various companies that occupied the building. A huge atrium with waterfall – very kitsch Carl thought to himself – but hard not to be impressed. The immaculately dressed receptionists matched their surrounds and were certainly selected for their looks rather than their capabilities. The receptionist who greeted Carl must have been no older than twenty but was already sporting a set of botox-enhanced lips and enormous silicon breasts. She handed over a security pass and sent him to the second floor.

As he entered Cherney's offices he was greeted by a burly security guard who looked every bit as if he'd walked off the set of a James Bond film. Thickset, with piercing grey eyes, furrowed brow and tight-fitting black suit, this fellow was no ordinary security guard. In fact he was almost certainly Cherney's personal bodyguard, there to meet and greet everyone that Cherney met or came across. Realising Carl did not pose any security risk, he nodded at him to go through to a corner office overlooking Barrikadnaya Square. Carl walked through and was greeted by a man in his 40s, medium build and height, with slicked-back hair and designer glasses, unremarkable.

Carl's initial impression of Igor Cherney was of a man who seemed in many respects quite ordinary, albeit slick, sharp. He could have comfortably fitted in to any law firm or senior executive's office.

Cherney's handshake was forceful, assertive. He looked at Carl for a few seconds before calling his assistant to bring coffee. Gesturing to Carl to be seated at a large oak table in the middle of the enormous office, he got quickly to business.

"I have some good news and some bad news Carl."

"OK, let's start with the good news," replied Carl, coolly.

Cherney smiled, tapping his right finger on the wooden table and taking out an Excel spreadsheet, putting it squarely in front of him.

"The good news Carl is that I have, on my spreadsheet," and he paused briefly, to ensure Carl was following the discussion, "the number which I can offer Falcon Capital for Kandinskiy's total liabilities to you."

Cherney took a sip of his black espresso and slightly theatrically placed it in front of him, putting it down at a perfect right angle to the Excel spreadsheet. He continued. "You see the process of 'sharing' Kandinskiy's assets among creditors has been handed to *me*." He paused again and took another sip of his coffee.

"Some very powerful people in this city have charged me with this task and I intend carrying it out to the very best of my capabilities. I cannot accept any dissension or dissatisfaction – everyone, *and I mean everyone*, has to accept the decision I have been entrusted to make."

At the end of his little speech, he shot Carl a look that suggested he really did mean business.

Carl took a breath, folded his hands in front of him and said to Cherney, "If this is the good news Mr Cherney, what is the bad news?"

"The bad news, at least for today's meeting," Cherney responded, a narrow smile coming over his face, "is that I cannot tell you how much I can offer Falcon Capital. You'll just have to take my word that it is the best possible deal I can offer you at this stage, considering the various competing forces in the mix and Falcon Capital's … *lack of bargaining power*."

At the end of this little discourse, Cherney, looking pleased with himself, placed the Excel spreadsheet back in a leather folder on the meeting table, as if to close down any discussion with Carl on the amount which he was prepared to pay Falcon Capital.

Cherney's use of the words, "lack of bargaining power", could not help but alarm Carl. Cherney clearly considered Falcon Capital the hundred-pound weakling he could push around with ease.

"Igor," Carl interjected, "it's going to be very hard to sell a deal internally when I don't even know the number you're prepared to offer. I'm going to look pretty foolish if I go back to the office with this."

Cherney, who was barely able to contain his displeasure with the upstart South African, decided to turn the conversation in a different direction. "I like your cufflinks Carl, they're very nice, where are they from?"

"I'm not sure this is relevant but seeing you're asking, they're Dunhill, Jermyn Street, a gift from a girlfriend, far more than I usually spend on a pair ..."

Cherney, cutting off Carl abruptly, continued, "That's nice, presents are always good, aren't they? I'm always curious about such things. Do you want to see what my friends gave me for my birthday?"

He went to a cabinet at the other end of his office. Carl noticed a large scar behind Cherney's ear that went all the way down his neck. Must be the handiwork of the kidnappers he thought to himself.

After carefully plugging in the combination for the safe, Cherney opened it and pulled out a huge pistol and an antique dagger with Arabic writing emblazoned over it in gold. He very ostentatiously placed both weapons on the large oak table in front of Carl.

"You see Carl, this is what my friends, or rather, associates, give me," and he let out a large, malicious grin.

"You may have heard about Ruslan Akhmatov and if you have then you certainly know the man he represents. They are very grateful for the work I am doing to ensure an *equitable* settlement for all parties. Despite our differences and the fact that we come from, how do you say ... *different worlds*, we essentially play by the same rules – we see an opportunity in the same way they do."

Cherney had a point. Despite their many differences with their Russian cousins, Akhmatov and the various strong men from Chechnya had very successfully penetrated into Russia, working their way into the upper reaches of some of Russia's most prestigious and powerful companies (mostly in the oil and gas sectors), and gaining enormous influence with the President, Prime Minister and some very powerful deputies in the Duma. They balanced quite brilliantly the murky relationship between business and outright criminality, applying mafioso principles to doing business and with great effect. That made them an extremely powerful, enigmatic force in Russian business. Carl had read and heard about their increasing influence. Now he was seeing it first-hand, courtesy of Igor Cherney.

"And that will be at the expense of Falcon Capital it seems," Carl said, almost to himself.

"That's likely the case Carl," said Cherney, offering no hint of sympathy whatsoever, his finger tapping emphatically on his desk, his face now wearing a look of slight impatience. It was the smile of someone who knew that his opponent would have to bend entirely and unconditionally to his will.

This was the moment when Carl was meant to flinch, but Carl recalled his childhood growing up on the rugby pitches of his native South Africa, when his coach would scream at any player who showed the slightest unwillingness to engage in physical battle, no matter how unequal the odds. Giving in was not in his DNA. He had no idea what were the consequences of standing up to Cherney. But he did not have the luxury of over-analysing them – Cherney was waiting for him to respond.

"You know Igor you have really left me with not much of a choice. Jason Rogers will never accept a deal like this no matter what the threats. He's seen worse in the nineties and I know he'll back me one hundred per cent in this.

"So let's consider we don't have a deal in the absence of … your number. We're not going to give up on our legal claims in international courts and our long-term plan is to fight tooth and nail until we get paid out, whether or not the other creditors like it or not.

"I'd like to think though that we can keep an open door for discussions going forward – you never know, we may well be able to help each other at some point in the future…"

Cherney looked up from his computer, not quite believing what he'd just heard. His mouth opened momentarily but rather than saying anything there was a long pause while Cherney calculated his response. Carl felt the tie around his neck had got a little tighter, his grip on the leather office chair a little harder, he had absolutely no idea how his refusal to play ball would be received.

After his moment of reflection, Cherney realised that no matter what his reputation or his contacts, he couldn't bludgeon Falcon Capital into submission, particularly if they wanted to be stubborn bastards about it.

They were small fish in a pond full of giant hungry sharks, better to let them keep swimming a little longer, they would eventually get eaten.

"OK, Carl, I let you leave this place in one piece, just this once, but I warn you, you are not dealing with nice western businessmen here, people who play by the rules and have big expensive compliance departments telling them what they can and cannot do."

Cherney looked at the pistol and dagger – still conspicuous in the middle of the meeting table, almost glistening under the lights of his office.

"You're in Russia now, not London or New York …"

"Understood Igor, I'm under no illusions regarding the people we're up against, none at all."

Carl got up from his seat and shook Igor's hand. He noticed that this time the grip was firmer and there was a definite absence of the charm and civility that had characterised his welcome only an hour or so earlier.

He breathed a sigh of relief as he left Cherney's offices and wandered out to Moscow's heavily polluted Garden Ring road. He jumped into the Chevrolet Tahoe to get to the offices at Moscow City as quickly as possible. Valentin revved the engine and the car sped off, throwing mud and rubbish in all directions.

The slightest opportunity to drive at speed had Valentin, his heart beating that little bit faster, revving up the powerful engine of the Tahoe and driving at speeds that would have him locked up in most cities. But this was Moscow, and a $50 bribe was usually enough to persuade an avaricious traffic cop that all should be forgiven.

As they flew into the car park at the Moscow City offices of Falcon Capital, Carl spotted Benny Goldsmith outside the enormous glass entrance, furiously smoking his fifth cigarette of the day, sipping on an espresso in a plastic coffee cup.

"Carl," he yelled out, "how did it go?" and gestured with a thumbs-up sign.

"Hard to say Benny, looks like we've got Ruslan Akhmatov among others to deal with which I am sure is going to go down badly here."

"Fucking A it will Carl, very fucking badly," Benny said, a look of near disgust coming across his face. The cigarette, espresso and Carl's latest revelation appeared to give him a little headspin. "Fuck, I need to sit down", he muttered to himself.

"Take it easy Benny. Let's grab a beer later. I'll sure as hell need one," and Carl patted his friend on the shoulder before heading into reception.

As soon as Carl got to his office and put down his things, Vadim Petrovsky wandered into his office, a look of grave seriousness pasted over his chubby face.

"What's the matter now?" was all Carl could say.

"Carl, it looks like the thieves from the tax office are planning a visit – the rumours are rife in the office this morning. The Russian staff are, how do you say, freaking out?"

Carl had heard rumours that sources in the "*Sledtsviy Komitet* " (Investigative Committee) were planning a raid. What was not clear was when it was going to happen and what was the trigger for it. Was it a simple grab for money or something more complex?

Rival companies with cash to burn frequently bought tax raids on competitors (the cost being anywhere up to US$200,000) to obtain highly confidential information or merely to disrupt the competitor's operations, intimidate its employees and make businesses that were otherwise solid appear fragile, impotent.

Employees and management would be paralysed in their offices for hours while tax police supported by Russian militia (the infamous "*Omon*") trawled through personal documents, and waved around semi-automatic weapons to intimidate and threaten them into complete submission. Confidentiality of documentation, legal privilege etc. all meant nothing to the investigators who would use a raid as an excuse to find out as much "*kompromat* " (compromising material) as they could about a company.

It had not taken long for Klaus Schwartz to realise that an imminent tax raid was his opportunity to shine and take control – he called a meeting of senior management to figure out a strategy.

Everyone in senior management, with the exception of Rogers, was assembled in the meeting room facing east, with views out to the Kremlin and the magnificent Moscow University and surrounding gardens of Sparrow Hills.

Schwartz, his face beetroot red with a combination of indignation and angst, entered the room like a generalissimo from a bygone era. All he needed to complete the effect was a riding crop and long black boots. He stormed to the head of the enormous wooden table in the centre of the room and sat down, the large leather armchair straining under his 110+ kilos of Austrian bulk.

Staring darkly at assembled management, Schwartz cleared his throat and barked in his thickest Austrian accent, "Some crooked fock has decided that it's a good idea to call a tax raid on us. I've spoken to our security guys," and he glanced over at Roman Lebedev who was seated calmly in the corner of the room, his face expressionless, his right hand supporting his chin, "and they are confident this is raid which has been paid for by someone in Russia with a bone to pick with us – fuckers!!!" Schwartz screamed, his voice shaking with anger.

He quickly composed himself and continued, "No matter what the motives are of these 'assholes', we have to take action and fast. We have information that we can't afford to let our competitors, or the government ever know about …" and he slammed his fist down on the table with such force at the end of his tirade that he sent his espresso cup – empty this time – plummeting to the floor.

Carl could only presume that Schwartz was worried about the innumerable offshore structures which he had put in place over the years, to hide dodgy schemes and minimise tax in a way that had sent other Russian businessmen to the gulags.

If the tax police could get their hands on this type of information, they would be able to extort tens of millions, perhaps hundreds of millions from Falcon Capital, or send the whole management team to Siberia's most dangerous penitentiaries.

Just as Schwartz was finishing his tirade, Rogers strode in to the meeting room, his blue eyes scanning the room to see who was in attendance. He had the demeanour of someone in complete control of the situation – neither relaxed nor anxious, just purposeful, every step measured, none of the flamboyance or self consciousness that characterised so many of his colleagues. Rogers had lived through so many crises in his turbulent career in Russia that dealing with them had become second nature to him.

Looking at all of the directors assembled in the meeting room, his large hands resting on the table in front of him, Rogers spoke calmly. "You've heard Klaus. This is an extremely serious situation. It is an assault on our integrity as an institution. If we allow these assholes to trawl through our systems and steal information then we're finished, we'll lose all fucking credibility in this town."

Carl noticed that when matters got a little tight Rogers' southern drawl would become a little more pronounced, as if he were reverting a little closer to his roots to address a common danger.

Rogers scanned the room to check that he had the undivided attention of his colleagues and continued, "I've been in this country for nearly 20 years now and every so often you get some filth from the government bureaucracy that wants to stick its nose into the trough, get their hands on the money and the revenues that you guys have worked so hard to generate.

"So what do we do?"

He paused briefly, taking a deep breath, "We tell them to go fuck themselves – no matter what the risk to us we push back. Why? Because if we don't then literally we will have people showing up at the door every single day until there is nothing, literally nothing, left of this business!"

The imposing Texan banker then got up from his chair and walked around the table, giving high fives to all of the assembled managers, bringing spontaneous applause to the elegant room looking out over the sprawling expanse of Moscow.

It was classic Rogers – a call to arms that energised and inspired his colleagues and had them brushing off dangers that would have most bankers running for cover.

As the bankers and traders filed out of the meeting, Carl noticed that Rogers had caught his eye and was clearly intending to speak to him. Rogers gestured to Schwartz and to Carl to follow him and they walked to another, smaller meeting room. This was the safe room – completely impervious to surveillance from the outside world. Rogers switched on a white noise machine and opened a large oak humidor containing 24 identical Cuban cigars. He took one out, cut it, lit it and settled back into a leather armchair in the corner of the room, the white noise machine emitting a dull hissing sound which was impossible to ignore.

But it did not seem to bother Rogers who drew back deeply on his cigar as he let his big shoulders fall back into the armchair. He muttered to himself "Fucking great cigar," and briefly closed his eyes, as if trying to block out everything around him, focus entirely on the aroma of the smoke that was enveloping him.

After allowing himself half a minute of tranquillity, Rogers opened his eyes and fixed them on Carl.

"What happened today with Cherney?" he asked, in an imperious tone, demanding an answer quickly.

"It wasn't exactly what I expected Jason ..." Carl began, cautiously. He ran Rogers through the exchange and did his best to recall every-thing that was relevant from the dismissive tone regarding Falcon Capital's chances of making a decent recovery to Cherney's ostenta-tious display of a gun and Chechen knife on his table in an effort to intimidate the South African.

It was the reference to the gun and knife that grabbed Rogers' attention and, Carl could clearly see, had the older man's blood boiling.

"This fucker is trying to throw us off the scent. Well he can go fuck himself. I've seen punks like this come and go. It's not the first time someone has tried to intimidate me, and it won't be the last. Screw him, no deal, he can stick his pistol and dagger up his ass!"

By now Rogers was sitting up straight in his leather armchair, his cigar waving backwards and forwards as he belted out his tirade, ash drifting towards the floor.

Carl thought hard about how best to respond to an irate Rogers. The temptation to say nothing was nearly overwhelming but he thought better of it.

"Jason, the complication this time is that we're not just dealing with Cherney and Moskvy Neft, but also – it turns out Ruslan Akhmatov – this changes the dynamic of the whole situation pretty significantly, it seems to me anyway …" and his voice drifted off.

He wasn't particularly enjoying their conversation. It had turned into a combination of stating the bleeding obvious and passing on bad news to management, which he had always felt was not his strong suit. The messenger more often than not got shot in such situations and he sensed that Rogers and Klaus were preparing to do just that.

Rogers bristled at being reminded about the risk Akhmatov posed to him and Falcon Capital.

"Carl, I know full well who this guy represents and frankly I don't care. We'll beef up security, get our contacts in the security services to keep an eye out for us and be more vigilant. Hell we've spent a fortune on them over the years, it's time they fucking well delivered!" he said, stubbing out his cigar in the ashtray, leaving a big plume of smoke to waft up slowly towards the ceiling of the meeting room, like a mushroom cloud from a mini atomic explosion.

However, for all the bravado and steely reserve, Carl sensed that Rogers had met his match in the form of Akhmatov. The Chechen brigade penetrating Russian business, social and criminal circles did not operate according to the rules observed by 99 per cent of the local population. They considered themselves neither legally nor morally bound to follow any rules.

Westerners behaving more or less along western lines, occasionally stepping over the divide but usually respecting business arrangements and norms of a civilised society, had little chance against people who viewed such principles as evidence of weakness to be trampled on at the earliest opportunity.

The cold, Machiavellian self-interest, not to mention a healthy dose of criminality in the form of intimidation, threats, bribes and other tactics meant that the businessmen from the Caucasus had the upper hand in the fight for the remains of Kandinskiy's empire.

The only hope for Falcon Capital was that local interests of the Russian state and other Russian businessmen who'd been screwed by Kandinskiy would be buffers against their rapacious cousins from the south.

CHAPTER 7

THE FLEET OF BLACK CARS WITH RED INSIGNIA OF the local Investigative Committee flew up the embankment driveway and into the car park of the Moscow City complex that housed Falcon Capital. Lights flashed and sirens wailed as the cars, stuffed full with tax inspectors escorted by heavily armed paramilitary ("*Omon*") dressed in camouflage and armed with semi-automatic firearms, screeched to a halt. The members of the Omon stormed into the building's ground floor reception and screamed at the receptionists to move away from their phones and computers and assemble alongside an exit door. The leader of the team of Omon, a man in his mid-40s, barked orders to the team through his earpiece and stopped to confer with another younger, smartly dressed man in a dark suit.

The younger man was the raid's supervisor, Tax Commissioner Yury Soloviev, a 40-something bureaucrat with a nose for tax evasion and an even greater appetite for bribes or "*vzyatka*" to finance his own luxurious and extravagant lifestyle.

Short, plump with thinning hair, dressed in a shiny grey suit, black coat and white leather shoes, physically he did not cut an impressive figure but he had enormous power and influence at his disposal. Those around him knew it or were quickly made to realise it. He could single-handedly transform up-and-coming businesses into bankrupt shells within months.

Soloviev and his team of paramilitary officers and investigative police took the lifts up to the 48th floor and Falcon Capital's reception. As the lift whizzed up the floors, Soloviev started to feel a buzz that came to him every time he raided a business. Satisfaction that he would be able to pocket a substantial proportion of the US$250,000 dollar bribe that a rival financial institution had paid for the raid, as well as the adrenalin that came when he knew he was about to scare employees and management witless with his heavily armed militia, the fear that he saw in their eyes quickly followed by the resignation of impending defeat.

But this time Yury Soloviev was in for a surprise. As he stormed out of the lifts into reception he was greeted by Schwartz, Roman Lebedev and the full retinue of Falcon Capital's security apparatus, standing in reception, as if they had received a special invitation in the post announcing the hour and location of the raid.

"Well what the fuck do we have here?" he yelled in Russian at one of his subordinates, also clearly stunned that their surprise raid was not such a surprise after all.

Schwartz, his arms crossed, standing as if he was ready for a fist fight to erupt between the rival parties, stepped forward and addressed an angry looking Soloviev in his near perfect Russian.

"Commissioner Soloviev, we have been expecting your visit to our offices today and are delighted to be able to show you around properly," and a large grin broke out across Schwartz's face. It was a theatrical moment and he had pulled it off perfectly.

Soloviev by this stage had turned red, almost purple with rage. His band of militia looked bemused and awaited orders from Soloviev.

"OK," he barked at them in Russian, "we start with the servers." Soloviev was desperately trying to re-assert his authority

"Of course," interjected Schwartz, "I'll take you straight to our IT centre," and he gestured to Soloviev and the goons to follow him to the floor below. Of course, Schwartz had ordered the offshore server to be cut off hours earlier so all that Soloviev and his investigators were left with was the Russian server which contained nothing that could expose Falcon Capital or its clients to any risks whatsoever.

This was quickly confirmed to Soloviev by a young IT operative wearing a shiny grey suit with a 70s style mullet. He shook his head with a mixture of fear and disappointment and told Soloviev in Russian that they'd not get any information, today at least.

Soloviev, who was boiling with rage, stomped around the office of Falcon Capital's IT department and punched one of the thin plaster dividing walls, sending bits of the wall flying everywhere and causing blood to pour from a cut on his hand. The raid was turning into an outright failure, and for Falcon Capital, a minor irritant but nothing more.

Whichever oligarch or member of the siloviki had ordered the raid would almost certainly request his money back, an unbearable outcome for Soloviev who'd already guaranteed members of his team a payment for this "additional service" they were prepared to perform.

"*Pizdetz*," Soloviev screamed, slapping the young agent over the back of his head with all the force he could muster, knocking him to the ground.

Soloviev, realising that his frustration had suddenly become the central spectacle, eventually composed himself and turned to Schwartz.

"Well Mr Schwartz, you were well prepared today but after today comes tomorrow and then after tomorrow the day after tomorrow. You have to be prepared *every day* for my return," and he gave Schwartz the half smile of someone who has been outsmarted for now but determined to get the final word at some point in the future.

"I am fully aware of this Mr Soloviev," Schwartz responded, his chest fully extended, a broad grin plastered over his face, "and we will graciously receive you at our offices next time you arrive!"

Soloviev and his band of tax agents and militia left reception and took the lifts down to the ground floor. As their procession of cars and Hummers snaked out of the driveway in the evening sun at breakneck speed back on to the road along the Moscow embankment, watched by Schwartz, Carl and a handful of colleagues from the meeting room on the 48th floor, Schwartz turned to Carl.

"Carl, today was a close call, we were lucky. These sharks will be back for sure and next time they will not fuck around and likely just plant something that shuts us down. We have to think of a plan B for this guy, we clearly have to get him off our back and figure out who is financing this show. We have enough problems without having these assholes compounding them!" he yelled at no one in particular.

Schwartz was being uncharacteristically philosophical thought Carl. In contrast to the inflated hype Falcon Capital repeatedly promoted to potential investors, things were not looking so rosy for the firm. Like a cold autumn wind blasting through the streets of Moscow, a reminder of the diaobolical winter that awaited, the Russian economy was starting to resemble more and more the awful stagnation of the Brezhnev era. The optimism and sparkle that characterised the early phase of the new President's reign had descended into what the Russian politician Viktor Chernomyrdin had once so beautifully described "We wanted the best, but it turned out as always."

Schwartz had been staring out of the 48th floor window, tracking Soloviev's cortege until it faded from view. He was overtaken by a thought which appeared to cheer him up.

"Screw it Carl, I'm sick of all this negative energy, these fucking Russians creating complications, what are you doing tonight? I think we need something to boost our spirits, and I know just the place," he grinned broadly, flashing his newly whitened teeth.

"I'm free Klaus, what did you have in mind?" Carl responded a little anxiously, not sure that he wanted to spend more time than necessary with Schwartz.

"Dreams, Carl, Dreams! There's only one place I know where we can really forget these assholes, we're going to drink some good champagne, smoke some great cigars and fuck some beautiful women ..." And Schwartz walked off to corral as many colleagues as possible into his nocturnal jaunt.

The portly Austrian, suddenly energised by the prospect of an evening of debauchery at the firm's expense, stormed around the office, sticking his head into the offices of colleagues immersed in their work and ordering them to come with him to Moscow's most notorious and celebrated bordel. "It will be fucking great, you'll love it!"

Carl tidied up his desk and packed his laptop into his bag. Before heading off with Schwartz and the others in the cortege of company limousines to Dreams, he popped his head into Vadim's office to brief him on the meeting with Cherney and the unexpected twist that the Kandinskiy debt recovery had suddenly taken, with the arrival on the scene of Ruslan Akhmatov and his band of Chechen thugs.

"*Bozha moy!* (My lord)," Vadim exclaimed when he heard the news.

"Carl I don't know how much you know about the Chechens but these guys don't play games, they're k-k-killers," he stammered, unable to contain his nerves. His round, chubby face was suddenly animated in a way that Carl had never seen before (and found a little unnerving).

"Vadim, I can tell management are shitting themselves about this problem, but we don't really have a choice other than to engage with Cherney. If we don't, we kiss goodbye to the two-fifty million and we're just not in a position to do that."

"OK, Carl but really, this is not ideal. I'm Jewish and don't want to be within a million miles of these assholes!' Vadim said, in a state of high agitation, his face a little redder than usual and his small feet shuffling nervously under his chair.

Vadim composed himself and went on, "Carl, OK, I hear you, the message is clear, maybe the best way to look at this is as just another complication, albeit a big one … we need to play around with our analysis a little.

"Our chances of recovery just got a little slimmer so we need to think harder about every potential angle, how we can get to Kandinskiy and his slimeball business partners and family. It will be tough but I am sure there is a weak link somewhere."

"Thanks Vadim, that's the spirit," and Carl affectionately slapped Vadim on the back.

CHAPTER 8

THE CORTEGE OF 4X4S AND LIMOUSINES SNAKED its way through the up-market Patriarshiy Ponds area. The procession arrived noisily at the entrance of Dreams. Located in a heavily fortified pre-Revolutionary building – the used-to-be residence of one of Russia's richest families, devout members of the Orthodox church, was now home to Moscow's most popular strip club and brothel.

Schwartz stormed into the entrance, greeting the guards warmly, discreetly handing out hundred-dollar bills to ensure that the evening passed off without a hitch. He surveyed the dance floor which was bustling with beautiful women in their early 20s and rubbed his fat white hands with undisguised glee.

Schwartz had reserved a large table at the end of the club dance floor, far from prying eyes but well enough positioned so that he could see the comings and goings of the clientele, many of whom were well known figures in Russian commercial and business circles. Within minutes of being seated Schwartz had waved across two of the prettier girls in the club and with a click of his fingers ordered two jeroboams of Veuve Clicquot. A dancer on either leg, Schwartz did all but dribble over them, not at all embarrassed by the fact that he was sitting there with colleagues.

"Isn't this city just fantastic?!" he yelled over the club music booming from a speaker near the table, "you can do whatever the fuck you want!" and he grabbed the left breast of one of the dancers whose ample cleavage was rubbing against his sweaty business shirt. She giggled and encouraged him to touch the other breast. Schwartz was in his element, the stress of Soloviev's failed raid now a distant memory.

The more the dancing girls fawned over Schwartz, and the more inebriated he became, the more raucous and indulgent the evening became. Black caviar, epic quantities of French champagne, and bottles of vodka covered the table that Schwartz had reserved for his team.

By 10.30 the table for fifteen was full, half being Falcon Capital people and the other half beautiful young women from just about every corner of Russia, Ukraine, and Belarus – they'd come to Moscow with nothing and were trying to make ends meet. All were vying for Schwartz's attention. Despite his age and girth they'd picked him out as the alpha male of the group and the one to cosy up to. He was loving every minute of their attention – he reciprocated happily by liberally distributing hundred-dollar bills among his beautiful admirers.

Fortunately for Carl, who was not particularly enjoying the spectacle of Schwartz's plump frame getting squeezed in a hundred different manners by the determined young dancers, his colleague Ronnie Allan had agreed to keep him company. Ronnie dropped him a text indicating he'd arrive any minute.

As Ronnie walked in, Carl could see that his friend was in a black mood. "Fucking bastards," was the greeting, which was not entirely unusual with Ronnie. "They have completely left me out to fucking dry …!"

"What are you on about mate?" Carl enquired, not particularly looking forward to the answer.

"The Bronsky deal is a complete, unmitigated fucking disaster, Carl," he whispered into Carl's ear, smiling broadly, trying to avoid attracting the attention of Schwartz and the other bankers seated at the table.

Ah yes, Carl thought to himself, the deal which Ronnie had been telling all and sundry about only weeks ago that was a one-way ticket to fast cash had suddenly lost its shine in spectacular fashion.

Congolese diamonds, expensive financing, equity upside, a toxic mix that was meant to make Falcon Capital millions if it played its hand carefully but one that ran huge risks if something went wrong – and going wrong was something Falcon Capital was doing with increasing regularity. The business had lost its edge, the fuck-ups were outnumbering the successes by a factor of 2:1.

Ushering Carl to an adjoining table, away from colleagues, Ronnie ordered himself and Carl a bottle of vodka and some Russian appetisers or "zakuski" – cornichons, dried horse-meat and lard. The two men hungrily devoured the plate of zakuski and quickly downed 250 ml of vodka each. The vodka coursed through their veins and within a few minutes Ronnie's mood started to improve.

Having loosened up, he decided to let Carl in on the latest excesses of his most profitable client.

"Bronsky operates on the edge, Carl, on the fringe, things we would never dream of doing – he does daily. He has this army of mostly local Congolese kids. They're there to terrorise the opposition, defend his workers from harassment. Anyway, they wiped out the workers at a rival mine, then killed all their women and kids in the neighbouring village. Bronsky is a bit cut-up about it, the guy isn't a complete monster but ..." he said, hesitating for an instant, "what the fuck was he thinking? The Americans have found out about it and now the President down there in Congo DRC – whatever his name is – is under pressure to shut him down – the whole thing is a complete fucking mess," he said with a touch of bitterness.

"It doesn't stop there Carl, there's photos of me all over his personal website meeting with him in DRC. In terms of PR it's the equivalent of having your photo taken with Idi Amin, Gaddafi and Bin Laden all at once!"

Carl took Ronnie's protestations with a little scepticism. In the world of frontier markets it was standard to be in close contact with dictators and warlords.

"I bet it's not bad for business Ronnie, and you know better than me, you'll be getting WhatsApp invitations from every dodgy fucker on the planet wanting to do business with you!" and both men laughed.

"Yeah, fuck it, you've got a point there, Carl," and Ronnie reached for his vodka glass, emptying its contents. He cracked his knuckles and looked around the club. Carl noticed a slight tremble in his hands. Maybe Ronnie wasn't as bullet-proof as he used to think. His thick brown hair suddenly looked a little whiter than before, his face a little more hollow, as if he'd lost weight. Life in Moscow eventually caught up with even the most physically and mentally robust. Working at Falcon Capital just added an additional level of stress – no wonder the bankers and lawyers there ended up looking so strung out.

As the night dragged on, Schwartz, who had returned from a visit to a private room at the back of the club, ordered a box of Cohiba cigars for the table. They were quickly snapped up by the bankers, the gaggle of nymphs around Schwartz opting for the more popular sheesha pipes that were a regular feature of Moscow clubs and bars.

Schwartz, whose shirt was open down to the waist, a steady stream of salty sweat pouring down his brow from the effort he had just expended in the antechamber of the club, puffed away on a cigar that had to be no less than a foot long. He had a broad grin plastered over his face – he was in his element.

But his mood quickly changed when he saw Carl sitting quietly at the table, flicking through emails. The spectacle irritated him greatly. He changed seats and sat next to Carl.

"Carl, you're too much of a pussy, you have to take the bull by the horns like me and that goes for the people in this country, they need to be fucked every now and then – they don't respect weakness, they have a physical aversion to it and want to crush weakness," he hissed, his hair an unkempt mess, a smell of booze and cigars radiating from him, enveloping everything around him.

Schwartz was getting sick of talking to his colleagues. They seemed to be disgusted by him and the feeling was mutual. Without saying anything further Schwartz grabbed two buxom Ukrainians and led them forcefully to a room out the back of the club.

"Fucking pussies," Schwartz thought to himself as he stormed off. The new brigade of expats who'd shown up in Moscow had only come after things got safe. They'd missed the bravura 1990s, when Moscow crims were blowing each other up and fighting over the spoils of perestroika Russia, stripped to bits by economic and social failures.

Schwartz had endured all of that, made money and become a respected business figure in the new Russia. Into his third marriage to a beautiful young Russian woman 30 years his junior, his libido had not slowed down one bit.

As he prepared to enter the vagina of one of the beautiful young girls who'd joined him in the club's private room he could not help but look at himself in the gold-framed mirror of the ostentatiously decorated room and feel his heart swell with pride. Here he was, 65, in the prime of his life, rich beyond his wildest expectations, screwing beautiful women young enough to be his grandchildren. He could tell that they loved it as well; they yelped, screamed and shrieked through their sessions so much he sometimes wondered whether he should be charging them for the honour of a private session with the one and only – Klaus Schwartz.

CHAPTER 9

YOLANDA WATCHED HER CLIENT, A HIGH-FLYING British lawyer to the powerful and the rich, snort what must have been his fifth line of cocaine that evening. It was 3 am. The private party in the Upper West Side of Manhattan had started at 10 pm and was by now in full force – a strange one in some respects. All the men were well into their 50s and 60s, all super rich, an assortment of Russians, Brits and Americans. The girls at the party, including Yolanda, were working girls from the Mid-East, Ukraine, South America and elsewhere.

Yolanda's client, Spencer, was likely her best ever. She had started to suspect that well-mannered, generous and incredibly loyal Spencer, an impeccably stylish Englishman in his fifties with wavy white hair, blue eyes and a penchant for Savile Row suits, had fallen for her. That made him incredibly vulnerable and her potentially very rich, assuming she could string him along. Her job was to convince Spencer that despite hers being the world's oldest profession she really did care for him, that their arrangement was unique, the first to go against thousands of years of mutual exploitation based on sex and money, one bound by love and not just one very long, extended, financial transaction.

From Spencer's perspective, Yolanda was the opposite of everything he'd known before. Married for twenty years to a very posh and proper girl from Buckinghamshire, he'd lived a life of complete, utter stability and, on paper at least, met everyone's expectations – his family's, his friends, his lecturers and mentors. Even his kids were perfect, accomplished students, well behaved and the opposite of the problem kids of most people he knew.

Yolanda came from Beirut. She had beautiful big brown eyes and a voluptuous figure that had men crossing the street to introduce themselves. Whenever she walked into a restaurant, bar or café with Spencer he would immediately sense that everyone in the room was looking at her, at them … and he loved the attention. He loved the feeling that every other man in their immediate proximity would give his right arm to swap places. That was never a feeling he came remotely close to experiencing with his loving, devoted wife Carol who had, rather unhelpfully, never managed to lose the weight she'd gained after their second child.

After emigrating from Lebanon to New York, Yolanda realised that getting by in New York was prohibitively expensive and paying for her studies through working at Burger King just wasn't going to cut it.

It wasn't long before she was spotted by a hustler from the Upper East Side promoting his brand new "modelling" agency. Except it wasn't a modelling agency in the conventional sense and very quickly she found herself dining with much older men in expensive restaurants around Manhattan, fawning over their every word, driving them crazy with desire as she flashed her generous cleavage. She loved the power she wielded over these much older men with unimaginable wealth.

Her initial disgust at the idea of being physically intimate with an older man eventually gave way to acceptance. After the first two experiences she found herself acclimatised, desensitised, almost comfortable with the flesh that hung off the bones of these older suitors, their dependence on little blue pills to get them going and keep them performing through mechanical, passionless sexual encounters. Before she knew it, she was the prized member of the modelling agency and the go-to girl for parties of the uber rich men who controlled that enormous, bustling metropolis.

Yolanda noticed Spencer deep in conversation with the host of the party, a Russian oligarch who she only knew as "Ari". Ari's parties were famous among the wealthy of New York. The best drugs, vodka and black caviar were in abundance as well as some of the city's most expensive working girls walking around in their underwear, adorned with gifts of Louis Vuitton bags and Hermes scarves. It was at one such party that Yolanda met Ari Kandinskiy and his lawyer Spencer Pearson.

◄►

On this particular night, Kandinskiy and Pearson had spent most of the night huddled together, drinking, smoking and snorting coke, not really engaging in the cavorting of the other partygoers.

Their occasionally animated discussion revolved around Kandinskiy's strategy for screwing his creditors, beating the courts and bailiffs hunting him in every corner of the globe. Spencer Pearson was possibly the best equipped lawyer on the planet to help him with that. He knew better than just about anyone anywhere how to frustrate creditors and render useless their efforts to get their money back.

Pearson was the master at creating enough distractions to throw plaintiff lawyers off guard. He knew which lies had to be told to get the better of judges who otherwise thought they'd seen everything and thought they could distinguish fact from bare-faced lie. The more Pearson worked for dishonest clients the more he realised, as did those closest to him, that he had changed, picked up the attributes of these crooked, ultra rich men who had spent their whole lives fabricating the truth, dealing ruthlessly with anyone who got in their way or had the audacity to challenge them.

"You see Ari, the bigger the lie the more the judge is likely to believe it. These English judges just have no bloody idea how corrupt and dishonest your countrymen can be!" and Pearson let out a chuckle of self-satisfaction.

Kandinskiy grimaced, finding the joke, at best, mildly amusing. He mostly found it insulting. While as a Russian he indulged in endless criticism of his countrymen he was completely intolerant of any foreigner daring to do the same.

The English courts had become relevant because a few international creditors, aided by the most expensive QCs (or "silks" as they were known) that money could buy, had managed to obtain what was known in English legal circles as "freezing orders", the sorts of injunctions that had the super-wealthy, who lived their lives with relative impunity, suddenly crapping in their Burberry trousers, Kandinskiy included.

"These fucking freezing orders are crushing me Spencer, you need to get them lifted pronto ..." Kandinskiy tapped on the wooden coffee table next to him, his nerves stretched due to a lack of sleep and the cocaine coursing through his veins.

"We'll take care of them Ari, don't worry," and Pearson greedily snorted the rest of the cocaine that was scattered across the coffee table and that he had now carefully collected with his black American Express card, one side of it now completely white.

Kandinskiy's best chance of getting the freezing orders lifted and regaining control of his finances lay in Pearson's ability to discredit Kandinskiy's creditors – implying that their claim to repayment of funds was tenuous at best and using every dirty trick in the book, telling every lie conceivable to throw off and disorient members of the judiciary.

And Pearson wouldn't stop there – he'd always find some way, however spurious, to get what looked like *"kompromat "* to a judge or jury and assassinate the credibility of Kandinskiy's adversaries. They'd regret the day they decided to go to court to get their money back.

At 5 am the party started to wind up. The wealthy partygoers headed out to chauffeur-driven cars that would take them back to their luxurious apartments and hotel rooms in other parts of New York City, in all cases with at least one beautiful companion from the up-market soiree.

In between animated conversation, lines of coke and glasses of Kristal champagne, Pearson had been furiously writing notes in his barely legible scrawl, a sea of squiggles, letters and numbers.

As he sped off into the night, Yolanda with him, Pearson felt a surge of contentment and satisfaction. He was about to sleep with one of the most attractive women in New York. He would make millions by saving the corporate empire of Ari Kandinskiy. He had his reputation, a loving wife and two perfect kids – he could do no wrong.

CHAPTER 10

WHEN PEARSON WOKE IN HIS HOTEL ROOM overlooking Central Park it was 9 am. Yolanda was by his side, fast asleep, the sheets draped over her in such a way that Pearson thought about spending the rest of the day in bed with her. He ran his hand over her soft, warm, voluptuous body. There was something about a woman's curves that he could just not help marvelling at.

Thoughts of a day spent in the enormous hotel bed, with silk sheets, shagging, were quickly replaced by an acute pain that started in his head and reached all the way down his neck and back, towards his lower spine.

"Christ," Pearson said to himself, audibly, waking the sleeping beauty next to him.

As he tried to deal with the pain that was almost certainly the result of excessive consumption of narcotics the night before, Pearson noticed his mobile phone flashing. He clumsily reached for it, straining every twisted muscle and nerve in his back to pick it up. Five missed calls from Kandinskiy. WhatsApp messages flickering across the screen. Something was clearly up.

It took Pearson a few minutes to stand up, put on his boxer shorts and wander to the coffee machine. It was physically and mentally impossible to form a coherent thought in the morning without first imbibing the strongest espresso coffee he could get his hands on. Kandinskiy sounded unusually stressed when he got through.

"The Chechens have taken Zelensky, my CFO," he said, his voice flat, without any energy. Kandinskiy was breathing heavily, exhaling forcefully, as if having a panic attack.

"Calm down Ari! Let's think this through," Pearson said, trying to reason with his client and friend.

"How the fuck can I calm down Spencer?" Kandinskiy yelled into his phone. "Zelensky knows everything – where all the money is kept, funds flows, the whole bloody structure of the group!! They'll beat the shit out of him to get access to this information and then leave him somewhere at the bottom of Moscow River." Kandinskiy sounded completely desperate. He hung up abruptly, leaving Pearson on his own to reflect on this latest twist.

Pearson sat himself in a large armchair in his hotel suite, next to a large window overlooking Central Park. He crossed his legs and started to ponder the situation.

This was a bold but very smart move by the Chechens. He had the impression that Akhmatov was more chess master than savage brute. Cerebral, strategic, every move was carefully orchestrated, impeccably executed.

A posse of menacing looking thugs from the "Stans" had arrived at a posh restaurant in the upmarket Patriarshiy Ponds area where Piotr Zelensky was enjoying a quiet meal with one of his mistresses (his wife and four children were at the country dacha).

The thugs cut menacing figures as they arrived at the front of the restaurant, sporting the familiar goatee beards; two stocky, smaller fighters and two more burly members of the crew in attendance just on the off-chance someone tried to intervene, or in the unlikely event that Zelensky tried to put up a fight. They breezed past the restaurant manager and security.

The leader of the crew, a wiry, intense-looking character wearing a black jacket and open-necked shirt, tattoos on hands and neck, approached Zelensky's table and calmly whispered into Zelensky's ear. He was asking Zelensky, courteously but firmly, to leave his meal and his mistress as quickly, and quietly, as possible.

Within a moment of being approached by the gang leader Zelensky realised he had an issue, likely a terrible one. As someone who had made his career in Moscow's opaque and murky business world, he knew better than most that a group of Chechens walking into a restaurant with no intention of sitting down to eat, spelt trouble. If he refused this man's request he was likely dead in a matter of seconds, a random execution in a chic Moscow restaurant, barely newsworthy.

Tall, thin, immaculately dressed and the picture of urbanity, Zelensky, still only 35, had a passion for numbers and offshore structures.

He'd very effectively helped his boss, Ari Kandinskiy, offshore much of his wealth through a complicated trading scheme with a major European investment bank, conveniently avoiding the attention of the piranhas in the Russian government (who were busily using the same elaborate scheme to steal as much of the country's wealth as they could get their own hands on – the higher up the food chain, the greater the numbers involved, the more brazen and hypocritical the behaviour).

In his late 20s, fresh from his MBA at a top US business school, Zelensky had been taken under Kandinskiy's wing. He was soon making money that was eye-watering by the standards of most young professionals his age – certainly immeasurably more than he could have hoped for when growing up in one of Moscow's grimmest suburbs.

Unlike so many of his contemporaries, Zelensky had never wanted to become a partner in a law or accounting firm, or even to join a big international company. He just wanted to get as close as possible to someone who was racing up the list of Forbes Richest Russians. His singular motivation was getting the confidence of one of the oligarchs, the mini-garchs or the uber rich living in Moscow – he knew this would be his ticket out of obscurity, away from life in the Moscow suburbs on a modest white-collar salary and a life expectancy of 60 (if he was lucky).

Zelensky had loyally served Kandinskiy and had started to take on the attributes of the nouveau riche in Moscow. A driver, fleet of expensive cars, a dacha in an exclusive gated community outside Moscow, girlfriends with expensive tastes and habits, first-class travel to increasingly expensive international destinations frequented by Russia's wealthy. It was all headed in the right direction for Zelensky until things started to unravel so badly for Kandinskiy.

Zelensky had thought about jumping ship and was probably only months, or even weeks, from doing so. But, unfortunately, he'd left his run too late – and this realisation came crashing down on him as he sat, wedged between two brutes in their black Hummer.

Despite his best efforts to control his thinking, his breathing and to stay rational, he could not help but start to panic. Thoughts of being bashed, tortured, flashed through his mind. He'd remained bizarrely composed as he was walked out of the restaurant but now the stress of the situation and the realisation of what was about to happen began to catch up with him. His hands and legs started to shake uncontrollably. He noticed he was sweating profusely. Would he ever see his kids again? His wife? Thoughts of his mistresses were long gone …

As they drove through tunnel after tunnel in the direction of west Moscow, Zelensky noticed that the Hummer was picking up speed and was actually part of a convoy of three, all Hummers, travelling in unison, through Moscow with impunity – little or no chance of getting stopped or pulled over, certainly not by any member of the Moscow traffic police.

A group of Hummers being driven by thugs in black from the "Stans" represented danger and unending bureaucratic headaches for the police if they happened to be connected to powerful politicians or businessmen in the area. The scruffy, corrupt traffic cops who lined the key junctions on the road out to west Moscow just watched as the cortege sped by at 100 kmh, grunting at their colleagues in disapproval, shrugging their shoulders as if to say "what is the point of trying to stop them?"

The commander of these Chechens, Murat Kabaev, had been a guard in the President's administration of Chechnya. He'd sworn his loyalty to the President and been rewarded with money, cars, respectability and free rein to operate in Moscow as he wished. The quid pro quo was that when called upon to protect his country's interests he asked no questions but just did what he was told.

Relaying information on a walkie-talkie to the other drivers, directing their every movement with precision befitting a Swiss watch, he was the consummate professional and leader of men. He had to be certain that the notorious FSB or "*Federalnaya Sluzhba Bezopastnosti* " (the successor agency of the KGB) had not been tipped off by a restaurant patron or disgruntled traffic cop and dispatched a unit to at least work out where Zelensky was going to be held, or killed.

As the cortege screamed out to the western suburbs of Moscow, Murat started to relay information to the person whom Zelensky presumed was the mastermind behind his kidnapping. Murat's demeanour and voice suddenly became very deferential when speaking to whoever was on the other end of the phone

As soon as the call was finished, Murat looked with undisguised menace at Zelensky, addressing him sternly.

"Do what we fucking tell you and you might come out of this in one piece. If you give us the slightest hint of trouble we go after your children, I swear to Allah."

Zelensky nodded affirmatively to Murat. He had no intention of making Murat's life difficult in any manner whatsoever. He had never in his life been more motivated to submit to the will of another human being. Breathing heavily, Zelensky could feel the air slip out of his lungs, and his heart felt like it was constricting so much he thought he'd have a heart attack there and then.

Zelensky knew as soon as he was ordered to come with his captors that they wanted access to his information on Kandinskiy's corporate empire.

He was the numbers man, with knowledge of every major asset, every major bank account, it was information that had long placed him at great physical risk – he knew in his bones that his chances of survival were very slim no matter how quickly he handed over everything he knew – he momentarily wondered if he was dreaming, but as the Hummer revved up and the grip of the goon sitting on his right side became ever tighter, he realised that this experience was all too horribly real. He'd waited too long to act, his opportunity to take the initiative and escape Ari Kandinskiy's crumbling corporate empire had come and gone …

CHAPTER 11

AS CARL FLIPPED THROUGH THE NEWSPAPERS that had been delivered to his office with his morning coffee, his thoughts wandered to the night before at the club. He had toyed with the thought of lying in bed for an additional hour or so but knew that this would just spell trouble on a day that was bound to be frenetic. His head was distinctly foggy from too much vodka, his voice hoarse from speaking to a very attractive performer over the music that blared like a 1980s rock concert.

Through the morning fog penetrating every corner of his brain he spotted an article about the disappearance of Kandinskiy's CFO. The article was nothing more than a few lines, halfway into the English language daily: *Moscow Times*. The lack of detail was not necessarily remarkable – businessmen were disappearing with increasing frequency in Moscow. But the connection with Kandinskiy made him sit up.

Before he had time to fully consider the implications of this latest development, Schwartz dialled his office phone.

"Carl," he barked into the receiver, "come to my office, there's something we need to discuss ..." and promptly hung up. Carl quickly downed the rest of his coffee, put the newspaper to one side and left his office.

As he strode towards Schwartz's office, he could see that Schwartz was seated at the small oak meeting table in his office with Jason Rogers, Roman Lebedev and a thick-set, stern-looking Russian man in his 50s, dressed in a shiny grey suit with white leather shoes.

Carl was ushered into the room by Schwartz and told to sit down next to Rogers. The men shook hands and then Schwartz got to business.

Schwartz cleared his throat, which was raspier than usual, and stank of whisky. "Carl, we've called you here today because things are getting serious with the Kandinskiy deal. They've just found the body of his CFO in a disused building site out in west Moscow – he'd been tortured very badly and had his limbs … how do we say, *removed*." Schwartz's voice trailed off, a bead of perspiration starting to form on his forehead – either the result of the previous evening's excesses or anxiety at this latest turn of events.

Rogers, who was immaculately dressed in a navy blue suit and a picture of concentration, in stark contrast to Schwartz who looked slovenly and exhausted, fixed his blue eyes on Carl and said "We think you've underestimated how dangerous this situation is Carl, we think we all have. This is not like getting things back from a business in the West, there's too much money at stake and thanks to the involvement of certain, how should I say it, *ethnic elements*, we have to tread very, very carefully."

"Carl," Rogers continued, "I'd like to introduce you to Yury Smirnov," and he nodded at the thick-set Russian man who showed all the trappings of being former Russian secret service.

"Yury is an old friend of the firm and has helped me over the years with *special assignments*; he is going to help us from an intelligence perspective, advise us what we can and cannot do here.

"He is particularly familiar with our friends from Chechnya and will finesse our approach so that we can keep all our fingers and toes, and stand a chance of getting our money back." Rogers let out a little smile.

Rogers then turned to Smirnov and nodded, inviting him to speak. In a shiny grey suit, with the neck of a heavyweight boxer, hands of a wrestler, Smirnov had the slightly clichéd look of a gangster.

While he spoke only rudimentary English, whatever he said was delivered in a precise and purposeful manner. Addressing Rogers, Schwartz and Lebedev, he placed his huge hands on the table in front of him, cleared his throat and said, "These people are very dangerous, they do not understand normal negotiation, you need to act careful, very careful. They kill for money and they enjoy it, most important, they have protection," and he gestured eastwards, towards the Kremlin visible in the distance. He exhaled and gave his shoulders a little shrug.

"I can help you – what you need is information or as we say here in Russia, "*informatzih*". It is everything, it is power, it will protect you all and protect your company. I will give Roman a list of my terms and start working, if you agree," and Smirnov, a man of very few words, particularly when not speaking his native Russian, nodded to Rogers that he had finished. With the stress of speaking

English his mouth had gone a little dry and he took a swig of the black tea he had been served.

Roman Lebedev unfolded his arms and addressed Smirnov warmly, "It's good to have you on board Yury Borisovich, we're very grateful indeed to have a man of your experience and *many talents* …"

No doubt old comrades in arms Carl thought to himself. Jason Rogers had most likely decided he needed someone with real brawn and an understanding of the new generation of hard men in Moscow. For all his old-world manner and diplomatic etiquette, Lebedev was very much a figure of a bygone era, when the enemies were external and scattered across the globe. Now, the enemies were deep inside Russian territory, and they would require an altogether different strategy to keep at bay.

As the meeting was breaking up, Schwartz shot a glance at Carl and asked him to remain in his office. He swivelled around in his chair and pointed his finger at Carl, barking in an accusatory tone "Carl, what is our fucking strategy with Kandinskiy, I need to know what you lawyers have planned – I'm sick of waiting for you to put together a fucking plan!"

But Carl was one step ahead of Schwartz. He calmly reached into his black Samsonite briefcase, picked up a manila folder and dropped it on the desk. "Klaus, you'll see we've been pretty damn busy on figuring out where to attack Kandinskiy. We've located company bank accounts in Jersey, London, the US and Panama. We've got a pretty decent picture of where he keeps a good proportion of his assets, but there's doubtless some stuff we are missing."

Schwartz grunted approvingly. His large fat fingers flipped through the pages, stopping at a photo of an elegant property sitting atop a rocky cliff.

"What the fuck is this?" he asked Carl aggressively.

"It's Villa Carnacina, Klaus, prime real estate in Monaco, one of the most expensive properties on the Mediterranean, if not the most expensive."

Thanks to his connections in the murky world of corporate investigations Carl had been able to obtain an aerial shot of the property, enormous in every respect, perched high on the Mediterranean coast, 10 kilometres from central Monaco.

Schwartz's mood improved and, sitting back in his enormous leather armchair, he asked Carl how much exactly it was worth.

"Hard to say," Carl replied, "probably well over 100 million, Klaus. It's a property with an interesting list of former owners. Idi Amin had title to it for a while but could never visit because he would have been arrested for 'crimes against humanity'."

"It was then owned by a prominent member of French industry with ties to the underworld before being sold to Kandinskiy. We think the terms of the transfer to Kandinskiy were far from transparent. He may have been hanging on to it for someone high up but that's not clear to us yet. Either way it's an asset we'd love to get our hands on. It's well over the value of our own debt. Who knows – it could even be a way of turning the whole exercise into a profitable one," and Carl looked at Schwartz who could barely disguise his glee.

"OK, get to work, I want you all over this property and the accounts wherever the fuck they are, we need to get injunctions up his wazoo pronto!!"

As Yury Smirnov's lift whizzed down to the ground floor he couldn't help thinking this latest client had no future in the new Russia. Falcon Capital had been very lucky to survive Moscow's corporate scene for this long without any proper "*krysha*" (protection), a second-rate security apparatus and declining profitability. It had benefited from the boom times in Russia when every start-up business was the next Russian equivalent of Apple or Facebook.

But as investors from both within and outside Russia started to figure out that their investments were often frittered away on private planes and grotesque villas, Falcon Capital as a champion of investment into Russia was screwed – the vultures in town would soon paw over the carcass of its business in an undisciplined feeding frenzy – it was just a question of time.

Nevertheless, Smirnov reckoned that Rogers and Schwartz would not give up without a fight – and that gave them a chance, albeit remote, of survival, at least for the foreseeable future.

CHAPTER 12

THE DAY AFTER HIS CAPTURE FROM LUNCH IN central Moscow, Zelensky woke up groggily in what he assumed was a basement somewhere in a residential house. He had a feeling of overpowering disorientation, as if he had consumed an enormous quantity of alcohol the night before.

It dawned on him very quickly that he had been drugged – with what he had no idea. His head throbbed, his heart was beating uncontrollably, he was suddenly overcome by an existential crisis. Every fibre of his being told him that his chances of leaving this place alive were remote at best.

The room, while clean and carpeted, was spartan, windowless, airless, devoid of any furnishings, almost cell-like. Zelensky heard the door open.

In walked Murat, the gang leader, walkie-talkie in one hand and clearly ready to get down to business. He gestured to Zelensky to follow him. Zelensky got up uneasily, his legs weak, the effort of standing upright almost too much for his poisoned body. He shuffled slowly behind Murat who was heading to a room down a long, dark corridor.

As he entered the room Zelensky was struck by how well lit it was. The effect on him was disorienting and he collapsed into the chair that had been placed in front of him by Murat. As he sat down and started to regain his bearings, a man of medium height, casually dressed, walked in.

Zelensky immediately recognised the man from local television – it was Ruslan Akhmatov, a Chechen businessman and reputed to be the emissary of the Chechen governor in Moscow. Having been married to a high-profile Russian Olympic swimmer, Akhmatov had shot to prominence within Russian society, but that had not tempered one bit the nature of his business affairs nor his propensity for extreme violence towards those who crossed him.

Zelensky felt his pulse race and the tremors which he was working hard to control in his hands were becoming impossible to conceal.

Akhmatov was however a picture of calm and good manners. His gestures were slow, careful and not in any way threatening or intimidating – his disposition was almost friendly. He asked one of the guards to bring Zelensky a glass of water and something to eat.

"Mr Zelensky, I am glad we can finally meet. I've heard quite a bit about you, all good things. You are clearly very good at your job. I would have very much liked to have had someone like you in my organisation."

Akhmatov sat down on a chair opposite Zelensky, his legs and arms crossed, with a thin smile etched on his face. "Let us say that it is circumstance which brings us together. You have information which I need, and I am sorry, but I had no option other than to bring you here, admittedly against your will. But if we learn to *work together*, this is for me just a temporary situation," he said in a reassuring tone.

Akhmatov continued, "I know your boss has very scrupulously hidden his assets in Russia and overseas ever since he started to make some money. I know that you are the person who has," and he paused briefly, searching for the right words, "*facilitated this process.*" He allowed himself a little smile.

"These recent months have clearly been bad for your boss but they have created opportunities, business opportunities for people like me. You see Mr Zelensky, Kandinskiy used to owe money to a friend of mine and that friend of mine has since sold his debt to me, for what we agreed was a fair market price."

Akhmatov placed his sinewy hands on the table in front of him and looked away from Zelensky. He then got up and started to pace around the room. His mind was clearly working overtime on an issue which was a major preoccupation for him. Zelensky took a sip, nervously, from the glass of water that had been served to him along with a cheese sandwich.

As if regaining concentration, "I do however," Akhmatov continued, "expect Kandinskiy to pay me back in full for my debt. My friend was probably going to be a little more, should we say, 'accommodating'," and he smiled briefly. "I am, however, from a part of the world where we are a little less flexible when it comes to recovering our debts, getting paid back money which we believe *is rightly owed to us* … I expect payment in full … and I am prepared to do *whatever* it takes to recover every kopeck that is outstanding."

Akhmatov, his sinewy hands now clenched into two large fists, took a brief pause and then continued. "I've been very, very pissed off that Kandinskiy has refused to engage with me, and fled the country like some schoolgirl – afraid of being held accountable for the consequences of his actions …"

Zelensky could not help but notice that Akhmatov's mood and demeanour had switched completely from that of someone eminently relaxed to tense, edgy and barely concealed hostility.

Indeed, Akhmatov was at first able to disguise the hostility and anger he felt towards Kandinskiy and everyone associated with him. Yet, the more he discussed Kandinskiy the more furious he became at the notion that this Jewish businessman had managed to get the better of him and evade Akhmatov's attempts to engage – until now.

Zelensky could feel sweat trickling down his back. As Akhmatov spoke, the terrible precariousness of his position hit again. Zelensky knew that it made absolutely no sense for him to be set free. A dead CFO was a far more compelling message to the creditors engulfing Kandinskiy's corporate empire than would be a CFO set free after an unpleasant overnight with Chechen heavies.

But Zelensky had not given up all hope. The sooner he divulged information about Kandinskiy's assets: the bearer shares being held by a powerful friend of Kandinskiy's worth US$500 million in a safe in central Moscow; the property near Monaco; the bank accounts in BVI and Panama where Kandinskiy still had US$200 or so million in cash stashed, the better.

Parting with the information might also bring on his premature death, but at this stage he had very few cards to deal.

Their conversation nearly at an end, Akhmatov stood up and extended his hand. Zelensky accepted, barely aware of what he was doing.

"Mr Zelensky, I wish you good luck, I'm leaving you in the capable hands of my team. I advise you to tell them everything you know, every minute detail. Once they have written everything down, they will come to me, we'll speak and if I'm happy we'll let you go. You can return to your lovely wife Ekaterina and your adorable children Misha and Sasha."

Akhmatov, like a predator toying with its prey, added finally, "It would be really awful if they had a sudden, terrible accident …"

As soon as Akhmatov left the room, Murat re-entered, a picture of seriousness, carrying a large black case. Over the next few hours with tremendous meticulousness he interrogated Zelensky regarding every aspect of his relations with Kandinskiy. He extracted all the information Akhmatov would need to get his hands on – the bearer shares, secret passwords to offshore accounts and even where Kandinskiy kept his fleet of vintage cars.

Murat's instructions were clear: as soon as Zelensky had divulged everything he knew regarding Kandinskiy's money and possessions, Murat was to leave Zelensky's body in a state that would send a message to Kandinskiy and all of his creditors that the Chechens were on the scene.

The beauty of the message was in its simplicity – fuck with us and there will be nothing in your life you regret more.

CHAPTER 13

IT HAD BEEN A FRENETIC WEEK. BY THE TIME FRIDAY evening came around Carl was completely whacked. All that he had left was the feeling of edginess that he would always try to neutralise through drinks with friends.

That was not unusual in Moscow – your average "Moskvich" started the commute to work on Monday morning, battled the metro, snow, the grumpy cohabitants, endless traffic jams all week till there was not a skerrick of energy left in them.

The weekend was a precious time to drink vodka with friends, nibble on the traditional Russian "*zakuski*" (hors d'oeuvres) and recharge their batteries.

Before he left the office, Carl remembered that he had several weeks previously accepted an invitation to a polo event in the countryside just outside Moscow. He'd at first thought of passing – who'd want to spend a whole day watching toffs on horses gallop around a paddock?

It came to him, though, on Friday evening as he was finishing up, that it would probably be useful to turn up at what was almost certainly going to be a high society event for Moscow's rich and famous.

Very likely there will be people who know Kandinskiy and potentially have an angle on the big news of the week – the kidnapping and murder of his CFO. So before leaving the office he popped in to see Vadim whom he found, looking a little dishevelled, poring through files on Kandinskiy.

"Vadim, I've got an idea for this weekend if you're free," Carl said. He was not sure whether his young protégé would be the least bit interested in what he had to propose.

Vadim sat back in his seat and smiled. "What is it Carl? The only plans I have are with my mother. That has been the same for how many weekends I don't dare to think."

"OK, great," Carl responded, "this might be a little more exciting than dinner with your mum. There's a polo event tomorrow just outside Moscow. It's being sponsored by some very posh English brands as well as some upmarket Russian ones. It could be a good opportunity for us to do something a bit different."

And then, wanting to be transparent, Carl added, "There is however a work angle to all of this. I'm pretty convinced that many of Kandinskiy's former associates will be there. It's basically going to be a who's who of Moscow business and social life. I also wouldn't mind trying to find out very subtly what the hell happened to Zelensky."

Vadim nodded approvingly, "Yes, there's almost certainly an angle for discreetly finding out what happened to him. But let's not forget such questions may not be appreciated by his former associates. We need to tread carefully there, Carl."

"OK, Vadim, got it. I won't say anything we'll regret."

Carl felt a little embarrassed that his protégé was concerned he would go off half-cocked and put them in an awkward position. But it was exactly this type of advice, this ability to orient one's way through the complexities of Moskvich society that made Vadim so valuable to him.

"Just one question Carl, what do people wear to the polo?" Vadim said, quizzically, his bushy eyebrows raised upwards as if to emphasise his curiosity.

"No idea Vadim!" Carl responded, amused by the question.

"Just try to look posh, maybe buy a copy of an English country gentleman's magazine to see what they wear – probably lots of tweed and a pair of leather boots, if you have any, can't go astray …"

CHAPTER 14

THE NEXT MORNING CARL WOKE EARLY, FEELING A little fresher than usual thanks to the first proper night's sleep in weeks. He grabbed breakfast with Vadim in the rooftop café at the Park Hyatt, overlooking the Kremlin, and spectacular views of the rest of Moscow. The weather was cool, but the sky a perfect blue, with a gentle breeze wafting through the city.

After Carl had finished his breakfast and downed his third ristretto, he phoned Valentin to arrange his pick-up. A few minutes later the Chevrolet Tahoe roared down Neglinnaya Street and came to a screeching halt in front of the hotel.

The hotel doorman Raymond greeted Carl warmly as he left the hotel.

"Off to the polo today Raymond," said Carl with a smirk.

"How very posh of you Carl, I'd expect nothing less!" and he let out one of his enormous belly laughs, slapping Carl on the shoulder.

As Carl jumped into the front of the Tahoe and Vadim into the back, he noticed that Valentin was in a buoyant mood, clearly excited by the prospect of hobnobbing with Moscow's elite. "*Davai,* let's go Carl!" Valentin said as he planted his foot on the accelerator and the Tahoe launched itself down Neglinnaya Street towards the Garden Ring and on to the northern suburbs of Moscow.

After an hour stuck in Moscow's dense morning traffic the Tahoe finally made it to the outskirts of Moscow, past the high-rise apartments that stretched for miles in every direction, constructed for the most part post World War II, in the 1960s and 70s to accommodate the hordes of Russians and migrants from Siberia and the Caucasus arriving to work in Moscow, the great metropolis which was the nerve centre of Russia and the greater Soviet Union.

Most of these buildings had by now become seriously dilapidated, the people living in them making do with lifts that barely worked, children's playgrounds stripped bare, shops that were for the most part boarded up or short on supplies.

Carl was struck by the desolation of these vast, unending rows of apartment buildings. But that was not his preoccupation today – just beyond these apartment blocks, in an immaculate birch forest, was Moscow's answer to an English polo club, with more security and firepower than Catterick or Salisbury Plain.

The vast sprawling estate of a Russian oligarch who held an iron grip on the country's packaging industry was complete with helipads that whizzed in wealthy Moscovites unwilling to brave the Moscow traffic, corporate tents full of the best vodka, caviar and wine, a car park full of Bentleys, Ferraris and Lamborghinis – it was a setting fit for a James Bond film.

Beautiful young women were everywhere, usually with men at least twice their age, and shown off like expensive accessories. All resplendent in the latest Italian designer clothes, sporting orange perma-tans – the cream of Russian society knew how to live life to the full and most importantly, how to show it off.

Carl and Vadim grabbed a glass of champagne each and started to wander through the crowd. Carl quickly spotted a familiar face, an American banker with Russian roots whom he'd met recently on a transaction he was promoting to interested investors. It had been a "high risk/high opportunity" transaction – it smelt, looked and felt like a proverbial dog turd of a deal.

In his 50s, tall, greying and 20 kilos overweight, Roman Bogdanov had grown up in New York, the son of Russian emigres who had left Russia in the 1950s. His parents had taken huge risks leaving the Soviet Union in the midst of the Stalinist repression when every defection was viewed as a crime against the country, and that would almost inevitably result in severe punishment being meted out to the families and friends of those left behind.

In the late 90s, when it was becoming evident that the opportunities in Russia were limitless for Russian speakers with US university educations, Bogdanov managed to persuade his young American bride that their future was not among the skyscrapers and wealth of Manhattan but in Russia.

It had been a fantastic career move – the young "repat" (as they were known in Moscow) had soon found himself clearing millions of dollars a year in income. Through shrewd business deals he had accumulated a portfolio of properties and assets in Moscow that were the envy of his friends back in New York.

Bogdanov was not the sort of wheeling-dealing banker to resist an opportunity to mix with the rich and powerful in Moscow society. So there he was, resplendent in tweed jacket, white open-necked shirt and Chelsea boots accompanied by his wife, a glamorous woman from New York. Married for 25 years, she'd worked hard to keep her man away from the legion of Russian beauties who circled around him like sharks.

She'd mostly avoided the temptation of plastic surgery to keep her looks, her one concession being a boob job at 45. She went to Russia's best plastic surgeon and paid well above the standard fee to have the best set of breast implants money could buy.

When Bogdanov saw Carl, he greeted him warmly, his whitened teeth glistening in the spring sun, "Carl, great to see you, fabulous event isn't it?"

"Absolutely Roman, the organisers must have spent a fortune putting this together, but I wouldn't expect less from the guy who owns this place …"

"Indeed …" Bogdanov replied, "he is one serious SOB. I've never seen so many rich assholes in one place, aside perhaps from New Year drinks at the Kremlin," and he laughed loudly, his chubby face creasing up like an old newspaper.

Carl, despite his desire to leave work behind for at least one social occasion that looked like being a lot of fun, found it impossible to avoid turning the conversation to Kandinskiy and the murder of his CFO.

"Roman, actually I'm very happy I bumped into you," and he paused momentarily, wondering how best to begin a conversation on a subject that he knew would be an uncomfortable one for Bogdanov.

"It's been a rough week, this Kandinskiy thing is causing me one enormous fucking headache – we're having a terrible time figuring out what we are meant to do next … but the bastard owes us a lot of money so," he said, scratching his head pensively, "I wonder if you have any thoughts on how we can get to Kandinskiy to have a conversation …"

Bogdanov's demeanour changed quickly. Gone was the air of frivolity and bonhomie. "Carl, I'll be honest with you – be very careful here. The people involved in this are serious players, right behind the president and the Chechen governor."

He gestured to Carl to follow him to another tent where drinks were being served from a huge bar covered in bottles of Moët in silver ice buckets.

Resting his hand on Carl's shoulder, he said out of earshot of the other guests, "This city is undergoing a profound shift – the days of the private Russian businessman are ... OVER!" and he gestured with his hands a little dramatically to emphasise the point.

Bogdanov was just getting warmed up. He looked around almost furtively and continued, "The people behind the president are encroaching on everything – you guys in your little western investment bank have absolutely no fucking chance here – they'll fuck you a thousand times over before they give you a penny."

Carl instantly regretted speaking to Bogdanov – the little sermon was rapidly taking the fun out of the polo. But Bogdanov, although he sensed Carl's discomfort, was not finished, his fat hands moving in an animated fashion, his index finger thrusting outwards when he wanted to make a point.

"Carl, I can sense storm clouds on the horizon. Just when things start looking good here it really means it's time to get out. For over a hundred years now this country has lived with political turbulence and upheaval. Finally we emerge from the abyss, start making some money, develop western-style institutions, in our own special way of course (and he smiled at Carl), but things just go back to the way they always were ..."

"I met the guy, the CFO," Bogdanov continued, "very smart guy. We pitched a few deals to him including how to restructure Kandinskiy's debts. But they were a little greedy, well Kandinskiy was anyway. We knew they had some assets they could have liquidated to pay off creditors but Kandinskiy just didn't want to.

"Anyway, now you know the story, this city is about to blow up due to the shit-fight between people trying to get their hands on what is left in Moscow," and Bogdanov's attention switched to a helicopter that was descending, no doubt bringing another well-heeled Moscovite to the event.

"Anyway Carl, I'd rather not spoil your day with this stuff. Please – enjoy yourself – life is too short to worry about business all the time! Go and find yourself a pretty young Russian girl who can keep you company tonight," and he laughed loudly, nodding to his wife to follow him as he moved on to the other tent.

Bogdanov was an enigma, Carl thought to himself, as he watched the Russian "repat" banker wander off. No doubt his advice was good. Carl knew that Bogdanov had an antenna for Russian politics and intrigue that few other people in the city possessed.

As Carl headed back towards the polo ground he saw that the first "chukka" was underway, horses and their riders darting around the field chaotically, like dancers in an impromptu tribal dance. The riders flew down the pitch effortlessly – the thoroughbred horses crashing against each other and generally behaving like impatient commuters in the Moscow metro.

One young competitor took a risk too many and found himself flying off his horse headfirst into the pitch. The second before impact he did, however, manage to stick out his hands to cushion his fall, the crowd collectively breathing an enormous sigh of relief. He was whisked off into an ambulance as a precautionary measure.

That first chukka ended up being much more eventful than the spectators had anticipated and everyone cheered raucously when the siren sounded.

As the alcohol flowed, the band of wealthy socialites in one of the corporate tents was starting to get into the party spirit, the polo a purely secondary consideration. Scantily clad women in their late teens and early twenties danced with men at least twice their age, moving around the dance floor effortlessly while their older, fatter companions struggled to keep up.

The barmen worked at breakneck speed to keep up with the orders of vodka shots, flaming sambucas, mojitos and Bloody Marys – all guzzled down by the enthusiastic partygoers, many of them at regular intervals slipping out to the mobile toilets at the back of the bar to top themselves up on cocaine and any other drug they could get their sweating paws on.

Carl spotted Vadim smoking a cigarette, sipping a glass of beer, looking a little out of place in his ill-fitting black suit.

"I tried to get some information on Kandinskiy and his CFO, but no one is opening up. Everyone is scared," he told Carl.

"I have the impression that we are not far from the truth of what happened, the killers may very well be here for all I know ..." and he stubbed out his cigarette on the grass underfoot.

At the other end of the field, which was now full of spectators pushing in divots to flatten out the playing surface, Carl spotted Igor Cherney. Resplendent in the finest tweed, accompanied by a very buxom blonde in a skirt barely big enough for a Barbie doll he could not help but feel a pang of envy.

What an impostor Carl thought to himself. His hair slicked back, as if to restrain his scalp, Cherney strode around the playing field kicking in the divots in his riding boots. His buxom blonde was anything but impressed and clearly irritated that her favourite pair of Jimmy Choos were getting wrecked.

"I didn't come her for this!" she barked at Cherney more than once. But he was completely impervious to her complaints, too engrossed in repairing the polo pitch.

When Carl spotted Cherney he was in two minds as to whether to say hello. But he knew that he couldn't pass up the chance to see what Cherney was up to, so he walked up to him and extended his hand.

Cherney shook it warmly. "Carl, good to see you," he said with genuine warmth. "I hope you realise that the other day I had my 'tough' face on. Today I am more focused on enjoying myself socially so I'm quite a different proposition," and he laughed, instantly putting Carl at ease.

"That's encouraging, Igor," Carl responded, "so I take it you're now willing to make me a half decent offer for the Kandinskiy loan?" and he smiled, a little pensively, unsure as to whether his half-joking query would be well received by the Russian. He hadn't noticed at their last meeting but Cherney had a small tic, a tremor which ran down the side of his face at regular intervals, causing a slight spasm in the left corner of his mouth.

But Cherney was not taking the bait and quickly switched gears. "Did you make any progress internally with that matter we discussed earlier in the week?"

"Not as yet Igor, I was more keen to establish what the hell happened to Kandinskiy's CFO – anything I need to worry about?"

Igor stopped for a minute, grabbed a glass of champagne and gestured to Carl to join him beside one of the less festive corporate tents where corpulent businessmen were sipping cognac and smoking shisha pipes, sprawled on enormous sofas.

"Carl," he began, "there is a major shift in power occurring in the hunt for Kandinskiy's assets. It's coming because our friends from the 'Stans' are pushing very hard for a piece of the action. They have worked their way into this deal – that's why I tried very diplomatically to reason with you in our meeting that the deal I was offering was a good one."

Cherney checked himself momentarily and took a look around. "Your management needs to realise that there have been seismic shifts in the power base in this city – the old bosses are gone – the new guys on the block are in their thirties, and they're much tougher, meaner and smarter than the old generation. I have to keep them happy as well as letting the more established guys have the feeling they're not getting shat upon ..."

A bead of sweat dribbled down Cherney's forehead and when he looked away across the polo fields Carl noticed that he suddenly looked tired and far less dominant and authoritarian than he had the other day in their meeting, when it was him, Cherney, dictating terms and making it clear who was boss.

Igor Cherney had found himself in a very uncomfortable position. He was hemmed in from every side. The Kremlin, Chechens, Dagestanis, oligarchs, investment banks, Russian companies all wanted their piece of the pie that had been Kandinskiy's corporate empire.

Juggling the various interests was proving to be an extremely complicated exercise, one which Cherney and even the heavyweight interests he represented in Moskvy Neft had underestimated.

"Ruslan Akhmatov was here today with his entourage if you didn't already notice," he said to Carl. "He showed up with his usual band of heavies – they scared the shit out of a few people partying – girls in skimpy dresses – too much for the organisers to handle. We thought they were going to abduct the girls at one point.

"Anyway, after security was called they eventually left, not that security could have stopped them. These people are extremely difficult to manage Carl. I'd strongly recommend you play ball and focus on making money for your investment bank ..." After a final and cursory handshake Cherney wandered off to see his girlfriend.

He'd clearly had enough of talking to Carl about the deal that was either going to mark his arrival on the Moscow corporate and political scene, or his demise.

Indeed, after the confrontation with heavily armed security guards, Akhmatov's cavalcade of Hummers had flown out of the polo grounds in north Moscow earlier that afternoon – kicking up dust, covering any unfortunate in the vicinity with dirt and exhaust fumes.

"Fucking spoilt Moskvich," thought Akhmatov as he gestured at Murat to get his contingent on the road and back to his residence in Rybolovka, the suburb of choice for wealthy politicians (*siloviki*) and oligarchs, not to mention the very luxurious and ever-expanding mansion of the President.

"Every fucking time I attend one of their high society parties they look at me like I'm some caveman who's came out to spoil their party!" Akhmatov yelled at Murat.

Murat was driving the lead car, a black V-8 Mercedes jeep, the preferred car of gangsters and drug dealers in Moscow. He pushed and agitated, revving the engine, flashing lights through the traffic jam leading all the way back to Moscow. He had a way of making traffic part for him that was unique and meant that Akhmatov would never have to spend more than 30-40 minutes getting to just about any part of Moscow, no matter how many *"probki"* (traffic jams) there were.

Murat was going to drop off Akhmatov and then take his comrades out for a well-earned night on the town. Murat and his gang were accustomed to walking into any popular nightclub, unimpeded by security, and watching while other patrons scurried out to avoid the violence and chaos that might follow.

As a devout Muslim, Murat would never drink, preferring to smoke kalian, or shisha pipe, popular with Moscovites and a fixture of just about any bar or café in his home town of Grozny, Chechnya. He would, if he could find the time, pray at least a few times a day – impossible with Akhmatov's routine to pray any more often. He never swore, and objected to anyone in the team using foul language.

However despite his religious piety, Murat was capable of carrying out the most violent, sadistic acts imaginable on the orders of his boss. Nor would he ever for a minute reflect on what those acts meant in the grand scheme of things or whether there was a moral boundary he had overstepped.

Zelensky's end was one of the worst in terms of callousness. He had screamed, sobbed, begged for mercy, squealing with pain at various stages and probably dying of heart failure before Murat had been able to finish sawing off his leg.

Murat left Zelensky's battered corpse next to an underpass out in far west Moscow, conspicuous enough to be discovered within a few hours by an unlucky passerby. With flecks of dried blood and Zelensky's hair on his hands and clothes, having deposited the corpse, Murat left the site with a clean conscience and positive disposition. He'd had a busy day, carried out all the wishes of his boss with immaculate precision – what more satisfaction could any working man want from his job?

CHAPTER 15

AFTER THE POLO CARL HEADED BACK TO MOSCOW through the *probka* that Murat had so successfully negotiated earlier that afternoon. A slow crawl back to Moscow, no less than two and a half hours. Torrential rain was followed by a few rays of sunshine and a more or less decent evening.

Vadim was asleep in the back of the car, the mix of hot, humid weather, free champagne and the occasional excitement at the polo match having taken its toll. Valentin was driving. He had spent the day talking to the other drivers about their conditions, their bosses, how much money their bosses made and where they ranked in the pecking order of Moscow society. It didn't bother him one bit that his boss was lower down the social hierarchy than just about everyone else there.

Valentin had driven for Russians. He swore that he would rather clean windows or clean toilets than put up with the constant humiliations meted out to him by his countrymen.

On the long drive back he grilled Carl about the various businessmen there, asking who held real power and made the real money. "There were a lot of those people there today Val," replied Carl. "But one thing to bear in mind, fortunes can change very fast, put your head too high above the parapet and it will get shot off – just look at Kandinskiy, we all have to be careful in this city …"

"I know," replied Valentin, "most of these guys have lied and cheated their way to the top, while people like me, from the middle of nowhere, have no chance of getting anywhere near them – we just keep our heads down, earn our money and shut up, and pray for a day when things will even out here, at least a little."

Valentin, who was in a reflective mood, continued. "You know Carl, my father was a war hero, he fought in the Great Patriotic War, survived for three years, and entered Berlin. He has enough medals to fill a wall, and yet he earns barely enough money now to pay for his heart medication. The pension has been cut back so much that he can barely feed himself. Under the old Soviet system, with all its problems, that was just unthinkable, we had a sense of camaraderie then, this new life dominated by *kapitalism* is killing the soul of Russia."

For Valentin, the latest preoccupation which kept him awake at night was the looming military service faced by his eldest son.

Russian military service was a brutal affair. Eighteen-year-old kids in Russia faced compulsory military service for two years.

In Valentin's time it had been more or less bearable. He'd been sent off to the Far East, near Vladivostok and very quickly put in charge of a contingent of young conscripts. His supervisors had warmed to him quickly. Despite the ordeal of being so far away from his home on the Black Sea, and unaccustomed to the freezing weather in the Far East, Valentin was physically strong and quick witted and this, along with a positive disposition, allowed him to earn his stripes quickly, and to rise rapidly through the ranks.

But things had changed in the Russian military since the fall of the Soviet Union. Often under-resourced and poorly equipped, the military had been sent twice to fight in Chechnya. The officers who served there had come back changed, brutalised men. The training of young soldiers had become an often-savage exercise, with military trainers embittered by falling salaries, lack of discipline and purpose, and angry about the selfishness and obsession with financial wealth that had taken over the rest of Russian society.

If the minister of defence and generals in the Russian army could live in extraordinary comfort and wealth, why should the real hard men of the Russian military, the soldiers who fought their wars and risked their lives for their country, get a pittance? If they were unlucky enough to die, or worse still, be maimed in some foreign conflict, thousands of kilometres from their homeland, their families would be left destitute.

The result was horrific "hazing" and brutalising of young recruits – episodes that could maim young men, even kill them. Valentin expected that his son Maxim, a sickly boy who'd not inherited any of the toughness and fortitude of his father, would last at best six months before he was thrown into hospital – or a cemetery.

Valentin had to figure out how to get the ten thousand dollars he would need to buy his son's exemption from military service. For him that was nearly six months' salary, wiping out the small savings he'd accumulated and was hoping to invest in a business plan to allow him to quit working as a chauffeur. He'd had various ideas, some legal and some not. Perhaps he'd be forced to ask help from Carl. But asking your boss for additional money was not something he wanted to do, no matter how good their working relationship.

As they made their way back to central Moscow, Carl got a call from Benny. "Whass up mate," he said in his distinctive, scattergun New York accent, "let's grab a drink somewhere, Jean Jacques?"

"Yeah Benny why not," Carl responded a little flatly.

Although thoroughly knackered from filling in divots, and questioning Moscow's high society on the latest brutal murder, Carl decided that a drink with Benny was exactly the distraction he needed from chasing debtors and avoiding the associated occupational hazards.

The bar Jean Jacques was pumping, full of its usual bohemian crowd and thick with smoke and the smell of old beer and wine. Litres of the stuff had infused every corner of the bar and restaurant over the past 20 or so years since it had opened. Benny was on top form, already on his fourth beer and in animated conversation with some cute student types sitting next to him. Carl pulled up a chair next to Benny and ordered a beer from the overworked waitress who was gliding between tables.

"These girls are right up for it mate, I'm tellin' ya," said Benny to Carl as he walked in. "Check out the blonde in the corner there, she has got some rack ..." Carl didn't bother pointing out to Benny that he was happily married with a wife and three adorable daughters. Like many married expat men in Moscow, Benny had fallen under the spell of the local beauties.

Some men managed to fight off temptation, but others succumbed, eventually taking things a step too far and falling into a trap they could rarely extricate themselves from.

"Benny, back to the topic my friend," Carl admonished, "I need your intel on the Kandinskiy thing – what are your sources telling you?"

Benny let out a deep laugh and said in his raspy New York accent, "Ah so now you want to talk to me! Finally the powers that be realise I'm someone to be listened to," he said half in jest and half seriously.

"Listen," he continued, "a little birdy told me that Pearson and Kandinskiy made it back to town this morning on Kandinskiy's jet. Which, and I don't need to tell you, is a very bold move given the fact that he is probably next on the list to get whacked. Zelensky's death was just horrible," he said looking away, "it's impossible to think Kandinskiy would fare any better."

"Why on earth did Kandinskiy come back?" asked Carl. "What's the point? I mean the guy is running a huge fucking risk … why is his lawyer here?"

Carl sat back in his chair and took a swig of his beer. He felt much better, the champagne had worn off and been replaced with a sense of fatigue, foreboding – the beer was now rejuvenating him – just what he needed.

"I reckon he's been asked to see someone really high up, the sort of person who doesn't go in for Skype, the sort of person YOU come and see, not the other way around," said Ari.

That made sense thought Carl – if someone in the Kremlin wants to ensure his cut of the action then the only way to be certain Kandinskiy is not going to screw him is to get him to come to town. Either way, whoever it is, must have some pretty damn good leverage with Kandinskiy for him to risk his life.

"OK, mate that is really good information. I don't suppose we're any chance to meet with Kandinskiy but I'll have to tell Rogers and Klaus – they may have some ideas. By the way who is 'little birdy'? I'd love to know where you get your information from."

"I can't possibly tell you that Carl – telling you would completely spoil the point of having a little birdy!" replied Benny, a broad grin over his face.

He enjoyed having something over Carl and his colleagues at Falcon Capital. It made him feel useful and needed in an institution where he'd started to feel redundant, like a piece of old unused furniture days away from being thrown into a dingy basement.

"What I can tell you is that I might be able to get some more information from this person, but I'm taking a risk here. I'd want Rogers and Klaus to 'look after me' if you get my drift."

Carl had been expecting this. No-one, even colleagues, ever did anything for free in Moscow. He couldn't blame Benny for wanting a few extra bucks, especially if he was putting his neck on the line.

"OK, I'll see what I can do. Just don't forget that no-one gets anything until we get a result – funds have to trickle back to us before we can start popping champagne corks and expecting payments offshore my friend!"

But Benny's attention had since wandered back to the table of young students he'd been flirting with. As the one with a generous cleavage started to get more and more flushed with wine and beer, her hair messy and eyes darting over to Benny at every opportunity, Benny realised that this was a chance too good to pass up and he made a beeline for her, beckoning the waitress to bring over a bottle of their finest French red.

Taking his cue, Carl wandered back to his apartment. The few beers he'd downed in Jean Jacques had brought a little spring in his step but he knew the feeling would be short lived.

The mood dampened when he saw his mobile ringing – Klaus Schwartz. As he picked up he could immediately sense Schwartz was in a state of high irritation, breathing heavily down the phone, seemingly struggling for oxygen. He must have just finished fucking some bimbo Carl thought to himself.

"Kandinskiy is here Carl, he's bloody here for some reason. We have to get a hold of him before he leaves the country – we've got to speak to him, get security on to it pronto!!"

"Klaus I'm all over it like a fly on shit," responded Carl, "Anyway we've got bugger-all chance of getting to him. He's come in a cavalcade of security and been escorted to the Ministry of Defence. He's probably on the way back to the airport by now, but I'll do what I can."

Carl knew his answer would send Klaus into a rage. Klaus only wanted to hear that things were being fixed, not that they were beyond hope.

"Just fooking do what I say," he said in his thickest Austrian accent.

Carl had noticed before that when he got angry Klaus lost any semblance of refinement and reverted to what he was – a thug from a provincial town somewhere in Austria, used to getting his own way and intolerant of failure.

CHAPTER 16

KANDINSKIY WAS NOTORIOUSLY CAREFUL WHEN IT came to security. He'd made it through the 90s by cheating and stealing from a whole range of people, some dangerous and some not, but he knew it took just one really disgruntled ex-creditor, for a modest fee, to retire you to some overgrown, grey cemetery on the outskirts of Moscow. So, since the chaotic 90s Kandinskiy had never left his house without a retinue of bodyguards, mostly Israeli.

His wife Anna had refused to be surrounded by her husband's security, fearing they would be there principally to spy on her for her husband rather than to protect her. Kandinskiy had heard rumours of his wife's nocturnal activities and liaisons but she had been incredibly discreet, far more so than him, so he felt he could never complain.

As he touched down at Vnokuvo airport that morning with a very pensive Pearson, he felt a shot of nervous energy and exhilaration as his plane made contact with Russian soil. What is it about his home country, he thought, that inspired such fear but that he couldn't resist returning to? Every other country he visited, and he'd been to more than he could remember, felt underwhelming by comparison. None had the drama, the history, the danger offered by his homeland.

For Pearson the sentiment was altogether different. Although battle hardened through years of defending clients against regulators, rival businessmen and hardened criminals, he felt unbridled anxiety about having to follow his client into this hornet's nest. Despite the extreme brevity of the trip (16 hours – they'd be leaving that evening), he realised the extreme danger they had put himself in.

If Akhmatov's men could get hold of Kandinskiy (and Pearson), at best they were a chance of a brutal beating and the theft of everything Kandinskiy had to his name – not to mention the end of Pearson's brilliant plan to make millions for himself.

But the Engishman had eventually succumbed to his client's entreaties to help him negotiate his exit from Russia –despite his instinct for self-preservation, he had to take this final risk, a risk that would be sweetened by a monumental payment to his offshore account if all went to plan.

Kandinskiy was being a little dishonest with himself in thinking that his temporary return to Moscow was driven principally by nostalgia for his home country. It wasn't the first time he'd convinced himself that his motives were entirely honourable. In reality he knew that the only reason that he'd come back was to meet with Igor Melnikov, the powerful Minister for Armaments who was on the rise, one of the key fixers in the government and, if all went to plan, a future prime minister.

Melnikov lapped up spare cash and ensured that wherever there was a big deal happening on Russian territory or between wealthy Russians, the right people in government got paid. It meant he could charge a generous commission for his services, by sparing more senior ministers direct involvement and potential embarrassment if discovered.

To get to this position the Minister had had to liquidate a number of pretenders to the same post. But Melnikov was always smart enough to put sufficient distance between him and the unfortunate victim of a home invasion gone wrong, or a helicopter accident that the investigating authorities could not explain.

As their motorcade left the airport, Pearson noticed that they were being followed by men in military uniform, in black 4x4s with distinctive red number plates. The escort was there on the orders of Melnikov who did not want any Chechen, Dagestani or member of the FSB to spoil his payday. Melnikov also had to watch out for Igor Cherney whose position at the behemoth Moskvy Neft was a direct risk to the Minister's access to Kandinskiy's remaining assets.

As they sped towards the Ministry of Defence building, sitting on Moscow River in the Khamovniki District, they passed the tall, thin birch trees that line the roads into Moscow. Kandinskiy was fidgeting nervously. Although he and Pearson had gone through the strategy for their meeting with Melnikov at least ten times, rehearsed every conceivable outcome, he could not underestimate Melnikov's ability to spring some demand on him.

As Kandinskiy saw it, the deal was going to be the following – he'd jotted it down after speaking to Melnikov on a secure line from New York the week previous:

- 25% of the shares in his failing property empire for approximately US$200m, much less than he'd wanted to accept but he knew that he'd never survive a restructuring of his business in Russia – so getting some cash out of the company he'd spent 20 years building up was not an altogether bad return;

- his wife would be allowed to keep her paintings, properties and all the other assets he'd transferred to her just before they divorced earlier in the year;

- protection from the siloviki, the Chechens and the other existential threats he faced in Russia;

- he'd be able to keep his properties in New York and Israel, but he'd have to give up the prized house near Monaco, the US$200m villa which had been owned by an African dictator and which he'd used to entertain the high and mighty, prominent businessmen, politicians and posh society types. (Whenever he'd been close to a big deal or needed the help of a politician to wreck the business of a competitor – or worse – he'd fly them to the villa. He'd entertain them with lavish parties; if they were into beautiful women he'd arrange for the most beautiful money could buy to spend a few days with him and his guests and indulge them in any manner they requested. He'd hand over bags of cash and gold to customs and trade officials who were spellbound by the opulence of the villa, the gardens and the infinity pool looking out over the Mediterranean).

But Melnikov could not guarantee him that he'd be able to keep the Chechens away forever. No matter how powerful Melnikov had become, Chechen influence had grown. Like a rapidly advancing cancer they had obtained their foothold in the Kremlin, penetrated deep into Russian business by taking positions in the country's best energy businesses, directorships on boards. They now wielded enormous power and influence, all supported and bankrolled by the local governor, himself very cashed up thanks to years of steady oil receipts. The Chechens' unpredictability and capacity for extreme violence meant that they could never be ignored or disregarded.

As the cortege got closer to MOD headquarters, Kandinskiy spotted people jogging and rollerblading down Moscow River, and the pristine boats of Moscow's top hotels dropping their glamorous, well-heeled guests off at the newly renovated Gorky Park just across the river. What he'd do to be with them now rather than going to meet Melnikov.

Kandinskiy momentarily missed the freedom associated with being anonymous and unknown – it had been such a long time since he could walk on his own without fear of being shot or blown up.

As he entered the building through MOD security he could not help but be impressed by the wall of precautions that greeted him. There were no fewer than three checkpoints, the guards at each one treating him with great suspicion. All in immaculate uniforms, at every checkpoint the security guard would take his and Pearson's passport, review it in detail and look each of them up and down, once satisfied just nodding that they were to go to the next step of the process. Pearson was doing his best to keep his cool but it was clear to Kandinskiy that the lawyer was finding this atmosphere oppressive.

Finally through the last checkpoint, the two men were made to walk down a very long corridor, at first very dimly lit and then, as if someone was playing with the lights, the corridor became brighter, oppressively so.

Kandinskiy and Pearson could see names on the doors of the windowless offices they passed but did not have time to take any of them in – the agent accompanying them was heading to the office at the very end of the corridor.

Once inside they were greeted by Melnikov, slick, well dressed, Armani glasses placed carefully on his long, angular nose. He was holding a cigarette in a small white holder, puffing away with an air of relaxed detachment. "Guys, great to see you," he said with a smile that Pearson found distinctly insincere. But he'd expect nothing less from a *chinovnik* who'd risen as far and fast as Melnikov.

Melnikov gestured to them to sit on the long, very expensive-looking sofa in the middle of his very spacious office, decked out with what looked like the latest Roche Bobois furniture, direct from Paris. On a coffee table sat an immaculate cigar box which Melnikov opened, offering his guests a range of expensive Cuban cigars. Kandinskiy and Pearson politely declined.

"Gentlemen, getting down to business," Melnikov opened in his thick Russian accent, speaking in English to accommodate Pearson, "it's good that you have been able to come here today. I have received an order from up high (and his eyes gestured to the ceiling) that we need to sign over the Monaco villa as quickly as possible. The rest of the deal will have to wait, the villa has become the priority," and he looked very deliberately at both Kandinskiy and Pearson who, despite their seemingly endless preparation, had not anticipated this development.

"Igor," responded Kandinskiy, "we came here today at great personal risk to finalise this '*matter*'. We have been working on an agreement for months, we didn't come here just to hand over the villa. I mean that's crazy," and he started to raise his voice, clearly angry that Melnikov had changed the parameters of their meeting so drastically.

Pearson, in an effort to subdue Kandinskiy, interjected, "Hey, let's give Igor a chance to explain every element of the deal on offer," and he nodded to Melnikov to continue.

Melnikov feigned surprise and slight offence at Kandinskiy's reaction. But given Pearson's prompting, he continued, comfortable in the knowledge that his guests were in no position to negotiate – they had lost all their leverage by showing up in the hornet's nest.

"The villa is but one part of the puzzle, but an important one. I don't need to tell you Ari Petrovich how much this place means to someone I am representing."

Kandinskiy had long feared that glossy photos of the Monaco villa would show up in the offices of the Prime Minister and that the lure of owning premier coastal property within spitting distance of the Mediterranean's most exclusive casinos would prove too much of a temptation.

Indeed, rumours abounded in Moscow society of the vast wealth which had been accumulated by this most unpopular and unprepossessing of men. Playing second fiddle to the President was not an easy job but with a hide like a rhino, completely impervious to criticism, the Prime Minister was ideal for his anointed role.

The villa would be a nice weekend get-away destination, assuming he could ever enjoy a life after Russian politics, given the numerous enemies he had accumulated over the years – on both sides of the political divide. Easy to protect, out of reach of the prying eyes of journalists, it would soon become a priority for the Prime Minister in the horse-trading over the remains of Kandinskiy's empire.

Melnikov started tapping his Mont Blanc pen on the coffee table. He watched both Kandinskiy and Pearson with great attention, waiting for the first of them to give up. He gently placed a short document in Russian and English before both men, asked them to review it, and if all was in order then Kandinskiy would sign, with formalities regarding the transfer of the Monaco villa to follow in the days to come as expensive offshore lawyers transferred from one offshore trust to another. The transaction would be handled with absolute confidentiality and, like just about any sale of super-expensive property in London or New York, no-one inspecting the title deeds would have the slightest idea who really owned the property in question.

Kandinskiy breathed in deeply and asked for five minutes with Pearson. Melnikov got up, grabbed his phone and escorted them to a neighbouring meeting room.

"I knew this son of a bitch would pull this stunt. We're fucked aren't we, there's nothing we can do?" he asked Pearson as soon as Melnikov closed the door of the meeting room. Pearson was doing his best to remain rational, aloof from the situation but it was extremely difficult.

"Ari, I can't imagine us getting too far if you don't sign. Certainly not back to Vnokuvo. So yes, on this leg we are pretty screwed. But we still have skin in the game, you have your shares and if he wants any part of that he needs to play ball. It may well be the truth that he just can't negotiate for the villa, he has to have it. Maybe we should have burned it down when we had the chance and collected the insurance …"

Kandinskiy punched the oak coffee table with his fist and grabbed the Montblanc pen that Melnikov had left for him. He hurriedly signed the paper and got up to return to Melnikov's office. The Russian Minister for Armaments had deftly exploited Kandinskiy's lack of leverage. But he had underestimated his older countryman's resourcefulness and appetite for a fight. Ari Kandinskiy would not give up that easily.

CHAPTER 17

COMMISSIONER SOLOVIEV WOKE AT AROUND 7.30 am, far too early, considering he'd got to sleep at 4 am. A stale taste of booze and cigarettes in his mouth, annoyed with himself for having had another blowout before an important day as head of Moscow's tax police, or 'nalogovy inspektor', he'd not been able to resist the charms of the muscular, olive-skinned twenty or so-year-old young man he'd spotted on the dance floor earlier in the evening.

He'd spent the evening at his favourite underground gay club. Located on the Moscow River near a complex of factories, abandoned at the end of the Soviet period, the club was sufficiently far from central Moscow to escape roving bands of homophobes keen to kick and punch the life out of the city's gay population, as well as being hard for the police to raid without giving good notice to patrons, who would fly out of the place, drugs in hand, at the slightest sign of trouble.

Soloviev had taken his regular table at the club, in the mezzanine overlooking the dance floor. He puffed away on cigarettes and kalian pipe, ordered bottles of champagne (Krug, nothing else) and would keep a predatory eye on the young men dancing below. He'd always come with heavies from the inspectorate. If he spotted someone he liked, his security detail would frogmarch the unsuspecting patron upstairs and he'd be forced to sit with Soloviev for hours, drinking, smoking and getting high. Then without exception these younger men would find themselves at Soloviev's ultra-modern apartment in one of the new skyscrapers at Moscow City, paid for out of funds embezzled from the Tax Inspectorate account.

Misha, the twenty-year-old aspiring actor from Vladivostok had been the target of Soloviev's desires the previous evening and he'd not disappointed. Misha had grown up in a poor family on the outskirts of Vladivostok. With an alcoholic father and a beaten-down mother who'd given up on life, as early as he could remember he'd wanted to get out of his home, away from his family and out of Vladivostok. With his striking Eurasian looks and a talent for acting which had been spotted in his local school, he'd realised at a very young age that his future lay in Moscow, not in the far-flung provinces.

He'd arrived in Moscow aged eighteen, shacked up with an older Russian woman who'd promised him entrée into the acting scene in Moscow, but just used him as a toyboy to satisfy her sexual desires.

A friend from his home-town who was also looking to break into Moscow's world of showbiz had advised Misha to seek a wealthy gay man as patron.

"They will do anything to keep you if you screw them well," his friend had advised. "Presents, watches, money, introductions, whatever the fuck you want … they're crawling all over the entertainment world and know all the stars, it's a fantastic way to get ahead."

Misha had taken the advice. He'd visited all the gay clubs but never struck it big. But his intuition had told him that things might be different this time with Soloviev. With a large retinue of bodyguards this guy had to be a player, he had to be someone important in Moscow and he likely had access, but to whom, and to what?

After an hour or two of boring conversation over champagne and the best cocaine money could buy, Soloviev invited Misha back to his Moscow City apartment where they screwed angrily, like mating chimpanzees for an hour before the effect of the alcohol and drugs became too strong to resist and they collapsed, together, into a deep slumber.

When he woke a few hours later, Misha saw Soloviev standing over him next to the bed with a coffee in his outstretched hand. Soloviev gently asked him to get dressed and leave the apartment. He had a busy day and had to put himself in the right frame of mind – staring at a naked Misha was not going to help him with that.

After a brief embrace, Soloviev asked Misha if he'd like to catch up again. He'd had the best fuck in recent memory. Misha ticked all the boxes, he was just the candidate for a short, passionate affair.

"Yeah of course, you let me know when and where," Misha replied, smiling with satisfaction that he'd made an impression on this man of influence. He handed Soloviev a piece of paper with his number scrawled on it. Soloviev carefully put it in his wallet, smiled and Misha left, taking the elevator down the side of the glass skyscraper overlooking Moscow River. "He must be seriously fucking rich if he can afford to live here," Misha thought to himself as the escalator sped towards the ground floor.

As Soloviev headed to the office in his convoy of black Mercedes, his personal assistant handed him a file on Falcon Capital. After the embarrassment of the recent raid Soloviev had realised he'd not done his homework properly on that company. This time he'd leave no stone unturned and he'd inflict as much financial pain as possible on the selfish, naïve expats who ran the operation, not to mention destroy the local Russians who'd decided to make their beds with them.

Thanks to connections in the FSB, Soloviev's Tax Inspectorate had been able to obtain some very confidential information regarding Falcon Capital's offshore operations, which, despite management's precautions, were not quite so secret after all.

As with just about every major company in Russia, Falcon Capital's phone lines were tapped. Nearly every senior person there was being listened to at some point or another. Management knew they were being listened to and execs were told to speak in codewords and riddles on sensitive matters to avoid incriminating themselves.

After a while, though, even bankers working on the most aggressive, compromising structures would get careless and have code names muddled up so they would inevitably provide people like Soloviev with information they craved.

It was clear that Falcon Capital had been very aggressive in their tax optimisation. Houses on Lake Geneva, yachts moored on the Côte d'Azur, supermodels, champagne, high-class hookers were all features of the executive lifestyle there and Soloviev was confident that if he could get his hands on some hard financial data, not the heavily doctored accounts signed off by internal management, he would have enough dirt on them to take them down and stick them all in a far-flung Siberian prison for at least a few years.

However, as the man who held the keys to protection from the tax authorities, he had a better idea – one that would benefit him far more lucratively.

If he could intimidate Schwartz and Rogers into thinking that they were toast, he might be able to drive them towards a "bilateral" arrangement that would cost them millions but would buy them protection from the tax police for a few years at least – maybe longer if Soloviev could hold on to his position for long enough.

Schwartz had, two years previously, decided to push the envelope a little on the company's tax bill to improve end-of-year numbers and feather his own nest a little. He had developed an "off balance sheet" scheme which was elaborate, even by his standards, and involved just about every shady offshore financial centre known to man.

The structure chart alone ran to no less than ten pages of graphs and detailed financial modelling – it was the kind of document that, if it got into the wrong hands, could put him in a Russian penitentiary for the rest of his life.

Nevertheless, it was a risk Schwartz was prepared to run. His lavish lifestyle had become increasingly difficult to finance – even with his already humungous salary and bonus. He was putting up two separate working girls in apartments in central Moscow, paying for their drivers, fur coats, gym memberships, Vuitton handbags, spa treatments and copious quantities of expensive champagne.

It only a matter of time before Soloviev would, like a bloodhound, discover Schwartz's dirty little secret.

CHAPTER 18

I T WAS NEARLY 1 PM ON THE DAY PEARSON AND Kandinskiy had landed at Moscow for their flyby visit. Just about everyone on the very long list of Kandinskiy's creditors was trying to figure out how they could get their hands on him. With extraordinary speed the news bounced around Moscow that, forced into a corner, Kandinskiy had signed over his villa near Monaco to powerful members of the Defence Ministry.

Indeed, Melnikov had played Kandinskiy beautifully by convincing him to return and sign what was meant to be an equitable settlement of all his outstanding liabilities. Instead of doing that, Kandinskiy had been bulldozed into transferring title to his magnificent Villa Carnacina to the avaricious Prime Minister and received a tepid commitment to a final settlement at some point soon when the "President had personally decided which direction this matter should take". Kandinskiy took that to mean "what he personally wanted out of the whole suite of assets up for grabs".

Kandinskiy couldn't quite believe that he'd been out-conned by a *chinovnik*, a government guy with no business acumen but someone who clearly understood the administration better than he ever could – and equally the new direction of Russia, albeit one carefully concealed by a focus on restoration of traditional conservative, Christian values.

The oligarchs and businessmen who had built up vast fortunes in the 90s were on the way out and it was just a question now of integrating into the new reality of modern day Russia – a complex web of competing interests – one misstep enough to put you in danger of losing everything with a snap of the President's fingers.

◀▶

As Carl entered the magnificent meeting room on the 48th floor, overlooking Sparrow Hills, Moscow University, Moscow River and the mighty Hotel Ukraine, one of Stalin's monumental "Seven Sisters", he observed Jason Rogers, white open-necked shirt, hands placed firmly on the oak table in front of him, in animated conversation with Schwartz and Lebedev.

Rogers swung around in his chair when Carl walked in and barked, "Apparently Kandinskiy has signed over the Monaco mansion and we think by the end of the day he will have signed over the rest of his assets. We'll be lucky at this rate if we can get our hands on his fucking watch collection!"

Despite efforts to portray a calm exterior, Jason Rogers showed the signs of someone under immense pressure. Rogers cracked his fingers nervously. Black rings had formed around his eyes, white hairs proliferated where previously there had been none.

Carl understood that if Falcon Capital collapsed it was Rogers' life's work down the drain. If it all went to shit, Carl knew he himself could get on a plane and find a job in London, New York or even back in his native South Africa.

Rogers, however, had spent the past 20 years working to turn Falcon into the premier emerging markets investment bank in the region, and eventually he hoped, the world.

Rogers continued, "We are not prepared to negotiate with Akhmatov and his Chechen goons Carl. That is a short road to oblivion for us. So you are going back to Cherney to 're-engage' with him. See if you can figure out what the fuck he wants to finally offer us. The sooner we lock in something the better. The longer we leave it the greater the chances that we will get picked off by these assholes from the Stans ..."

Without wasting another minute Rogers left the meeting room with his bodyguard Viktor in tow. Carl noticed dark black clouds forming on the horizon, threatening to transform Moscow's sunny skies in dramatic fashion.

CHAPTER 19

RUSLAN AKHMATOV LOOKED AT HIS HUBLOT watch, an elegant if garish Swiss timepiece. It showed 11.33 am. He reached for his phone to call Murat. He had spent the morning as he did most mornings, trawling through Russian newspapers for information on the goings on in Moscow. He kept a keen eye out for a story, or anything to do with a business competitor, that might give an insight into someone of power or wealth who found themselves in a vulnerable position and was now open to exploitation.

At 11.25 he had been called by an informant in the Ministry of Defence that Ari Kandinskiy and his British lawyer had just left the building in a cortege of cars, headed back to central Moscow.

"He's here, Murat," Akhmatov said perfunctorily into the telephone. "Kandinskiy's just left the Ministry of Defence and he's somewhere in Moscow.

"He won't be staying long, he'll be heading off via one of three or four exits out of Moscow, this evening I am sure, probably Vnukovo. He's a chance to visit his wife before he leaves – or that young Ukrainian he's been screwing. Check both addresses. If we can get him then we win, it's simple," and he looked again at his Hublot. "So get going Murat, '*davai!*' " he screamed into his phone.

Murat, who had taken the call mid way through morning prayers, picked up his mobile phone, car keys and revolver and called his two top lieutenants into a meeting room at their heavily fortified hideout in the Moscow burbs.

He stretched a large map of Moscow on to a rectangular table and pointed to the main arteries leaving central Moscow, plotting the route that he and his drivers would take to ensure Kandinskiy had little chance of escaping.

The veins in his neck and head had started to pulsate with the adrenalin that was now coursing through his veins. It was a hunt and he was the hunter. Kandinskiy was his prey, a decadent, dishonest businessman from an earlier age. Murat wanted to deliver him to Akhmatov – unharmed but scared, frightened out of his wits.

The office in the hideout turned into a sea of thugs in leather jackets barking orders to crews operating in Moscow, getting agents out of mosques, hotels and safe houses across the city. Getting them to act uniformly with one common purpose was going to be a huge logistical challenge but one at which Murat would excel.

He put on his leather jacket and black boots, slipped a laminated photo of the family back in Chechnya (his good luck charm) into his top pocket, and jumped into the black Escalade. That fired up with a loud rumble. Specially reinforced with steel plates and practically indestructible, it was the pit bull of cars – fast, manoeuvrable and perfect for scaring all and sundry on Moscow's congested roads. The Escalade cruised menacingly out of the garage into the streets of Moscow.

CHAPTER 20

ARL WAITED PATIENTLY AT THE BAR OF THE Ritz-Carlton, sipping on a coffee, checking his email every few minutes to see if there was any news of Kandinskiy.

Rogers had placed a call to Cherney's boss, a junior energy minister in the Kremlin, to have Cherney meet with Carl to run through the fine print of Falcon's "payment" as part of the distribution of Kandinskiy's assets.

Carl was anything but hopeful though. In fact there was no cause at all for optimism. Melnikov had made off with the chateau in Monaco (by all accounts on orders from the sharks in the Kremlin).

Cherney may not even be able to promise Carl anything. The game of musical chairs was now, like a Tchaikovsky ballet, going at full speed, the principal dancers all in perpetual motion – fortunes changing minute by minute.

Or Carl thought, the Kandinskiy matter had started to resemble an enormous game of chess, and playing the Russians at chess was, Carl knew, bound to end badly.

Cherney showed up looking like a man who had not slept in weeks. Although as always immaculately dressed, slicked-back hair, the most expensive glasses money could buy, not to mention a diamond-studded Breitling watch, it was obvious to Carl that he'd lost the arrogance and unbridled confidence of his earlier meeting.

The burly bodyguard had entered the lobby moments before, scoped out the area and nodded to Cherney that he could jump out of the enormous Bentley he'd arrived in and was now blocking the driveway of the Ritz-Carlton. Cherney was not taking any risks and was preoccupied with his own safety.

As he entered, Cherney looked at Carl and realised the effect his near state of exhaustion must be giving. "You know Carl this has not been the easiest few weeks. But I've been through this shit before. I suspect your security guys have already told you about the abduction I went through five years ago ..." and he fixed his dark brown eyes on Carl's.

"Yes, I'm aware Igor, must have been awful, I can't even begin to imagine ..."

Before he could finish the sentence, Cherney snapped back, "Yes there's no way you could imagine ..." and his voice went very quiet but calm, "so what you must realise is that I have got what it takes, I will deliver this fucking deal and it will work. Your shitty investment bank of fat foreigners will get its money, and you'll not even realise how lucky you are to be getting a penny back and keeping your arms and legs in the process."

Cherney's brief tirade broke the calm, polite atmosphere of the hotel lobby and distracted the pianist who had been lost in his thoughts, playing away, causing him to miss a few notes.

Cherney quickly regained his composure, corrected his tie and placed his hands gently at his sides, after taking a short sip of the black ristretto he'd ordered.

"I'm sorry I get a little carried away sometimes."

"No problem I ..." and before Carl could finish his sentence Cherney cut him off again.

"Let's be clear about one thing though – from now on if you guys want to recover any money at all you listen to me –do what I say and when. I don't want you to go off piste and try to create your own 'innovative legal strategy'." You stand no chance against the Chechens and Melnikovs of this world – they'll eat you up and spit you out," and he snarled at Carl.

"Take this piece of advice from me Carl," Cherney went on, his voice menacing, "keep your head down. You're exactly the sort of prime target for the lunatics we have all over this deal now. Being an expat is not such an advantage these days. Everyone is fair game. So be prudent – if you have security, take him with you, at least until this is finished."

And Cherney got up to leave, his bodyguard striding in front, surveying everyone who came within twenty feet – as menacing as a pit bull on steroids.

After Cherney left, Carl got on the phone to Schwartz. "Just spoke to Cherney. He thinks he's still in a position to do the deal. He's pissed off but if he's behind this we'll get something. Clearly, he's worried, and I suspect it's Akhmatov and his Chechens that have thrown this thing off balance. He also suggested I get security."

"We don't have the fooking budget for you to get security so you can fooking well forget that," Schwartz barked into the phone.

"Good news though that he's not reneging – we stand some chance of getting something, I'll speak to Rogers," and he hung up.

Bloody great, thought Carl – I mention the need to get security and all that Schwartz is worried about is cost.

The stress of recent weeks was starting to take its toll on Klaus Schwartz. Never in the twenty years he'd spent battling with adversaries in Russia had it been quite this hard.

Despite the new demands on his body and mind he still dragged himself out of bed every morning for a gruelling gym routine with a buxom young blonde called Olga. There was no greater motivation he thought than trying to impress a beautiful woman less than half his age. So he arrived at his gym sessions on time, lifted weights that much younger men would never dream of lifting, drenching himself in perspiration that was as much H_2O as alcohol from the previous night's festivities.

In recent days though he'd noticed that the sessions were getting harder, the weights he was able to lift lighter and lighter. He thought his blood pressure might be going up but refused to get it checked. "Doctors are for pussies," was his motto.

Olga too noticed that her older protégé was showing the strain. He had the unmistakable signs of being old, signs he'd managed to disguise previously but now were apparent. The tremors, fatigue, red eyes – Schwartz was falling apart at just the wrong time. All he could hope for was that Rogers wouldn't notice and decide to replace him with someone newer, younger, perhaps even hungrier to succeed.

CHAPTER 21

WHILE MURAT WAS SCOURING MOSCOW FOR signs of Kandinskiy and Pearson, Akhmatov was getting ready for an unannounced meeting with Yury Feltsov, a powerful oligarch and an old business partner of Kandinskiy's. Feltsov had won the cigarette wars in the 90s, laying waste to his competitors in every sense of the word. Still in his early thirties by the time the wars had ended, Feltsov had taken an unassailable position as king of the Russian cigarette empire. The challenge for the remainder of his life would be to hold on to his vast fortune, fight off parasitical government officials trying to muscle in, and avoid getting shot by someone bent on avenging a dead relative or business partner.

Feltsov was a fitness fanatic and led a relatively spartan existence. Despite the opulence of his apartments and residences he didn't drink, kept in perfect physical condition, read extensively and was earnestly trying to make the transition from thug businessman to cosmopolitan man of the world.

It was, however, this transition that left him open to challenge. Gone were the menacing hitmen and bodyguards in Russian-made Volgas who had helped him in the 90s –replaced with more urbane looking thugs in Mercedes and Audis.

While in captivity, waiting for his legs to be sawn off, Zelensky had started furiously recounting everything he'd ever known about Kandinskiy. He gave a crucial bit of information he'd held on to until the very last minute, the information that he'd hoped would one day make him a filthy rich mini-oligarch – the whereabouts of the bearer shares for Jozhneft, a medium-sized oil company Kandinskiy had set up with Feltsov and others.

The two oligarchs had worked assiduously to keep Jozhneft "under the radar" – profitable enough to justify the investment made by the various business partners but not so profitable or large as to make it an essential target for the voracious chief executive of the country's state-owned oil company, which was so deliberately and steadily eating up the private oil industry.

Oil and gas had become too valuable to the Russian government to be left in the hands of wealthy private Russians, notably the oligarchs. Not only did the government get to keep proceeds from the sale of the nation's oil and gas but most importantly it provided extremely lucrative wealth creation for well placed *siloviki*. Able to siphon off cash through capital investment at inflated prices, employment contracts at grossly inflated salaries, "consultancies" that never consulted, the *siloviki* who could find their way into such corporate groups could achieve wealth their parents and grandparents had never dreamed of in the Soviet era.

Jozhneft had so far avoided this "silovikisation" and Akhmatov realised immediately what a lucrative prospect that made it. Zelensky had confessed that Kandinskiy had left his bearer shares with Feltsov but that Feltsov in turn kept them in his apartment in Moscow City, an impregnable fortress on the 60th floor of one of the complex's highest skyscrapers. He had security positioned in the lobby and on both floors of the apartment he occupied. Short of blowing up the building or ambushing him while en route to a meeting, it was going to be near impossible to steal Feltsov's bearer shares.

But Akhmatov had not come this far only to be put off by "logistical" issues. His appetite for brutality, his Chechen cunning and a willingness to go a step (or two) further than his opponents, had allowed him to overcome all manner of obstacles before – this time would be no different.

As he looked at himself in the mirror that morning before jumping into his car, Akhmatov could not resist thinking he looked good. The new Italian suit he'd had tailor made fitted like a glove. With his million-dollar Breguet watch and Armani glasses he was the very image of a wealthy European businessman – not a stuffy Brit in a pinstriped suit with bright coloured shirt and tie, but a much more elegant figure.

He was going to enjoy this meeting with Feltsov. He had meticulously prepared his strategy. He was looking forward to seeing the reaction on Feltsov's face when he, Ruslan Akhmatov, makes the wealthier, more respectable Russian businessman, an offer he cannot refuse, in true Godfather fashion.

It was a chilly October morning and he felt a blast of cold air between the door of his residence in Rybolovka and the Maybach limousine that was waiting. Today he'd be travelling lightly and economically – one car and one bodyguard. He'd leave nothing to chance though. He carried a gold-plated Beretta pistol with him everywhere, a present from his friend, the Governor of Chechnya, for his 40th birthday.

Engraved with quotes from the Koran and a message of brotherhood from the Governor, Ruslan liked to bring it to a meeting and ostentatiously place it on the table if he was unhappy with how a discussion was progressing and wanted to make his displeasure obvious.

Ruslan also knew that Feltsov was no ordinary rival. He had survived the brutal cigarette wars of the 90s – no mean feat even by Russian criminal standards. Akhmatov was proposing to steal an asset that Kandinskiy had entrusted to Feltsov – he knew there was no way that Feltsov was going to give in easily.

It would take more than a gold-plated Beretta engraved with platitudes from the Chechen governor to intimidate him.

At precisely 8 am Akhmatov's Maybach arrived unannounced at Feltsov's building in Moscow City. Akhmatov had been tracking Feltsov's movements in Moscow since his return from the US days earlier. He knew Feltsov was there and could almost certainly not refuse a meeting.

One of the unpleasant aspects of being a Russian oligarch was the life of luxury being punctuated by encounters with people like circling piranhas who wanted to take everything you owned. The more you had, the greater the paranoia.

Akhmatov walked into the lobby of Feltsov's apartment building. He was immediately recognised by Feltsov's minders, and a man in his late 40s, wearing a perfect-fitting black suit with open neck collar, came out to greet him.

"Good morning Ruslan Ramzanovich, it's our pleasure to have you here," and the man gave Akhmatov an icy smile, flashing bright white teeth. Civilised in every respect but obviously one of Feltsov's key henchmen, Akhmatov sensed the minder had a distinctly KGB air about him.

The man led Akhmatov and his bodyguard to an opulent meeting room next to reception. Akhmatov and his bodyguard waited for a few minutes before the man returned and said that they would have to follow him to the 60th floor to meet Feltsov. Akhmatov had the impression Feltsov had been expecting a visit from him – everything was going a little too easily.

As they went up in the lift Akhmatov noticed four cameras in the ceiling of the lift. He suspected Feltsov would be watching so he let out the broadest smile he could muster.

As the lift reached the 60th floor and came to a stop, Akhmatov and his bodyguard walked into a short corridor. They turned right and came to a vast living room of 400 or so square metres, complete with ultra-modern furniture and fittings, giant screens and a spectacular 360-degree panoramic view of Moscow.

Feltsov was seated on a giant sofa near the window sipping a coffee. As Akhmatov entered, he got up and walked deliberately to greet Akhmatov, staring at Akhmatov directly and extending his hand to offer a stiff, perfunctory handshake.

"*Strasvitsa* Ruslan Ramzanovich – good to finally meet after all these years. I've heard a lot about you."

"And so for me Igor Stanislovich, I have heard many great things about your business success these past years – if I could build up a corporate empire like yours I would be very happy indeed."

Feltsov smiled and tapped nervously on his leg.

"Thanks Ruslan for the kind words," Feltsov continued, "I am however quite sure you're not here to exchange compliments with me on this Monday morning."

He beckoned Akhmatov to take a seat in front of a large oak coffee table next to a window looking into a neighbouring skyscraper at Moscow City.

Akhmatov paused for a moment, and took a deep, long breath, as if to settle himself. "That is indeed true Igor," he said nodding in agreement. "I've not come to waste your time – actually you have something I need and I suspect you know what it is."

Ruslan flashed a menacing look at Feltsov, the first indication that with civilities now over he was eager to lay his cards on the table.

"The Jozhneft bearer shares no doubt," Feltsov responded. The moment Feltsov's men had identified Akhmatov he understood what the new adversary was after.

Feltsov and Kandinskiy had met at university in the early 90s. Then, after finishing their degrees in applied physics, they launched themselves as young entrepreneurs in the chaos of Moscow corporate life. They had watched each other's backs, and in the process prolonged their professional careers longer than many contemporaries who'd not made it to the end of that violent decade.

"Yes, exactly, how did you know?"

"Not too hard to figure out Ruslan. After your men slaughtered Zelensky, that was the one piece of information of real value that he alone had. Ari was stupid to have let him in on that one."

A sinister smile came across Akhmatov's face.

"Yes he was stupid Igor, very stupid," he answered, "I need those shares now to recover the money which your old comrade Kandinskiy owes me. The greedy son of a bitch has refused to engage with me and instead is flying around the world like a frightened animal," Akhmatov's voice began to rise.

But Feltsov was also now overcome with a sense of indignation. "Ruslan, the value of those shares far exceeds the balance of Kandinskiy's debt to you. Anyway this is an issue you need to discuss directly with Kandinskiy – not with me!" The older man aggressively thumped the table with a clenched fist, unable to restrain his emotions any longer.

But his Chechen tormentor had no interest in discussing the merits of the two men's respective positions on the subject of the bearer shares any further. He ran his hands through his slicked back hair and straightened his glasses.

"I'll make this easy for you Igor," Akhmatov continued. He asked his bodyguard, who had been patiently waiting at the entrance to the vast living room, to bring over a mobile phone.

The bodyguard, a hulking bear of a man, walked deliberately towards Akhmatov. He reached into a black leather bag and pulled out a black mobile phone that he then carefully handed to Akhmatov.

Feltsov was trying to figure out the next move of his adversary but had no idea what stunt the malevolent man from the Caucasus was about to pull.

Akhmatov had a brief conversation with someone on the phone. He then swivelled in his chair and handed the phone to Feltsov. "Take it Igor, it's your son, I'm sure he'd love to hear some reassuring words right now."

Feltsov, a battle-hardened veteran of some of Russia's worst corporate battles, thought he was going to drop the phone so badly did his hands tremble when he heard Akhmatov utter those words. But he managed to take the phone and speak into it.

"Papa, it's me …" said his son Maxim into the receiver, out of breath and clearly terrified.

"It's me Maxim, don't worry, I'll make sure you're OK. There's nothing to worry about." Feltsov tried to speak in an assured tone but his nerves were impossible to disguise and Akhmatov aggressively grabbed the phone back from him.

"Igor, I am sorry to have to do this but you know I have my reputation to think of. I can't fuck around with people who don't pay their debts," Akhmatov said to the trembling oligarch rather clinically.

Feltsov's 15-year-old son was a student at one of England's most prestigious boarding schools. The presence of other wealthy Russian and Middle Eastern students meant that it was better protected than most schools but it had been a relatively straightforward exercise for Akhmatov's men to whisk young Maxim from his morning run around the school grounds.

They kept him in the boot of their Toyota Landcruiser while they waited at the local village for a signal from Akhmatov's meeting in Moscow. Their orders were clear, scare the younger Feltsov but not to the point of causing him any physical harm. He had to be able to reassure his father he was OK, still breathing and alive.

The men Akhmatov had hired were from a Chechen family which had settled in Dalston, north London, in the 1990s during the first Chechen war. They were no less brutal and determined than their brothers back in Chechnya and had developed a fearsome reputation in the London underworld.

Akhmatov was keen to conclude his appropriation of the bearer shares and gestured to his bodyguard to hand him a small black steel case which he placed in front of Feltsov. "Igor you know that if you want young Maxim to be safe you have to give me those bearer shares. If I leave here without them you will never see him again."

Feltsov nodded. He understood that Akhmatov would deliver on his threat. Slumped in his chair, a feeling mixed between resignation and utter terror consumed him. He noticed that within minutes he had tremors passing through his muscles, the arteries in his neck and arms dilated along with his pupils. Feltsov was like a boxer who'd been knocked out for the count, every vestige of power and aggression stamped out of him.

Akhmatov tapped a Montblanc pen on the wooden coffee table while he waited for Feltsov to react. Tapping slowly at first, the taps grew faster and faster as he waited, the noise becoming more and unbearable for Feltsov who realised he had no choice but to hand over the shares.

In years previous, before having children, it would never have entered his mind to give anything up to a rival no matter how great the personal cost. In his mind back then everything was dispensable if it meant retaining power and wealth. With the arrival of his eldest son Maxim, followed by a succession of sons and a daughter with his wife and mistress, his attitude to life and business had changed. Now, thanks to Akhmatov he realised just how vulnerable he had become.

As Akhmatov left Feltsov's apartment, bearer shares safely secured in the bullet-proof black case carried by his bodyguard, he could not but help to feel a blast of euphoria.

He'd entered Feltsov's place a rich man on the up and left several hundred million dollars better off. His corporate empire was secure beyond his wildest dreams. More importantly, this money would give him the capital to rise a rung or two up the social and business standings in Russia, within spitting distance of the men who were his nemeses, the fat, ageing oligarchs – in today's Russia, like so many dinosaurs.

CHAPTER 22

MUSCLES ACHING WITH FATIGUE, JASON ROGERS turned to do the last lap of the basement swimming pool he'd installed at his palatial residence on the outskirts of Moscow. It was not yet 7 am but he had nearly finished his daily routine of 40 laps of the 25-metre pool.

When he had started on this morning's swim, he told himself that he still had the energy and aggression to mix it with men far younger. He'd been through more than all of them put together, seen off more rivals, done more deals, lost more money and made more enemies than all of them put together.

But as he completed lap after lap of the pool his mind wandered to the plethora of problems that were preoccupying him – he could feel his natural optimism and bullish mood wearing off. Every stroke was hard work. By the end of the swim, he was completely spent – not a kilojoule of energy left in him.

Jason Rogers eventually got out of the pool, put on a dressing gown and walked slowly towards the kitchen where his morning breakfast was being carefully prepared by the Russian housekeeper who attended to his every need.

"Thanks Ludmila," he said warmly.

"*Pozahlyusta* Mr Rogers," she replied with a mixture of deference and warmth. Ludmila had looked after Rogers like her own son when his Russian wife left with the kids and half his assets several years previously. She cooked all his meals, ironed his shirts and ensured that in those rare hours when he was not either working or travelling he was well looked after.

Sipping on a double espresso while he waited for his visitor, Rogers scanned the daily newspapers for anything connected to Falcon Capital and anything that may give some information on his latest obsession – recovering much needed money from Ari Kandinskiy.

Getting his hands on the money owed by Kandinskiy could be the difference between making it to Christmas and into the New Year or having the lights literally turned off and the office furniture turfed into the parking bay in front of the Falcon Capital office.

The maid came into the kitchen and announced that Klaus Schwartz had shown up for their breakfast meeting.

"Jason," Schwartz barked as he entered the kitchen, throwing his briefcase under the large table.

Without exchanging any formalities Rogers asked Schwartz to sit down.

"What progress Klaus? I need the fucking money from Kandinskiy. This is taking too bloody long," he said, impatiently tapping his thumb in a mechanical action against the wooden table, making a rat-tat-tat sound a bit like a machine gun.

"Jason, this is a complicated process. We have a team of our best people on the case. But it's proving very hard to track Kandinskiy down and figure out who exactly is calling the shots – one minute it appears to be Cherney – the next Melnikov – you know the corrupt government minister for armaments – and then we have Akhmatov in the mix as well. He's messing the whole thing up, running around and scaring the fookers – it's like musical chairs –"

Rogers cut him off, "Yep musical chairs all right Klaus. But we have no fucking idea who's sitting where or where we're meant to be sitting …" His southern accent seemed to accentuate – his manner towards Schwartz borderline hostile, aggressive even.

But Schwartz wasn't to be intimidated easily – he knew that he was right, it was just a question of time, of wearing down the opposition.

"True, but this is Russia Jason – we've been here long enough to understand that things can be unpredictable. We just have to keep going and apply the pressure, there's no other way."

Rogers started tucking into his breakfast of eggs and bacon – what is the point of continuing to argue with Schwartz he thought to himself. He more or less ignored Schwartz for a few minutes while he ate.

Then half way through his third espresso for the morning he turned to Schwartz and said, somewhat philosophically, "Actually Klaus I'm getting fed up with this place, the returns are crap and I've realised that the parasites, the *chinovniks*, the *siloviki*, the mates of the President are just growing bolder and bolder, stealing more and more."

"Klaus, do you know the difference between a parasite and a parasitoid?"

Schwartz, who'd never known Rogers to show any interest in anything scientific, stared back at Rogers with a puzzled look.

Rogers, his blue eyes focused on Schwartz, went on, "A parasitoid is an organism that lives within a single host organism; unlike a parasite, however, it ultimately sterilises, kills and consumes its host … what we're dealing with is not parasites skimming from the sides but parasitoids who will ultimately bring this system and this country to its knees."

"And the head parasitoid is the President. He's created a system that works entirely to his advantage. The edifice is showing signs of cracking and when it does, heaven help those who have hung around for the end of the party."

Schwartz, unused to such moments of reflection from Rogers, could only mutter, "What do you mean? Are you thinking of giving up? We've come too far, achieved too much to let these bastards win now … haven't we?"

"I think I'm done here Klaus. Now, I'm focused on new markets – Africa, Asia – where people are keen for growth. They want to transport themselves out of poverty, into the 21st century.

"What we need to achieve in Russia is liquidate our positions, sell up, use the cash to establish ourselves in a country with a future. The money from Kandinskiy is part of that plan. We need to get that fucking money back …" he hissed at Schwartz.

"OK, Jason, I hear you …" Schwartz responded, this time with a degree of resignation. He grabbed his jacket and brief case and said a curt goodbye to Rogers.

As he jumped into his chauffeur-driven Mercedes, Schwartz was overcome with a feeling of deflation. A big part of Schwartz did not want to leave Russia, just yet. He'd led a fabulously luxurious life there, had as many girls as any man could want in one lifetime, been courted by businessmen and politicians and risen up the ranks to be one of the key foreigners in the city.

Packing up his things and moving to another emerging markets jurisdiction, to start all over again, was not something Schwartz had had in mind.

"Fook," he thought to himself, "fooking hell."

Still feeling a little disoriented and under huge pressure to deliver, he hit his speed dial to reach Carl.

Carl groaned when he saw who was on the other end – but he had no choice. He picked up. "Klaus, before you start, please just allow me to give you an update on where we are."

Carl rattled quickly through a series of successful freezing orders he'd managed to put in place over assets held by Kandinskiy in a range of countries. While not counting as dollars in the bank, the freezing orders over a hundred or so million dollars of bank accounts had effectively ensured that Kandinskiy could not dissipate assets to his cronies or pay off preferred creditors. It gave Falcon Capital some leverage, a little window of opportunity, that it did not have before.

Barely taking a breath he then he went on to detail the intelligence he'd obtained from an Israeli agent he'd hired for info on Kandinskiy's assets in Israel.

Like any good Russian oligarch of Jewish heritage, Kandinskiy kept a proportion of money in the homeland. Kandinskiy always said that if the world went to shit and decided to turn on the Jews again the only place he and people of his kind would be safe was Israel. He was probably right thought Carl, and digging around there was likely to yield results.

When the rundown of events had finished, Schwartz let out a gruff, "OK, thank you, so when the fuck do we get the money?"

"We won't be getting it in a hurry but we're still in the game."

Schwartz hung up abruptly, not appreciating Carl's answer one bit.

CHAPTER 23

COMMISSIONER SOLOVIEV'S FOOT TAPPED nervously on the floor of his luxuriously decorated office. He puffed on his cigarette.

He had been distracted all day and the combination of late nights, poor returns on recent tax raids and an increasingly hostile business community – less prepared to dish out "*vzyatka*" or bribes, to keep him off their back – had seen his bank balance growing at a more modest rate than he'd ever thought possible.

Like everyone in Moscow in the 2000s he'd profited directly from the exponential 7–8 per cent growth that he expected to last forever. Businessmen didn't get too pissed off if he showed up at their doorstep with his hand out for money.

Soloviev could also, until now, rely on the less reputable members of Moscow's business community to pay for tax raids on their competitors. Usually $200,000 a pop, the raids were a perfect supplement for Soloviev and his team's paltry state income.

With a few such raids every quarter they could go out and buy the most expensive watches, invest in property in France, travel to Ibiza on holiday. Not bad for low- to middle-ranking bureaucrats in the tax department.

But it wasn't just the financial pressures he was facing from falling revenues – his new squeeze, Misha from Vladivostok, had stopped taking his calls after a tempestuous few weeks together. And that was driving Soloviev crazy.

Things had ground to a halt after Misha had asked for $50,000 to invest in a film project with contacts in Moscow. They were going to make a low budget movie with Misha as the lead actor. It was his shot at stardom – his contact from film school had the equipment and the actors all ready to go. Like everyone starting off in film, though, the contact just didn't have the funding to get the project off the ground.

Misha had given his all physically to make Soloviev fall for him hook, line and sinker. And so enamoured was he of his new, handsome young protégé, Soloviev had practically stopped going home to see his wife and kids.

When Soloviev showed signs of dithering over the investment, Misha did the only thing he knew he had to do to get Soloviev to pay – he ignored him. Misha knew that at best Soloviev would last a week without seeing him – but not longer. It would be the most expensive fuck in Soloviev's life but he wouldn't have the choice, his testosterone would get the better of him.

And his testosterone did. Soloviev cursed himself after making the call and instantly worried how he was going to fund the growing ambitions of his new "friend" – not to mention the life of absolute luxury his wife had grown accustomed to and that bought Soloviev some freedom in his personal life. He'd woven a deeply complex and tangled web of friends, lovers, business associates and rivals, people who wanted him dead and people he wanted dead.

Soloviev's best chance of making some quick cash was Falcon Capital. Bleeding cash and mortally wounded by competition from the state-backed banks, the risk was that if he didn't get in fast there may be nothing left to get his hands on. Just another thing to worry about he thought to himself as he ashed the cigarette in the Hermes ashtray that adorned his kitchen table.

CHAPTER 24

K ANDINSKIY STARED OUT OF THE WINDOW OF HIS suite in the Ritz-Carlton in Tverskaya. He could see cars whizzing past at speeds well in excess of 100 km per hour, as if they wanted to fly past the Manezh and make it directly into the heart of Red Square.

As he was preparing to leave the Ministry of Defence earlier that day, an old friend from the underworld had tipped off Kandinskiy that Akhmatov planned to apprehend him before he could get out of Moscow.

Kandinskiy reflected quickly on his options. He understood that Melnikov would not mind seeing him liquidated now that he had got his hands on Villa Carnacina.

So Kandinskiy decided that his health and wellbeing meant rethinking his departure from Moscow later that evening. Pearson had protested furiously, insisting he be allowed to leave alone, by commercial airline. But Kandinskiy overruled him.

"Spencer, you have no idea who you are dealing with. These guys are monsters. They're not even remotely like anything you've dealt with before – alone you're a prime target and you'll end up like … Zelensky," and he looked warily at Pearson.

"Of course there's lots of good lawyers out there Spencer, lots of scumbags who will do what I tell them and take the money, but you're my scumbag Spencer, and I need you too much," he said, smiling at the increasingly angst-ridden Pearson, almost affectionately.

"Great, thanks, after all these years I've risen to the rank of well-paid scumbag," and both men laughed.

"But seriously Spencer we have to take our next steps very, very carefully. Neither of us can afford to make a misstep and let that prick Akhmatov get his hands on us."

"I've been in touch with Melnikov but he's not making any promises. The fucking liar convinced me to come – and now he's dumped us like, how do you say in English?"

"A hot potato," answered Pearson ruefully.

Kandinskiy's principal bodyguard, a great bear of a man called Andrey, tapped on the door of Kandinskiy's suite.

Kandinskiy gestured him to come in.

Speaking in his rough brand of prison Russian Andrey informed Kandinskiy that it was still too dangerous to venture outside.

"There are Chechens in the lobby – we don't know if they're Akhmatov's men but we can't take the risk. It's safer if you stay here. We have enough firepower on this floor to look after you.

"We are speaking to the hotel's security guys to figure out who the fuck these guys are. But they're scared and don't want trouble at the hotel – the hotel's owners also don't want to give Akhmatov any shit. They're Kazakh and not keen on getting involved in this shitfight, they're terrified of the Governor …"

Kandinskiiy nodded to his bodyguard and turned to Pearson.

"Spencer, you probably didn't get a word of that but we're not going anywhere in a hurry – it's time for me to call in a favour or two from my Jewish brethren …" and he reached into a large black leather bag he carried just about everywhere and pulled out a gold telephone.

"Avram," Kandinskiy said into the receiver, "I need your help …"

Kandinskiy had reached out to Avram Budinsky, a Russian Jew who had emigrated to Israel in the 1980s before the fall of the USSR. Budinsky had soon realised that Israel had the climate, girls and fun to make for a jolly lifestyle but wasn't going to sustain his business interests and stimulate him in the same way Moscow had when he was a kid growing up.

A born gangster, Budinsky had learned the tricks of organised crime very early and had quickly progressed to executing hits for clients on business rivals, political enemies and anyone unfortunate enough to have aroused the ire of one of those clients. A life of crime had made him a wealthy man.

Most of his business was done at his villa in Tel Aviv. In his garden lined with palm trees, a 50-metre swimming pool and a retinue of beautiful women on his speed dial, Budinsky led an idyllic life for a 50-something bachelor. At 120 kilos and a diminutive 160 centimetres, venturing out only in Hawiian shirts and baggy shorts, his arms and legs covered in prison tattoos, he cut a formidable figure as he lounged around Tel Aviv's outdoor cafes and bars with a retinue of bodyguards who looked like gangsters out of a 90s Russian movie.

"Ari, how the fuck are you!! It's been years!" he screamed in Russian into his mobile phone, turning heads on the trendy terrace bar where he had spent the afternoon.

"Not too good Avram! I am in deep shit my friend, where do I start …" and he proceeded to give Budinsky a rapid-fire summary of the jam he and Pearson had found themselves in – Chechens marauding all over Moscow, unsettling the delicate balance that had existed since the bloody wars of the 1990s – the *siloviki* trying to absorb private businesses into government enterprises so they could bleed them dry (why go through the pain and effort of growing a business when you can just suck the life out of an existing one and become a multi-millionaire in the process?).

Budinsky muttered a few obscenities and then launched into a tirade, "These fucking Muslims get a bit of money from oil and now they're the fucking kings of the world – we should go back to Chechnya and blow the shit out of Grozny, and Dagestan while we're at it. OK, I hear you Ari, I've got lots of clients complaining about the same shit."

As Budinsky was speaking, every square centimetre of his substantial frame was wobbling in an agitated manner. His mouth was practically dribbling foam and to the people sitting in the posh terrace bar he had the distinct look of a man suffering from a bad case of rabies.

He had fought hard to make his first million and he cherished his connection with the motherland – Russia. That it was now being overrun by Muslims from Chechnya was too much for him to bear.

"Ari, my brother, I'll be on the next plane out of Tel Aviv. I should be in Moscow by tomorrow morning at the latest. I'll come straight to the hotel – I am coming with my best men – they're all former Mossad so they won't fuck around with these assholes."

"Great Avram, I knew I could rely on you," and Kandinskiy hung up.

"What the fuck was that about?" asked Pearson in his plummy, upper class English accent.

"The Jewish cavalry are coming tomorrow Spencer. Get ready. Moscow won't have seen anything like it for years."

But rather than comforting Pearson, Kandinskiy's reassurance had the opposite effect. Pearson could feel a bead of sweat beginning to trickle down his forehead as the realisation dawned upon him that he was soon to find himself in the middle of a religious war in the heart of Moscow.

CHAPTER 25

A BLAST OF COLD AIR FILTERED INTO THE LOBBY OF the Ritz-Carlton. Murat had been there for nearly 24 hours, sipping espressos patiently, waiting for his prey to come out and attempt a break for the airport.

However, Kandinskiy and his security men had not taken the risk. They'd waited patiently for Murat to make the first move, which he could never do without the approval of Akhmatov, and in turn something he could never do without a green light and protection from the powers that be in Grozny. Their own affair had reached an impasse, but life in the hotel went on around them, seemingly unaffected by tensions between the two camps.

Businessmen arrived for their meetings, and conducted them right next to Murat and his goons, completely unaware of the potential danger they represented. Waiters served coffees, high-end prostitutes came in and out of the gold and marble-plated lobby (enough gold to decorate a pharaoh's tomb in Egypt) with their clients before heading upstairs to "seal the deal". The pianist played an enormous Bosendorfer piano by the bar, never pausing between pieces, completely lost in his own thoughts, trancelike.

The wait was beginning to frustrate Murat and he was tired of pacing up and down. "Fuck this place," he muttered to himself. His colleagues noted his dark mood and knew to keep their distance.

Then Akhmatov called. After a short conversation Murat picked up his jacket and informed his key lieutenant to hold the fort while he left for a few hours. Akhmatov had let him know that the Kremlin had decided it had had enough of the peregrinations of the vultures clambering all over Kandinskiy's business empire.

The powers that be could not afford gun battles in prominent hotels, CFOs being chopped into bits and prominent foreign lawyers being effectively held hostage with their Russian oligarch clients.

"They're fucking weak Murat. These Russians piss themselves at the first sign of trouble. I think they're just worried we're climbing out of the shithole they've kept us in all these years.

"So we have to meet at Sanduny banya this evening. Melnikov has organised a private room. No guns, we're in towels and sandals …"

"What about Kandinskiy?"

"We keep an eye on him of course. I want Ahmed on top of this – you come and pick me up and we go in together."

Ahmed was one of Murat's most loyal and effective lieutenants. He had fought in Afghanistan, Chechnya and a range of other war zones. A frightening combination of terrorist and gangster, he'd given up on his political beliefs or at least learned to suppress them in the interests of making money. His face scarred by battle, physique hardened by years of war, body-building and fighting, he was the human equivalent of a pit bull. The only person in Akhmatov's retinue who could exert authority over Ahmed was Murat. Ahmed admired Murat's appetite for brutality and his piety –a man he respected and could work for.

Carl's Chevrolet Tahoe crawled along the congested road that ran along the embankment of Moscow River, weaving its way through the heart of the city, past the Kremlin and out towards the skyscrapers of Moscow City.

"It's 'pervih sneg ' (first snow) Carl," said Valentin, a look of both mild irritation and expectation coming over his face. *Pervih sneg* meant horrible traffic jams but it also meant that parks and gardens would be covered in snow, kids could pull out their toboggans and any bit of plastic they could slide on. Moscow would be transformed from a grey, miserable city into one which was for a brief period quite beautiful and almost pristine in its cleanliness. Perfect white snow would sit atop the wall that ringed the Kremlin as well as adorning the onion domes of the Orthodox churches that dominated the skyline of Moscow.

The snow brought with it massive traffic congestion. But the movers and shakers of the city who had "*migalkas*" (flashing blue lights), were able to bullock their way through the monumental traffic jams with impunity. They could run the Ladas and Volgas off the road and scare the hell out of anyone else brave or stupid enough to venture on to Moscow's roads at this time of year.

The incessant demands associated with pursuing Kandinskiy's rapidly evaporating assets had taken their toll on Carl. He decided the moment had come for some form of extra-curricular amusement away from the office. Without it he'd end up in hospital or needing to see a psychiatrist.

By good fortune, he'd kept the phone number of the Dreams nightclub's prettiest dancer, a beautiful girl from far-east Siberia called Oksana.

She'd grinded over him and let him touch every square inch of her svelte figure for the better part of an hour, then fallen into a long conversation about her life, where she'd come from, why she'd ended up working surrounded by old, fat men who looked at her like she was an object and would throw her away once they'd had their moment of titillation.

Carl arranged to meet Oksana at a restaurant above the prestigious Lotte Plaza. With views all over Moscow, it was a notorious pick-up joint and up-market restaurant all conveniently wrapped into one. Clients puffed away on their shisha pipes, glamorously dressed single women scoped the restaurant for rich men (single or married it didn't matter).

Carl spotted Oksana at the end of the bar, elegant in a black dress, Bloody Mary in hand – what a cliché he thought and felt a pang of regret mixed with embarrassment at having invited her on a date. Oksana waved as soon as he arrived, her gestures natural and normal, putting him instantly at ease.

"*Privet* Carl," Oksana said warmly, "where do you want to sit?" as she planted a soft kiss on the side of his cheek. Carl was struck by her easy, unpretentious manner. She was even prettier and more engaging than he'd remembered at the club. She had none of the hard edges, the narrow obsessions, of so many ambitious, self-absorbed socialites in Moscow.

"You know I wasn't sure you'd come Carl. I've met men like you who get cold feet at actually spending time with someone like me," and she gave him a little smile, flashing her immaculately white teeth.

Carl hesitated for a minute before answering her. "I have to be honest with you – this is a first time for me as well," and he let out a nervous laugh. "I'd had a *lot* to drink, my memories were a bit of a haze afterwards but I do remember thinking that we'd had a great conversation," and he let out a little laugh, before continuing, "about what exactly I don't know other than your personal story was quite fascinating.

"You see where I grew up in South Africa things were not so straightforward either, my family life was very, very complicated – that much we have in common," and he noticed that her dark brown eyes were looking at him intently.

The DJ at the bar started to turn up the Kylie Minogue song "Can't Get You Out of My Head" and was gently bobbing his bald, egg-shaped head from side to side, his enthusiasm for this old disco classic infectiously gripping other patrons who started tapping their feet and shifting from side to side in their chairs.

"You know you Russians never do things by halves – everything is so intense, so extreme – it's exhilarating but so bloody exhausting sometimes," Carl said to Oksana, with a slight sense of exasperation.

"Carl," she said in her Russian accent, a broad smile coming across her face, "we Russians can't do things in moderation, it's not in our nature. We have the dial permanently switched to 'maximum'. I wonder sometimes why we can't be more like you westerners, do things, more ..." and she searched for the right word, "gradually, there, that's what I mean!"

"Where I am from in Siberia men don't have jobs, well a lot of men don't, and they just go crazy with drink and boredom. That's why I left, I'm too smart to work in a factory, I wanted to do some-thing with my life ..."

As she spoke, the restaurant was starting to fill up, waiters glided between tables with cocktails, patrons did their best to look good, nonchalant, natural in a setting that was anything but natural.

The DJ was effortlessly shifting between disco classics, his bald head still bobbing up and down, arms swaying from left to right, oblivious of everything around him, concentrating on the music as if his life depended on it.

Men and women chain-smoked long kalian pipes, sending great plumes of apple-flavoured smoke up into the air. Thick-set security guards, dressed in their trademark black, wandered up and down the bar, making it very clear that trouble was out of the question. Whether that was meant to be menacing or reassuring, Carl wasn't quite sure.

As the restaurant filled up so did the atmosphere intensify, and before they knew it Carl and Oksana were deep in conversation, genuinely enjoying each other's company. One cocktail became two, three, four and then Carl started to lose count.

Their body language became less and less inhibited, limbs started to loosen up and Oksana's magnificent figure started to show itself underneath her very elegant black dress. They spoke a lot about their lives and backgrounds.

Carl couldn't remember the last time he had enjoyed a date so much. Oksana's thoughts were the same. She'd dated Russian guys and some foreigners but their objectives were without exception very primal and one-dimensional. She thought that just maybe Carl was different.

But Carl's moment of fun was under threat as he noticed his phone ringing endlessly – almost certainly Schwartz's assistant trying to track him down. Fuck it, he thought to himself, this is my night off. I'll let Schwartz figure out what the fuck he's going to tell Rogers. He put the phone on silent.

"Work bothering you?" asked Oksana, "or perhaps some girl-friend, or wife ..." and she smiled.

"Work fortunately or unfortunately as the case may be," responded Carl. "I'm stuck trying to recover money off some fat-cat oligarch and getting a lot of pressure from people high up in the bank where I work who think you can just click your fingers and make things happen – unfortunately in corporate Russia I'm learning things are very, very complicated," and he reached for his vodka martini, his third, the first two having the desired effect while the Beluga vodka coursed through his veins, dulling his sense of fatigue.

"Don't worry, I completely know what you mean – you know life in a nightclub is probably not too different from an investment bank. You get lots of money but you have to give every inch of your being," and she stared at him, her smile temporarily replaced by a look of resignation.

Carl took the opportunity to move closer to Oksana on the sofa at the back of the restaurant and give her hand a gentle stroke, not overly provocative but just enough to make her understand that he was fond of her.

It was strange in some ways that he felt obliged to be so careful and discreet. They'd thrown themselves at each other the previous week in the club. But this time the dynamic was completely differ-ent. The relationship of patron and performer had been reversed, this time he desperately wanted to be with her and it was entirely her decision whether to acquiesce or send him home alone.

The evening concluded as well as Carl could possibly have hoped. He and Oksana drank and smoked shisha pipe until 2 am, laughed so loudly they got on the nerves of patrons sitting next to them and then retired back to Carl's apartment in Patriarshiy Ponds, the swank quarter in central Moscow, with tree-lined streets and late night cafes that were full of Moscow's young and upwardly mobile. They staggered up the stairs to his apartment, arm in arm, laughing raucously.

As soon as they made it to his apartment Carl opened a bottle of French red wine, his favourite from the Pécharmant region near Bergerac. "Try a glass of this," he said to Oksana, "and tell me it's not the best glass of red you've ever had!"

"Carl," she replied in her thick Russian accent, "I think you could give me cat's piss at the moment and I'd be happy," and she let out a peal of laughter.

Carl woke five hours later, his alarm buzzing, and as he saw the voluptuous figure of Oksana lying next to him, he had a sudden feeling of exhilaration which was quickly overcome by a steep descent into the reality of what the day most likely had in store for him – battling the effects of a horrific hangover and likely to be dealing with an irate Schwartz as his first item on the agenda once he made it into the office.

"Fuck," he said to himself – why couldn't I just have a moment of peace and tranquillity?

CHAPTER 26

TWELVE HOURS AFTER TAKING THE CALL FROM Kandinskiy, Avram Budinsky's private jet was getting ready to touch down at Moscow Vnukovo airport. He was accompanied by five men, all former Israeli army and Mossad. They brought with them an arsenal of weapons, explosives and ammunition – enough to start a mini-war on the streets of Moscow if Budinsky felt like it.

Budinsky was dressed in a black suit, with gold chains – and rings between the jail tattoos that covered his fingers and hands. His two front teeth were 18-carat gold and it would be an understatement to say that he cut a menacing figure as he walked down the narrow, rickety staircase off the plane.

Of course, arriving in Russia with an array of heavily armed men was not something which would usually escape the attention of local immigration and customs.

His remarkably easy passage into Russia was facilitated by an enormous "*vzyatka*" or bribe that he had paid to the deputy head of Russian immigration and the General Prosecutor to ensure that he and his team would not be given any interference when they touched down on Russian soil.

What happened between Vnukovo airport and central Moscow was completely up to them. Most importantly the little army had 36 hours to conduct whatever business they intended, on the proviso that they did nothing which would arouse too much attention.

Both the General Prosecutor and head of immigration had sweated over Budinsky's proposal. But the prospect of a pay-off of two million dollars per man proved a temptation too great to resist. The money was to be wired in two parts, the first instalment upon successful arrival in Moscow – with the second instalment upon successful exit from Russia. As with all *vzyatka* in Russia the payments themselves had to be shared across the multitude of officials who would have to turn a blind eye to the ensuing violence.

As soon as Budinsky and his men stepped out of the plane they were greeted by a cavalcade of black Hummers and Escalades, driven by an array of goons with shaved heads. It was nothing less than a Vegas-style convention of thugs. The Israelis carrying large black bags offloaded them into the back of the 4x4s and jumped in.

The leader of the cavalcade, Ari Goldman, was an old associate of Budinsky's. They'd met in prison as youngsters and ever since watched each other's backs and made money together – lots of it. The next 36 hours was to be no exception.

Goldman, who carried a gold-plated Beretta with him at all times (legend was he slept with it under his pillow) greeted Budinsky warmly. *"Privet moy dryg!"* (hello, my friend) he yelled in his coarse, scattergun Russian. Budinsky gave Goldman a giant bear hug, practically lifting him into the air. He appreciated being able to call upon his boyhood friend in a difficult situation. The niceties were however quickly replaced by business.

"Avram," Ari began, "we have intelligence that there is a meeting of Kandinskiy's creditors tonight, including Akhmatov, at Sanduny banya. This is our best chance to get Kandinskiy out of the Ritz – there'll be a reduced contingent of Akhmatov's thugs there.

"Akhmatov's number-one guy will escort him to Sanduny. We will have our chance to create a distraction and get Kandinskiy out and knock off a few of Akhmatov's guys in the process – a nice result for us and for you." He slapped Budinsky's shoulder and handed him a map of the hotel.

Budinsky's large head, shaped like a volleyball, nodded as Goldman outlined his strategy for saving Kandinskiy. He said relatively little as the cortege of vehicles weaved through Moscow's outer suburbs at blinding speed. Then, as if suddenly waking up he screamed, "It's time we kicked the shit out of these Muslim fucks and reasserted ourselves like we used to in the 90s. Since when was Moscow dominated by these men? It's fucking outrageous!"

Goldman patted Budinsky on the shoulder and said, "Avram, be patient my friend, *'shag za shagum'* (one step at a time)!"

The streets were relatively calm as they passed through the outer suburbs of Moscow – past kilometre after kilometre of dilapidated apartment buildings.

Soon enough they got to the giant cauldron that is central Moscow – that imposing beast of a city – the very heart and central nervous system of everything that happens in Russia.

CHAPTER 27

ACROSS TOWN MURAT WAS TRAVELLING IN A convoy of black 4x4s to pick up Akhmatov and bring him to the meeting at Sanduny banya, the exclusive sauna in central Moscow that was the meeting place for everyone from prominent politicians and businessmen to the gangsters and crooks of Moscow.

The different groups brushed shoulders, sweated and drank vodka in close proximity. Like an ancient ritual which had to be observed with deference and complete respect for age-old traditions, Russian men and an assortment of foreigners would shower before entering the steam room, take birch sticks and whack the skin off each other's backs, endure heat that would fell a horse and then recover in ice cold water, freezing extremities and slowing hearts. Then they'd repeat the exercise all over again until their skin, bright red from the session, would not be able to take any more.

Murat felt a deep sense of unease at the prospect of bosses meeting in such a bastion of old Russia. Like every Chechen he shared his countrymen's profound dislike, hatred even, for the Russian military and political elite. Melnikov was a slippery combination of both, a man who had lied and murdered his way to the top and would think nothing of crushing Chechen interests in order to pursue an agenda of self-enrichment and aggrandisement.

Murat had no cause for anxiety though – his boss, Ruslan Akhmatov, had a very keen antenna for the duplicitousness and unreliability of his Russian brothers. Akhmatov knew that ultimately the Russian establishment could turn against him and his boss, the Chechen governor, at any time. It might mean another war in Chechnya but there was an inevitability to that anyway. For hundreds of years his countrymen had been fighting invading armies. That would not change. This time, with oil, they had some money and independence. That would buy them time …

As Akhmatov's cortege pulled up at Sanduny, they noticed a sea of black 4x4s stretching around the corner out of Neglinnaya Street – there were bodyguards in numbers surprising even by Moscow's standards.

"There are more guards here than at the fucking Kremlin," Akhmatov said to Murat.

CHAPTER 28

J ASON ROGERS LOOKED OUT OF HIS OFFICE WINDOW
on the 52nd floor of the Falcon Capital offices. He'd spent the
morning studying the group's numbers.

"Fucking terrible", "catastrophic", "complete and utter annihi-
lation" were the words he fired like verbal hand grenades at the
directors, including Schwartz, assembled for their usual Thursday
morning meeting to discuss group finances. He'd spent nearly 15
years building up Falcon Capital – now, he was watching it slowly
and inexorably evaporate into obscurity and felt completely powerless to do anything about it.

Schwartz had looked uncomfortable, even exhausted during
the meeting. The others in this collection of expat managers and
Russians looked similarly depleted. They'd seen their business
model destroyed by competition from local – Russian – banks. The
Russians appeared to have unlimited capital, were willing to offer
huge loans at competitive interest rates without showing any particular interest in the credit profile of their borrowers. They just had
to be a "name", someone recognisable to the Kremlin masters. Even
better if the borrowers were politicians in the Duma or apparatchiks
working directly in government.

These were loans that would never be repaid, like a gigantic gravy
train being willingly lapped up by anyone with access to the President or his network of very powerful friends from his hometown.

"Jason we can't compete with these guys," said Schwartz. "They
don't know anything about banking and they don't want to know –
they're just transferring huge amounts of wealth from the Russian
state to their friends."

Rogers stared at Schwartz, his eyes locked on Schwartz's. His
moment of frankness with Schwartz a few days ago about giving it
all up and wanting to move to Africa was all forgotten – it appeared
now he wanted to hold out and put up a fight.

"Next question," Rogers asked the assembled directors and security guys. "What the fuck is going on with that son of a bitch tax inspector who keeps paying us visits?"

The room turned towards Roman Lebedev who, immaculately dressed as always in a dark Hugo Boss suit, poised and confident, addressed Rogers and the directors in his near perfect English.

"We've been following Yury Soloviev for a few weeks now – we think we have a potential weak point but we have to be extremely careful. This man is extremely vain and dangerous. We understand he's liquidated businessmen before, lower ranking but nonetheless we have to be careful.

Soloviev has affiliations with the General Prosecutor, another man who as I've told you before requires extreme caution, given his role as boss of one of the most aggressive and greedy gangs in Moscow. We expect Soloviev will be visiting us again soon. He needs the money apparently and the Russians are now not paying him because of the economic slowdown of recent months."

Rogers turned around to face Lebedev and said, "What's this weak point? Where did you get this information?"

"We got it from Yury Smirnov, the private investigator we hired – former KGB. Apparently the FSB have been following Soloviev for years. For various reasons they haven't done anything about him … yet. The information is that Soloviev has, how do you say, creamed a lot of money from targets of the inspectorate.

"We knew he was corrupt but we underestimated just how corrupt. There's another angle, more personal – he has, how do you say, a very complicated love life."

"This is interesting," Rogers responded, "go on."

"Soloviev has been preying on young men for years – how do you say, 'seducing' them and getting rid of them when he got sick of them or when they tried to interfere with his family, extort money off him etcetera.

"That as you know is not a problem for someone of his position in this country but he has been (and Roman paused for a moment), a little extravagant of late. We understand he may be on the verge of doing something again soon with a new lover he has on the scene.

"If we're ready then we could potentially discredit him, generate a little scandal in his department and you know, get him off our back … I don't need to tell everyone in this room how dangerous this information is in the wrong hands …"

"Quite," was Rogers' response, and he scratched the back of his neck, as if uncomfortable with this latest revelation.

Then Rogers turned to Schwartz. "And what is the status with Kandinskiy? From what I hear half of the world's crooks have shown up here in Moscow to rip him into fifteen different pieces."

"That's not far from the truth Jason," Schwartz said, addressing the directors. "From what we understand he's holed up in the Ritz-Carlton, defended by a number of security guards and possibly supported by hotel security as well.

"We've heard that the Chechens, and by that I mean Ruslan Akhmatov, have their own guards, pretty ferocious people, stationed there as well, just waiting for Kandinskiy to make a move. If they get hold of Kandinskiy then there's very likely not going to be any return for us at all, except for what we have blocked in overseas accounts – ten million bucks at best.

"We've also heard that there's a meeting tonight of creditors, just Russians invited, no foreign creditors, but we're not exactly sure where and what the context is. Either way we're in the dark there," and he looked at Rogers who momentarily closed his eyes and exhaled deeply, the unending flow of bad news almost too much even for him to bear.

Rogers stood up and looked out the window overlooking the impressive Moscow University, housed in one of Stalin's "Seven Sisters". He could see, as well, kilometre upon kilometre of the thick green forest of the area known as Sparrow Hills.

Rogers spoke to Schwartz, "Klaus, it sounds like we have our backs to the wall – the only way to win from here is to think very, very strategically. We'll need to ramp up our intel on the situation with Kandinskiy's overseas assets. And Roman, I need you to get personally involved with what is going on here in Moscow. I need you to dig into your reserves of intel, get Yury Smirnov in for a meeting – ideally first thing tomorrow morning."

With that Rogers banged on the wooden table to signal that the meeting was over and made a quick exit, his bodyguard in tow.

CHAPTER 29

FROM THE MOMENT AKHMATOV AND MURAT entered the very elegant and historic building housing the Sanduny banya they were filled with a sense of unease.

Escorted by a burly security guard they moved away from reception, down a long marble staircase and then past a large swimming pool adorned with marble statues, towards one of the larger rooms in the banya.

They passed groups of men sitting by small tables, huddled in conversation, feasting on plates of horse meat, *salo* (pig's fat), salty Russian cheese and fresh tomatoes from Azerbaijan and other remote corners of the former Russian empire – all the while knocking back shots of vodka and drinking black tea provided in huge ceramic pots. The waiters dressed in uniform passed between the tables effortlessly, carrying trays laden with food and drinks for their impatient clients.

Eventually Akhmatov and Murat were shown to a private room adjacent to the public area. They were instructed by the guard to undress and prepare themselves for the banya.

"Mr Akhmatov, your party is ready to receive you, everyone is in attendance …"

"This doesn't feel good," Murat said to Akhmatov.

Akhmatov patted Murat on his shoulder to reassure him. "I'll be OK," he whispered in Murat's ear.

Akhmatov was ushered into the private room dressed in a gown and sandals. Murat was shown to an adjoining room where ten bodyguards sat with bored expressions on their faces, all looking warily at each other, none engaging in conversation. One of the men, Murat noticed, was a former champion heavyweight boxer from the days of the Soviet Union. He had a nose that must have been broken a dozen times, a face hardened and calloused from being hit repeatedly over a distinguished career, fists the size of baseball gloves and squinty eyes that looked at Murat with undisclosed hostility, hatred even.

Murat could sense him thinking, "Fucking Chechen, fucking Muslim dog ..." Murat chuckled to himself as he wondered which part of this human colossus he would dismember first if ever given the chance.

As Akhmatov entered the ornate, gold-plated private room that had been reserved for his meeting with Melnikov he saw six men, all Russians, one of whom was Igor Cherney, sitting around a large, marble table in their dressing gowns and sandals. All bore angry, disapproving expressions. It was clear they had been in animated conversation that had been suddenly cut short when Akhmatov, the Chechen interloper, showed up.

Igor Cherney stood up to greet Akhmatov, shook his hand, nodding politely, without any particular warmth. Carefully positioned at the centre of the table, and convener of the meeting, was Melnikov.

"The slimy, slippery son of a bitch," Akhmatov thought to himself.

Next to Melnikov were seated representatives of Kandinskiy's other main creditors including a prominent Russian oligarch, a member of the Russian senate who had made a fortune in illegal weapons sales and bought himself a seat in the governing party (and respectability in the process), and a wealthy school friend of Kandinskiy. All of them had clearly made the same mistake of trusting Kandinskiy to invest their money wisely.

"Hello Ruslan, it's great to finally have you here," said Melnikov, his face pushing out a forced smile, doing his very best to come across as sincere. However, his discomfort was clear and he could barely disguise his distaste at having to allocate so much of his precious time to Akhmatov.

"Igor, yes, a pleasure to see you again," responded Akhmatov, his cold dark eyes, expressionless, fixing on Melnikov's.

After Akhmatov was seated, Melnikov cleared his throat and commenced. "My dear friends, the purpose of today's get together in a ... convivial environment is to discuss the situation we have with Kandinskiy, and how it will be resolved to the benefit of all involved, in a mutually respectful manner."

Melnikov's eyes moved from participant to participant, beads of perspiration forming on his large, white, protruding forehead.

"It's fair to say that Kandinskiy's business practices have been," and he paused for a while, taking a deep breath as if the effort of reflecting on the oligarch was a source of some physical effort, 'unsound'.

"He's brought us to this rather unfortunate situation through his reckless disregard for the norms of proper business behaviour, his mad excesses in every sense, including personal, his crazy projects without having conducted any clear business case and, in the process, losing us all a lot of money."

Like any good Russian, Melnikov knew how to disgrace and discredit an adversary, adding a moral dimension to vindicate his sense of righteous indignation. Of course, Melnikov was nothing other than a terrible hypocrite but he would never allow that to get in the way of sticking the boot into Kandinskiy at every opportunity.

Once his short introductory statement was over, Melnikov ushered the men, at this stage wearing nothing but large woollen hats to keep their heads cool, into the private banya adjoining the room. Each man took a spot on the pine benches in the small private banya, which by now was excruciatingly hot thanks to the efforts of a burly employee, with arms the size of a wrestler's, who had kept applying water to the hot stones in the centre of the room. There is enough heat here to melt the polar ice-caps, Akhmatov thought to himself.

Melnikov, once settled on to a bench, sweat starting to form on his brow and beginning to drip at his feet, continued.

"The issue we have, gentlemen, is how to ensure equity," and he emphasised the word "equity", saying it very deliberately and slowly, "between all of us here."

Without his glasses, which gave him an air of gentrification, Melnikov's face looked pudgy and common. He had clearly gained the initiative by gathering together Kandinskiy's rival creditors. Arguably, Cherney was as well, if not better, placed to call the meeting – given his backing from the state-owned gas giant and their own very considerable debt to Kandinskiy.

But while Cherney had been prepared to let his rival Melnikov take the initiative on this particular occasion he was waiting for Melnikov to make the slightest slip, the smallest transgression.

"I couldn't agree more with you regarding equity," Cherney said to Melnikov, not willing to let his rival do all the talking. "However it seems to me that it's the other parties in the room who have begun to, *prematurely*, acquire Kandinskiy's assets despite our strict understanding that this was to be an orderly process left to the end, once we'd … silenced Kandinskiy completely," and he stared directly at Melnikov, his lips curling up in a sign of displeasure.

"The villa in Monte Carlo for example, worth, what, US$250 million, maybe more, maybe less – you," and Cherney, his eyes still fixed upon Melnikov, continued, "you had Kandinskiy sign that over to your 'interests' last week according to my sources."

Melnikov didn't challenge Cherney but instead stared at his own chubby, alabaster-coloured feet which were now also covered in perspiration.

Turning his attention to Akhmatov, Cherney said "Ruslan, we're also aware of your little detour down to Feltsov's apartment last week and your … how do I say, 'offer which couldn't be refused'."

He took a sip of his tea and continued, "We know that you guys from Chechnya play by certain rules and take a slightly more aggressive approach than us, your Russian brothers –but those shares represented 500 million dollars! What on earth made you think this was yours alone to keep?" By now Cherney was wearing a barely disguised look of deep displeasure, his right index finger waving at Akhmatov in an animated fashion.

But before Akhmatov could respond, a waiter pushed open the door of the small private banya and announced that their supper was ready. The men then left the excruciating heat of the banya for the adjoining salon, where the waiters had laid out for them a platter of cold meats, hot tea, ice-cold vodka and vegetables from Azerbaijan.

Despite the cooler surroundings in the salon, the mood at the gathering of Kandinskiy's creditors remained tense. Akhmatov's greed and inability to play by the rules had, in the minds of the other men there, got the better of him. The macabre execution of Kandinskiy's CFO had only exacerbated matters. Extravagant violence of this type was a throwback to the 90s, unsettling the delicate balance of recent years.

But while his Russian brethren were trying to intimidate him, Akhmatov was having none of it. Sipping quietly on black tea, chewing a large slice of cured horse meat, he cleared his throat and focused his gaze on Cherney, staring at him for a good twenty seconds before beginning to speak. It was a look that would intimidate most men … make them retreat to the furthest corner of the globe.

"Igor," he said, quietly, his voice tightening a little, "I don't know what to say. You guys invite me to this … what do I call it, rehearsed meeting and then choose to accuse me of bending the rules." And he shot each of the men sitting around the circular table an icy look – a mix of cold hostility and contempt.

But despite the bravado, Akhmatov could not help but feel a little on the defensive. He was alone among his mortal enemies, the Russians, and he knew that every step, every move in this increasingly complicated saga, had to be very carefully choreographed to avoid falling into one of many carefully laid traps.

"Like all of you here today, when I bought up Kandinskiy's debt *I earned a seat at this table* ..." and he picked up his cup of tea, taking a sip, placing the gold-plated cup firmly back on the corner of the wooden dining table.

"There's nothing that differentiates any of you here from me, other than that I have chosen to use my legal, contractual right in a (and he searched for the right word) more *strategic* fashion than perhaps you would have contemplated – but that is your choice. Your caution has created a vacuum and in so doing an opportunity for me which I have chosen to exploit."

Akhmatov's fists tightened, his pupils dilated, his brain and mind were now working overtime to process the many angles that he needed to assemble in his mind to formulate the right response.

"All of you sitting here now have arrived at your position of wealth and influence through playing your hand. I'm playing the hand that was dealt to me, nothing more, nothing less. Occasionally I have to provide a little gentle encouragement to arrive at the right result," and he smiled at his companions.

"But I see that as my legitimate right (and by this stage the veins in Akhmatov's neck had started to pulsate and his voice started to rise slowly and inexorably), I repeat, am doing *nothing more and nothing less* than each of you would do in the same situation ..."

Melnikov clasped his hands around his chair and, looking to retake control of the discussion, interjected, "Ruslan, you're hacking legs off accountants, that's hardly a case of just enforcing contractual rights, your ... *activities* have been getting a lot of attention, made it into the papers, made people like me look foolish. The *boss*" (and Melnikov gestured in the direction of the Kremlin) "is apparently very unhappy that things have got so out of hand – he's started taking a personal interest in the matter, which means that we need to be much more diligent in how we conduct our affairs."

Melnikov paused a moment to wipe off sweat that was streaming down the side of his plumpish face, and continued, "The most senior people in the presidential administration are keeping an eye on things. They prepare a note for him weekly which he reads, annotates and that leads to a hundred separate questions. I am sure that you want to avoid any problems for you and *your boss*."

Akhmatov looked completely unfazed by this revelation, but Melnikov suspected this was probably a very unwelcome development for Akhmatov. The more he interfered with the local political scene, the greater the likelihood he was going to draw the Chechen governor into the quagmire.

In the other room Murat waited patiently, completely cut off from the outside world and from his boss without his phones, sipping on green tea, watching the other bodyguards who'd started to chat to each other. The guard who'd bought them to the waiting room was seated in front of a small monitor connected to the banya's security cameras. He spoke from time to time into the earpiece which Murat assumed connected him to Melnikov's security detail parked outside.

The guard spoke in short, sharp, staccato sentences, punching out orders like a commander-in-chief. His perfectly shaved head sat atop a neck that was twice the size of that of most men. He had the torso and physique of a heavyweight boxer and Murat assumed that as someone connected to the Ministry of Defence, he was almost certainly a former soldier, very possibly an active participant in the Chechen wars and if so had undoubtedly blown away his fair share of Murat's countrymen.

Back in the bosses' private room, it was left to Igor Cherney to lay down the law to the clearly unrepentant Ruslan Akhmatov.

"Ruslan, we need you to start behaving yourself and we need you to return those bearer shares to us – they are part of the pool of Kandinskiy's assets, not yours alone to pilfer. We can offer you a generous share but not exclusive ownership – that is, how do I say, *non-negotiable*.

"Consider this an ultimatum. We won't come crashing down your door today but you'd better hand them back within the week," and Cherney looked over at Melnikov for approval. He simply nodded in agreement, his cheeks by now a crimson red, his whole body drenched in sweat.

Akhmatov didn't say anything for a few minutes then stood up and gestured to the guard at the entrance of the banya that he wanted to leave. The guard looked at Melnikov who nodded and said "*Davai*, let him leave."

CHAPTER 30

WHILE AKHMATOV AND MURAT SWEATED IN THE heat of Sanduny banya, Avram Budinsky and his men showed up at the Ritz-Carlton in a cavalcade of Hummers, Cadillac Escalades and Chevrolets, jumping the pavement and practically parking in the lobby of the elite hotel.

It was an impressive sight. Moscovites and tourists alike walking along Tverskaya Street could not help but be slightly overawed by the scene which was a throwback to a bygone era of rampant gangsterism and lawlessness.

Budinsky jumped out of his car surrounded by his cohort of Israeli mercenaries and strode purposefully, his huge shoulders and girth moving from side to side, into the lobby of the hotel. He was in his element, back in Moscow, his homeland, about to liberate his Jewish brother from the hands of a bunch of Muslims from the "Stans". He scanned the lobby and immediately spotted Ahmed and his troupe of guards sitting conspicuously along two sofas, leather jackets thrown over the backs of the sofas, concealing a small armoury of weapons.

Ahmed spotted Budinsky and his Israeli bodyguards straight away – the jail tattoos of Budinsky emblazoned on his hands and neck left Ahmed in no doubt about the risk he posed.

As Budinsky approached, Ahmed put down his coffee and fixed his black eyes on Budinsky. Without standing on ceremony Budinsky sat himself down aggressively opposite Ahmed, like an MMA fighter ready to beat the life out of his opponent. Breathing heavily, he cracked the knuckles on his immense hands.

"Time for you guys to fuck off. I'm taking Kandinskiy with me and there's two ways we can do this – peacefully or I unleash my comrades," and he looked around to the burly mercenaries who'd escorted him into the lobby.

"... on to you and your men, there's another twenty of these guys waiting outside – ready to join the fight if necessary. We have enough weapons to kill every single person in this hotel ten times over. It's your call," and Budinsky smiled, exposing a mouth full of gold teeth. He was, at that moment, in complete control of the situation, perfectly prepared for either alternative.

But before Ahmed could muster a reply to Budinsky's ultimatum, a defeaning blast seemingly ripped open the atmosphere, smashing windows of the hotel, sending glass, metal, dirt and what must have been human body parts, flying through the hotel lobby.

Hotel guests were thrown violently to the floor by the terrifying force of the explosion, deafened by the roar of the bomb which had detonated outside in Tverskaya Street. The bomb was a highly sophisticated device placed with great care and loving attention by Budinskiy's men beneath the wheels of a large black Bentley that was always conspicuously parked outside the front of the hotel, for the use of VIP guests. The grandiose two-tonne Bentley proved a perfect weapon of mass destruction for everyone and everything nearby.

Ahmed lay incapacitated and prostrate on the ground from the force of the explosion, disoriented and unable to make sense of the unfolding events around him, other than the awareness that he was the victim of a bomb attack. Budinsky stood over him, the broad grin still plastered on his face, the gold teeth showing, the ear plugs carefully in place to muffle the sound of the bomb.

He placed his foot over Ahmed's neck and with all the force he could muster pushed it down until it had crushed Ahmed's larynx and left him minutes away from death. After the blood from the crushed larynx poured into his throat and started dribbling out of his nostrils, and into his lungs, Ahmed coughed and choked involuntarily, losing consciousness. Budinsky observed his eyes roll back gently inside his head. Budinsky abruptly released his foot from Ahmed's larynx and wiped the blood off his Sergio Rossi black boot on to the Persian rug he was standing on. Piercing screams and groans started to penetrate through the acrid smoke billowing into the lobby from the wreck of the Bentley.

Kandinskiy and Pearson had been thrown to the floor by the impact of the explosion as a piece of the Bentley's roof careered through the enormous window of their hotel room. The flying metal had shattered the window with such efficiency that every square centimetre of glass became immediately airborne, themselves becoming tiny flying objects of pain and destruction.

Kandinskiy and Pearson were blinded by the tiny shards of glass that filled the room like snowflakes – only after a few minutes were they able to struggle to their feet. The roar of the bomb echoed up and down Tverskaya Street, into Red Square and then back up to the Mayor's building at the top of the hill.

"Are you OK?" Kandinskiy yelled to Pearson.

"I think so," Pearson replied, assuming that if he could hear and formulate a response he must still be in the land of the living.

As they were staggering to their feet, picking fine particles of glass out of their eyes, the door of their room flew open and Budinsky entered triumphantly, with a broad grin, eyes alight, his arms raised like a champion boxer who had just knocked out an opponent.

"Quite an entrance Avram!" and Kandinskiy let out a chuckle which strained his rib cage and the left side of his face that was injured either in his fall or from the flying glass – he couldn't tell which.

"You look like shit Ari!" and Budinsky let out a huge, guttural laugh. He grabbed Kandinskiy like a rag doll and threw him over his shoulder. He gestured to one of his men to pick up Pearson. "We've got to get out of here fast Ari, before the cops come – and they're coming. We've got cars downstairs, we'll be at the airport in no time, you just watch!"

As Pearson was carried out of the hotel room he noticed a long trail of blood on the ground which never stopped and which appeared somehow to be connected to him. He realised that his ear was hanging awkwardly on the side of his head, not in its usual position. "Fuck Ari there is something really fucking wrong with me," he screamed in his plummy tones at Kandinskiy. But before Kandinskiy had time to respond he had passed out and was hanging completely limp in the arms of the Israeli mercenary.

As Budinsky and his men sped out of Tverskaya into Moscow's side streets they followed a route to Vnukovo airport which had been meticulously planned as the quickest and least likely to encounter resistance from police or Akhmatov's men. Pearson's ear was bandaged up and as he regained consciousness, he was given painkillers to dull the blinding pain that came as soon as the adrenalin started to wear off.

Kandinskiy grabbed Pearson's hand reassuringly and said, "Not far now my friend, we should be back on the plane soon, it was a fun trip wasn't it?" and he gave Pearson a broad grin. Pearson could only mutter a faint, "Fuck you Ari ..." before slipping back into unconsciousness.

Murat was driving away from the banya, down Neglinnaya Street in the direction of the Ritz-Carlton, when he saw a fleet of police cars flying down the main ring road outside the Kremlin. There were military helicopters whizzing overhead. He'd not been able to reach Ahmed and he instantly had a bad feeling, "Ruslan, this doesn't look good ..."

"No, it doesn't," responded Akhmatov, peering out the window at the fourth military helicopter to pass overhead. "It really doesn't."

Before Murat and Akhmatov could drive into Tverskaya Street they were blocked by an enormous cordon of police cars. Paramilitary units jumped out of large wagons and were arresting anyone and everyone in the vicinity.

"Let's get out of here!" Akhmatov barked at Murat. Akhmatov punched the roof of his car in frustration.

"This is the last time we let ourselves be distracted by the Russians Murat. I swear in the name of Allah!"

"Allahu Akhbar," Murat responded, although in a slightly despondent tone.

CHAPTER 31

I T WAS NOT IMMEDIATELY CLEAR WHO HAD KILLED the tax commissioner Yury Soloviev. What was clear was that he had died in spectactular fashion – murdered in a chic restaurant in the Patriarshiy district, in front of his wife and kids. A bullet into the back of his head sent his face into a bowl of borsch, his brains indistinguishable from the red cabbage pouring over the white table cloth in front of him.

The assassin had shot from the roof of a building across the street. The impact had covered his wife and children in his blood. His head had been struck by a series of bullets, at least three, fired with immaculate precision, exploding, as they had been designed to do, upon impact with human flesh, putting beyond any doubt the survival of the target.

Soloviev did not even have time to utter a final goodbye, his face having been effectively lifted off his head and deposited on to the table in front of him.

A second gunman had simultaneously walked up to the black four-wheel drive parked ostentatiously outside the restaurant and fired directly into the windscreen, killing the driver and all three bodyguards inside. The windscreen was knocked to the road by the force of the bullets. For good measure the gunman fired at least fifty rounds into the passenger doors on either side of the car.

From the killers' perspective it was an extremely well executed operation. Although Soloviev had made numerous enemies in Moscow, neither he, nor members of his gang operating within the tax inspectorate would have expected his death to come so quickly. Executions of prominent public servants had significantly diminished in recent years with the rise of the *siloviki* and the omnipotence of the Kremlin – immune to challenges from civilians, or business – and a wider society that had sunk into a state of near perfect acquiescence.

The news of Soloviev's assassination reverberated around Moscow. It was Schwartz who called Rogers to let him know what had happened. He rang Rogers at home late Sunday evening.

"Don't worry Klaus, I'm well aware of what's gone down – one less thing to worry about. Let's start focusing on getting our money back from Kandinskiy. And let's stay off the phones for twenty-four hours … you never know who might be listening."

Schwartz was at first taken aback by Rogers' complete lack of surprise at the bloody demise of Soloviev. He wondered how Rogers could possibly have known of these events even though the attack had only taken place an hour or so before.

"Oh fuck," Klaus thought to himself as he put down the receiver. "He's fooking had him whacked."

Despite their long association – years working 24-hour days together, eating, sleeping and breathing Falcon Capital – there were still aspects of Jason Rogers, the man, that were a complete mystery to Schwartz. There were also certain things, such as this sudden, violent and stupendously bloody demise of a major irritant to the business, that Rogers would never confide in Schwartz.

As Rogers put down his mobile phone, he got back to carefully assembling the cash he had meticulously counted in his counting machine, all US$100,000 – the second and final payment to the man who had carried out the hit on Soloviev earlier that day.

Rogers would travel out to a heavily guarded building in north Moscow to hand over the money. Accompanied by his bodyguard and driver, he trusted only himself to ensure the payment went smoothly and without any screw-ups. This had always been his modus operandi.

The need to vanquish rivals had diminished in recent years as the business world in Moscow had started to show signs of gentrification. Paying for a bunch of corrupt cops, tax police or government officials to raid a rival's centre of business operations was now seen as a more economical, civilised way of gaining a necessary tactical advantage over a rival than having his brains scattered all over a restaurant. This was one of those exceptional situations where Rogers felt circumstances militated in favour of the latter, more grisly approach.

◄►

Dmitry Ovchinnikov was the quintessential man of the shadows, even by Russian standards. Tall, bald and gangly, he had grown up a two-bit thug in a Siberian town that had produced munitions during the Soviet era. Like so many one-industry towns, the fall of the Soviet Union had been a catastrophe, because the main factory – the town's only source of income – shut down. Every man within a 30-kilometre radius of the factory found himself unemployed and practically destitute overnight.

As gangland battles raged in Moscow and Saint Petersburg and the newly appointed government struggled to figure out what to do, cities like the one Ovchinnikov grew up in started to disintegrate – the men reverting to alchoholism, families collapsing, kids forced into a brutal new world without order or respect for human dignity or life. It was in this world that Ovchinnikov came to excel.

Lucky to have survived several vicious beatings in the epidemic of gang violence in his town, he formed a small gang of thugs intent on making a name for themselves through stealing from the endless trains that crept past their town, transporting cargo across the sprawling Siberian expanse to Moscow and western Russia.

Dmitry's skills included intimidating other gangsters, and running a variety of drug-selling, standover rackets and other illicit pastimes.

After successfully establishing his operation, wiping out opponents and effectively buying control of the local politicians and police force, Ovchinnikov realised at the young age of 30 that his life's dreams and ambitions were not being met in the far-flung provinces of Siberia.

On the few occasions he'd been to Moscow for business he'd noticed the smirks of the Moskvich he'd encountered in bars and restaurants and in the street. With his black boots, black coat, tattoos and toothless grin, not to mention his very distinctive Siberian dialect, he realised that he came across as a clichéd version of a Russian gangster from the middle of nowhere – much the same as a hillbilly from the Appalachians showing up in New York.

He'd returned to Siberia and not been satisfied, growing frustrated with his band of gangsters. "You're all a bunch of fucking nobodies in this shitty little outpost. Moscow is where it's all happening," he had taken to shouting at them before launching a punch or reaching for the nearest vodka bottle to throw at them.

So, he took the decision to up sticks, hand over control of the provincial operation to his best friend – a less ambitious local but just as vicious and conniving as Ovchinnikov– and move to Moscow.

He quickly realised that to live at a standard that would earn him respect – as a gangster operating in Moscow, able to support at least one bodyguard – he would need to get to work fast.

Ovchinnikov had been introduced to a young foreigner who was making tracks in Moscow's business world but had ruffled feathers and was now under threat from a few locals who had not appreciated this upstart.

Jason Rogers had fallen out with a former Russian business partner, Rudi Kuznetsov – Kuznetsov had turned out to be a drunk and a crook, only interested in Rogers' ability to attract foreign capital (which he'd figured out a foolproof technique for embezzling).

Rogers' suspicions were aroused long before Kuznetsov had time to issue the securities on Russia's debt capital markets – these, so Kuznetsov imagined, would form the basis for an elaborate fraud that would make him an extremely rich man.

Rogers could have challenged Kuznetsov. But he knew the Russian's connections, particularly with Moscow's prosecutorial service, would make him a formidable enemy – the sort to have Rogers out of Russia on a one-way ticket.

And so, Roman Lebedev, Rogers' old head of security, introduced him to Ovchinnikov.

Ovchinnikov grabbed Kuznetsov from his parked car in a quiet street near Gorky Park in Moscow. Before Kuznetsov had the time to say – maybe even think of – any final words, Ovchinnikov deposited four bullets deep inside his brain, each one having the desired impact, atomising his brain and killing him instantly.

Rogers and Lebedev had calculated, correctly, that Kuznetsov's hit would not be attributed to Rogers. A foreigner, banker, someone who got around with limited security did not arrange hits on Russians, unthinkable! For years Ovchinnikov was Rogers', and Lebedev's, dirty little secret, called on to liquidate Rogers' enemies but only when circumstances dictated, in Rogers' mind, that he was left with absolutely no other choice.

Soloviev had been one such individual. His avarice, greed, personal vices would likely know no bounds, require unlimited funds to satisfy and once he had a captive target, Jason Rogers knew he was going to suck more and more blood out of them to feed his enormous ambitions and extravagant lifestyle.

Ovchinnikov had a curiously moralistic approach to Soloviev's killing. He had been handed an extensive file by Lebedev and could pick from a number of different locations to determine Soloviev's place of death.

"It won't be with the boyfriend," Ovchinnikov eventually told Rogers, "but with his family. I want his kids to see him in bits, to see what comes out of living such an immoral existence …"

At first, Rogers had struggled with numerous inner demons as a result of Kuznetsov's liquidation. What the fuck was he thinking? He'd become nothing better than the men he'd initially despised in Russia – the gangsters who'd penetrated Russian business courtesy of their win-at-all-costs mentality, running organisations that did not create viable businesses, but just stole the businesses of more honest competitors who'd toiled for years to create something viable in Russia's unforgiving and brutal corporate landscape.

With the passage of time, however, Rogers had come to terms with his actions. He'd been able to keep his business empire together, grow it even, thanks to his willingness to be as mercenary as his Russian counterparts.

At every new gathering of Falcon Capital, when he'd been able to celebrate the latest deals, the latest awards from "Banker of the Year", he felt his "arrangements" with Ovchinnikov were well and truly justified, even morally so if you looked at them from a certain perspective.

CHAPTER 32

THE KREMLIN WENT INTO OVERDRIVE TO MANAGE the fallout from the explosion earlier that day in Tverskaya Street. The President's spokesman, Dmitry Samudorov, a tall, mercurial Russian with a magnificent command of English, was quick to blame the attack on Chechen dissidents.

"The Chechen rebels, scum that they are, have attacked innocent women and children again but we reassure our fellow citizens that we will track down the criminals who perpetrated this heinous crime. No stone will be unturned, we will avenge the deaths of all the innocents today, you mark my words."

At the end of his tirade Samudurov's voice was shrill, full of indignation – it was a stellar performance.

However, despite the Kremlin's attributing blame to Chechen separatists, and its PR machine having gone into overdrive, rumours abounded in Moscow that the attacks sprang from a commercial dispute between rival criminal gangs. As the dead and wounded were ferried off to hospitals in central Moscow, oligarchs, *siloviki* and everyone of influence called on their contacts and security personnel to figure out what had really happened and whether it had any implications for them.

Carl sat at his desk going through a briefing sent by security on the events of the past 24 hours – three pages of densely written script, an awkward translation from Russian into English, in parts hard to fully decipher. But the overall message was more or less clear.

It had been mayhem in Moscow in the past 24 hours – Carl had never seen anything like it. Kandinskiy had managed to avoid capture by the Chechens with the help of a conveniently timed "terror attack". And the latest nemesis of Falcon Capital, the ever-corrupt tax commissioner, Yury Soloviev, had had his brains sprayed all over an up-market Italian restaurant in a chic part of town.

Carl was temporarily overcome by a sense of deep unease, fear even, that he was tied up, inextricably, with the events which were unfolding – a dangerous place for an expat with no real backer, or "*krysha*", to find himself in.

As well as the fear though, he could not deny to himself that he felt a sense of exhilaration at the thought that he was a part of this deeply complicated, violent story taking over Moscow.

As he sat back in his reclinable office chair, sipping away at his third espresso of the morning, Carl knew that Kandinskiy getting away would not help his efforts to recover the outstanding loans from the fleeing oligarch.

Carl's only hope lay in outsmarting the opposition, thinking of avenues and strategies that were normally the preserve of their Russian rivals.

Panama. It was in that far away haven for the rich and despotic that Carl felt the chances of retrieving Kandinskiy's cash were probably best. Roman Lebedev had received a tip-off that Kandinskiy had been spotted earlier that year at the gaudy Trump Tower hotel in Panama.

Carl had asked Vadim to take a trip out there to see for himself and do some digging, but as he half-expected Vadim point-blank refused.

"I hate hot countries Carl, you know that. It's bad for my blood pressure – and my mother will freak out if she hears that I've gone somewhere like Panama!"

"OK, I'll ask Natalia to go," Carl said matter of factly to Vadim, hoping to engender a little jealousy that the more junior Russian lawyer would be getting such an important assignment.

He'd recently hired Natalia Ivanova, a bright young lawyer from Irkutsk in Siberia to help with his impossible workload. Statuesque, beautiful, the intellectual equal of anyone she came across, Natalia had quickly exhibited a tenacity that pleased Carl no end. He knew that he could throw the most complex legal problems at her and she would find a solution. She was also completely impossible to intimidate – her male Russian colleagues were quickly put in their place if they tried on her the chauvinistic behaviour that was characteristic of most offices in corporate Russia.

Before Carl had even finished asking Natalia if she was prepared to make the trip, she volunteered herself for the exercise.

"I need to get out of Moscow Carl, and anyway, I'm much better at digging out information than Vadim – we all know that," and she let out a laugh.

Vadim shrugged his shoulders and smiled awkwardly, not entirely sure Natalia was joking.

"Don't worry Vadim," Carl said, "you'll get the trip out to Grozny once we've worked out who we need to speak to there to get Akhmatov off our back."

"Not funny Carl, I am Jewish!"

"How could I forget Vadim?" Carl replied.

"OK, Natalia," Carl continued, "I can only let you spend a few days there – we have too much going on here. Two, three days of looking around, speak to the biggest law firms, the corporate administrators. They don't like to give away information but if you're onsite you're a chance they'll let something slip."

His faith in Natalia's forensic abilities was justified. After a little bit of research she'd realised that the key man in town was the senior partner of Panama's most prestigious law firm, Roberto Suarez. Suarez was the epitome of chic – always immaculately dressed, with long flowing grey hair, he had a penchant for expensive, bespoke Swiss watches that cost more than most Panamanians could earn in a year. He was indeed the country's mover and shaker, the man who would very likely ascend to the presidency unless someone was brave enough and well connected enough to take him on.

That he'd agreed to meet Natalia in his palatial office in the exclusive quarter of Panama City was a major coup and Carl had no doubt that Natalia would make the most of the opportunity. As soon as the meeting was confirmed she'd raced home, hurriedly packed her bag and sped out to Sheremetyevo airport to take an Aeroflot flight to Miami. From there she'd be on one of the shuttles out to Panama, ferrying wealthy clients for meetings with their private bankers.

Within minutes of arriving in her hotel room in downtown Panama City she showered and prepared herself to meet Suarez later that afternoon. Fastidiously punctual, she had arrived at Suarez's offices a good 15 minutes early and walked around the block a few times to familiarise herself with the area. The building was heavily guarded, no doubt in part due to Suarez's clientele who ranked among the wealthiest people on the planet and had a pathological obsession with ensuring their money was kept as far away as possible from the tax man in their home countries.

Natalia had been allocated a maximum of 30 minutes with Suarez, his secretary informing her over the phone that as a very busy man he could not possibly devote any more time to what appeared to be on the face of it an obscure Russian matter.

As Natalia entered the building, she noticed the classical, colonial architecture, the high ceilings, fans and South American artefacts hanging on the walls. She was greeted by a tall, elegantly dressed guard who walked her slowly towards the first-floor reception.

"Miss Ivanova, Mr Suarez is expecting you, he'll be ready in approximately five minutes. Ramon will walk you to his office."

Ramon, all two metres of him, discreetly looked Natalia up and down and guided her down a long corridor towards a large door, outside which stood an equally large and muscle-bound security guard.

"This place is more secure than the Kremlin," Natalia thought to herself.

The burly guard knocked on the door of Suarez's office and beck-oned Natalia to go in. As she entered, Natalia saw a man in his early 50s, dressed in a tailor-made light blue cotton suit, hair slicked back in perfect order, with dark brown eyes. He exuded self-confidence – a man who was clearly very much at ease with his place in the world.

"Miss Ivanova, it's very nice to meet you, please sit down," Suarez gestured to the leather armchair in front of his enormous mahogany desk. He could not help but be impressed by Natalia, tall, svelte and immaculately dressed in a revealing black suit with Jimmy Choo high heels – she was much younger and prettier than the rich old men and women who constituted 99 per cent of his clients.

"Coffee?" he started.

"Yes, thanks, double espresso," Natalia replied.

Suarez smiled, "Double espresso, just like me – Ramon get us two double espressos, *vamos*!"

His eyes fixed on Natalia's, Suarez got down to business.

"Miss Ivanova, how can I help you? My assistant mentioned you were interested in an old client of mine, Ari Kandinskiy."

"Yes, Mr Suarez, it's fair to say that Mr Kandinskiy has become a particular source of interest for Falcon Capital, the financial entity I work for." Natalia paused very briefly. She could tell she had the undivided attention of Suarez. He sat a little forward, his hands placed carefully on the table in front of him, his eyes fixed on hers, a narrow smile across his face.

For Roberto Suarez this meeting with a beautiful young lawyer from Russia was an unexpected surprise. He was instantly fascinated by her poise, her confidence. There was something so terribly attractive about her and for an instant he had to tell himself to keep his cool.

Natalia smiled and continued her little monologue. "Mr Suarez, we are a creditor of his and – how can I put it –matters have become relatively delicate as far as he is concerned. I realise that he is still a client of yours and it may be difficult for you to divulge any information you may have regarding his movements and assets here in Panama ..." she let the sentence drift off unfinished, keen to gauge Suarez's reaction.

"Miss Ivanova, Ari Kandinskiy *was* a client of mine but we have had a ... falling out ... he decided to play hardball with the Panamanian government and with me. He decided to engage in activities that were going to get Panama back in trouble with our powerful friends in Washington, and we can't have that. This country has been through too much to risk our reputation and stability for someone from your home country like this gentleman – if indeed he can be called a gentleman. We learned quite a few things about him in our subsequent investigations that suggested he conducted his business affairs in a rather unsatisfactory manner."

"Mr Suarez, I can assure you – our experience is entirely the same, that's why we have invested so much time into locating his assets ..."

Suarez nodded and started to speak, with a gentle wave interrupting Natalia, "to save you any further time and effort," and he let out a broad smile, "I'll hand over everything I have to you, details of where he kept his accounts, corporate names, director names, whatever you need. I just have three conditions – one is his legal fees be paid, I think at last count he had nearly half a million dollars outstanding, a not inconsiderable sum for my practice, and, more importantly, you agree to let me take you out for dinner this evening ... and, finally, please, call me 'Roberto'," and he smiled again, this time the smile of a man who knew that this was an offer which he didn't expect to be refused.

Natalia let out a little laugh and then quickly composed herself. "Roberto, of course we can take care of your fees if this information allows us to recover moneys owed to us. We can discuss details in due course. As for dinner, yes that suits me well, I imagine you're a very good person to have as a host in this city," and Natalia smiled again, just enough to give Suarez some encouragement but nothing more.

"Great, I'll have my driver pick you up at eight o'clock at your hotel. We'll do a little tour of the city and then go for dinner at around ten o'clock if that suits. I know a very good club on the outskirts of town with a Michelin-star chef, the views are great and you will leave Panama having seen the best this city has to offer.

"Tomorrow my secretary will hand you the information relating to Mr Kandinskiy. She will just need a little time to put it all together."

Suarez stood up to shake Natalia's hand, not letting her grip leave his for a few seconds. Natalia enjoyed the attention and did not for a second regret that this older man clearly wanted to sleep with her. It gave her a sense of power and control that suited her current purposes.

As Natalia left Suarez's offices, slightly exhilarated, she called Carl with the good news. "Suarez was very accommodating Carl, seems Kandinskiy has pissed him off by not paying his fees. I think we'll get what we want tomorrow, I'll be back in Moscow in a few days at the latest."

"I don't know how you do it Natalia. Well done – that is just one giant fucking relief," and Carl exhaled deeply.

After weeks of toil with endless setbacks and wrong turns, finally there was a little bit of good news – perhaps the turning point for Falcon Capital's attempts to recover funds and survive for just that little bit longer.

"Don't ask how I did it, Carl. I have to go out with Suarez this evening for dinner, so you owe me big time!"

"OK," Carl responded with a degree of curiosity and intrigue. "Be careful, remember this is Panama, not Moscow! I need you back here in one piece, first thing Thursday morning, with the paperwork, all of it."

He put his headset down and stared over the Moscow skyline. Couldn't be further from Panama he thought. What a long way to go to hide your money. In the end – not far enough.

CHAPTER 33

RUSLAN AKHMATOV BRUSHED THE FINE HAIRS OF his Staffordshire bull terrier Ramzan, a present from his patron in Chechnya – a beast of a dog, bristling with muscles and bursting with nervous energy – teeth big enough to rip through just about any living being walking the planet.

In his dog, Ramzan, Akhmatov saw the qualities he valued most: blind loyalty and a terrifying singularity of purpose that humans almost never had, being too often distracted by petty concerns and physical needs.

The dramatic escape of Kandinskiy and the slightly humiliating nature of the encounter with Melnikov and his Russian brethren had made Akhmatov angry, very angry.

Akhmatov's standing in Moscow had been challenged. What had been a vertical ascent into the business and power elites in Moscow had suddenly arrested in a dramatic and public way. He'd been outplayed by both Kandinskiy and Melnikov due to distractions, his failure to anticipate the ever-shifting dynamics of business and criminal life, inexorably intertwined in modern Russia. He knew he had to return to his old ways – more of Ramzan and less of Ruslan Akhmatov the Moscow socialite.

As he sat alongside his basement pool, lights shimmering on the salt-water lit by enormous gold chandeliers that he'd imported from Rome, Akhmatov watched the morning news on the enormous flat TV screen stretching almost the entire length of one wall.

The female news presenter sported a Soviet-style hair cut so popular now in the new Russia that had in every sense given up on its rapprochement with the West. Russia was returning almost subconsciously to the moral purity and sanctimoniousness of the Soviet period.

The presenter pointed out the latest injustices provoked by Washington and London before switching to an interview with Vladimir

Zhinskiy, the firebrand and Russian Duma deputy. He denounced everything western and urged military confrontation with the "inbreds and halfwits" in the US and Europe.

As Zhinskiy railed on about the West, the female presenter nodded approvingly as he listed the various injustices perpetrated against the Russian people. Abruptly, she switched topics and asked Zhinskiy about the latest terror attacks that had terrified Moscow – the indiscriminate metro and hotel bombings by the feared "black widows", the wives of Chechen terrorists killed by Russian or Chechen forces.

The black widows from Chechnya and other parts of the "Stans" as the neighbouring republics were known, wearing kilos of powerful explosives strapped under their hijabs, would arrive at hotels or Moscow metro stations and blow themselves up along with every man, woman and child in the immediate vicinity. Nails and ball bearings strapped into the suicide belt would travel hundreds of metres and maim for life anyone far enough from the initial explosion to survive the blast but unlucky, on that day of their life, to be within striking distance of a black widow.

"These bastard black widow bitches," Zhinskiy screamed, "they're good for nothing like the whole damned Caucasus. We should close the border and tell them to fuck off. We don't need the terrorists and we don't need the bastard lackeys who run the place now and come up to Moscow in their Humvees and Bentleys looking for our girls and beating the shit out of our boys …"

The cameraman switched from Zhinskiy to the sanctimonious newsreader who was starting to go a crimson red, impossible to hide her embarrassment that what was meant to be a straightforward denunciation of the West, and music to the ears of her employer and their bosses in the Kremlin, had turned into a racist rant against the powerbrokers in Chechnya, the very people the Kremlin had for many years cultivated and tried to keep onside.

"But Mr Zhinskiy, you must accept the good work done by the Governor of Chechnya in bringing stability and peace to the region since he was nominated to the governorship …"

But before she could finish her sentence, Zhinskiy, clearly enraged by her question, launched into an expletive-filled answer that had her editors reaching for the station's plug. Akhmatov's TV went dead – all he could see was the reflection of his pool, the tranquil ripples contrasting with the mad rhetoric of Zhinskiy.

"Reactionary asshole," Akhmatov thought to himself. Yet he knew that Zhinskiy spoke for an increasing proportion of the Russian public. He was expressing views that people were too scared to utter in public – opinions that the average man in the Moscow metro just whispered discreetly with an accompanying nod as if to say "you agree of course, it's just a self evident truth isn't it?"

A few minutes later one of Akhmatov's mobile phones, the one reserved for his most important contacts, lit up. The boss in Grozny must have been watching the same TV show as he saw the name flash up.

There followed a series of expletives and curses in Chechen, all said very calmly but there was no hiding the fact that the Governor's patience with Zhinskiy had reached its limit.

"I think it's time we resolved this problem Ruslan. Zhinskiy has finally signed his own death warrant."

As he listened to the governor, Akhmatov stared at the ripples of his underground swimming pool. Ramzan the bull terrier lay at his feet, on the verge of dozing off, a little pool of drool forming on the ground.

Akhmatov stayed silent as he listened to the governor – he was not entirely comfortable with the thought of liquidating this very public foe of the Chechen people. On the governor's orders he'd killed journalists hostile to the governor – and while he could more or less act with impunity in Moscow (the chances of criminal prosecution almost non-existent) he could not control the international media circus that now accompanied every newly executed journalist.

Killing a prominent far-right politician was likely to bring a wave of international and domestic attention that he felt ill-prepared to control.

But the governor, completely unchallenged in Grozny, effectively ruling for life, surrounded by 50,000 lackeys and soldiers ready to do his dirty work at the drop of a hat, did not feel the constraints and limitations that Akhmatov had to deal with as his emissary in Moscow.

"Come to Grozny, Ruslan. We'll sort out details and hang out together. I've missed you. The family would love to see you."

"OK, boss, that sounds like an offer too good to refuse. I need a break from the shit going on here. I'll fly out tomorrow."

Akhmatov hung up his phone and again stared at his swimming pool, transfixed by the gentle ripples across the surface.

By the time his call with the governor had finished, the TV station had resumed coverage but was showing an old movie from the Soviet period about a heroic Russian soldier who almost single handedly saves a small village of old ladies and tiny children from a battalion of demented Wehrmacht soldiers and SS officers.

Akhmatov chuckled to himself.

CHAPTER 34

THE NEWS OF NATALIA'S GOOD FORTUNE HIT Falcon Capital's offices like a thunderbolt. Thanks to her success in locating Kandinskiy's funds in hidden accounts in Panama, and the assistance of Suarez in ensuring the judges hearing the sequestration of Kandinskiy's accounts offered no opposition to their seizure by Falcon Capital, Falcon had managed to get its hands on US$130 million, over 60 per cent of the debt outstanding.

Natalia's three-day trip to Panama had turned into two weeks. Carl wondered how Natalia had managed to obtain such extraordinary assistance from the shady Suarez but decided against ever quizzing her on specifics – who cared, he thought to himself – the thing that mattered was they'd got back so much money. She would be looking at a spectacular bonus when the time came – probably three to four times her annual salary.

Schwartz and Rogers exchanged high fives when the news filtered through to their adjacent offices on the 49th floor. They went straight to the cigar room on the executive floor where they cracked open a 60-year-old bottle of Caol Isla whisky and cut the finest Cohiba cigars they had in the mahogany cigar box, reserved for special occasions.

"This is better than fooking a supermodel," Schwartz said to Rogers who chuckled approvingly.

"It's about fucking time we scored a win Klaus, we've been on the back foot too long," Rogers said as he took a sip of the smokey Scotch – it trickled down, warming his throat and stomach.

But Rogers knew that while the little victories were critical to the survival of Falcon Capital, getting some money back from Kandinskiy would simply shore up the company's finances for the next few months and reverse what had been a string of losses caused by impossible competition from the state banks – not to mention the avaricious behaviour of the *siloviki*, tax inspectors, oligarchs and just about every shark in Russian corporate life. He took another sip of his whisky and puffed away on the Cohiba cigar that Schwartz had just handed him.

"Got to enjoy these little pleasures," he said to himself as Schwartz grinned broadly, patting Rogers on the shoulder, barking, "Enjoy the moment Jason, we may not get many more of them!"

When the news hit Kandinskiy's camp that his cash accounts in Panama had been seized and emptied by Falcon Capital there was consternation.

Spencer Pearson took it as a personal affront that his carefully orchestrated efforts to conceal Kandinskiy's money from creditors had been so spectacularly blown apart by a bit of deft investigatory work and initiative from the upstarts at Falcon Capital.

Within minutes of being informed of this latest twist, an enraged Pearson ordered his assistant to reach out to Carl.

"Get that fucking South African on the phone now," he bellowed down the phone

The fifty-something assistant Deborah, from Guildford in Surrey, a taciturn and slightly religious woman, was shocked to hear her normally very polite and reserved boss suddenly descend to language she heard from the less well-to-do boys around her neighbourhood.

She knew exactly who Pearson was referring to though, and skimmed through her list of phone numbers to the name Carl Fitz-maurice. She dialled the number and transferred the line immediately to Pearson.

As soon as Carl picked up the phone he was greeted by a furious Pearson, his voice shaking with rage.

"Carl, it's Spencer Pearson, counsel to Ari Kandinskiy. Get to our firm's offices in Dmitrovka within the next thirty minutes. There are some extremely serious issues that we must discuss immediately but in a confidential manner – the lines are encrypted at the Dmitrovka office. You and your colleagues have really fucked up this time!" and he slammed down his phone, the line going dead on Carl.

Carl was a little taken aback but not entirely surprised by Pearson's tone – it was the tirade of someone under tremendous pressure, one step away from complete professional and personal disaster.

"I wish someone would finally finish off this pompous asshole," Carl thought to himself. But Pearson's demise showed no sign of coming any time soon, and Carl knew that he would have to speak to Pearson at some point – better to have that conversation sooner rather than later he resolved.

He called Valentin and asked to be picked up.

"Where to boss?"

"Dmitrovka, have to talk to an English '*kriminel yurist* ' (criminal lawyer)."

Valentin laughed, "You seem to know a lot of them Carl, why couldn't you get a job in a nice firm somewhere safe in England?"

"I'm asking myself that question a bit these days Valentin, but first we have to fuck this guy so let's get there pronto," and Valentin let out a loud, guttural laugh. He liked it when his boss talked tough. The instant Carl jumped into the Tahoe, Valentin planted his foot and they sped off eastwards.

As the Chevrolet passed the red brick walls of the Kremlin, Carl, as always, was awed by their vastness, their length. Constructed centuries ago to repel foreign invaders, including the Mongol hordes who terrified Russia for several hundred years, the Kremlin had since become a fortress for those who held the reins of power.

Like a small red planet – windowless – its own world at the heart of Russia, it symbolised the complete centralisation of power in the hands of those fortunate enough to occupy it. There was a long-standing tradition that whoever occupies the Kremlin would never willingly cede that power. Either the usurpers had to kill them or there had to be a wave of popular discontent so vast, so overwhelming that they had no choice but to pack up their bags and leave.

When Carl eventually arrived at the offices in Dmitrovka, central Moscow, of the English law firm Pearson represented, he noticed that security was unusually heavy for an international law firm, even one operating in Moscow. A burly security guard in an ill-fitting suit was stationed at the front door – hand on an earpiece – and giving anyone within 10 metres of the office a menacing look. As Carl walked up, the guard thrust out his right hand and asked Carl to announce himself.

"Carl Fitzmaurice, here to speak to Spencer Pearson via videoconference," Carl responded manner-of-factly in Russian to the burly guard who promptly waved him through.

"They must have bitten off more than they can chew," Carl thought to himself – a law firm crawling with bodyguards was a sign that the partnership felt under physical threat.

Maybe their association with Kandinskiy and the peripatetic, risk-taking Pearson had brought the practice undone. But these were secondary considerations as Carl prepared himself for the verbal outburst that he was certain would be coming from Pearson.

He was led into a windowless meeting room with thick reinforced walls and a telephone sitting in the middle of a small round coffee table. The phone lit up and he answered.

"Carl, it's Spencer Pearson here, you have really fucked up so badly this time. I can't begin to tell you the trouble you're in."

Pearson's voice shook as he began his little diatribe. Then he steadied himself and continued in his posh English accent.

"Do you realise Carl what Ari is capable of doing to you guys? This whole process has been so carefully managed, to the *very last detail*. Your colleague's little trip to Panama has disturbed the equilibrium which we had worked so hard to achieve. I won't be able keep Ari and his dogs at bay – I'm sorry ..."

Pearson's little speech was full of indignation and self-righteousness – he clearly felt terribly aggrieved at being made to look impotent in the eyes of his client. He also couldn't resist mentioning the risk of physical violence to put Carl in his place, remind him that this wasn't just a battle of legal tactics, or of wits, but of brawn and raw power, as was almost always the case in mother Russia.

Rather than unnerving Carl, Pearson's pomposity, air of superiority and conviction that he, as the older, more experienced lawyer, would always get the better of the younger man from the Antipodes just grated and brought out the fiery boy from the suburbs of Cape Town. Long ago, the South African had learned that the only way to respond to a challenge was with a kick to the face of that opponent.

"You know Spencer," Carl said calmly, feeling himself very much in control of the situation, "I think you'll find that Jason Rogers doesn't take too kindly to threats. As you now well know we've taken most, if not all of your client's cash in Panama.

"I think it's also fair to say that you and your client are little chance of ever setting foot in Russia again. That is probably not a problem for you, given your near death experience here in Moscow. But I doubt Ari Kandinskiy feels the same way ..."

Carl was enjoying every moment of their exchange. He relished being in a position of strength on this one occasion, no longer the whipping dog for more powerful domestic interests and toffs like Spencer Pearson.

Pearson went silent for a little while, breathing heavily into the receiver. He realised at that moment that Kandinskiy had put him in an impossible situation by refusing to negotiate with the multitude of creditors and adversaries who were lining up to tear his empire to bits.

But Pearson was not going to allow the upstart from South Africa to upset him.

"OK, Carl, suppose you're right. What on earth makes you think that we won't tip off the Chechens and the other players that you've been dipping into Kandinskiy's offshore assets? They will literally show up at your door tomorrow to fuck you senseless."

Pearson smashed his fist down on the desk in front of him, giving the trainee lawyer who shared his office at the firm's plush City offices a little fright.

"Fine Spencer, then make that call. We're ready," Carl said finally, putting down the phone.

There wasn't much point in continuing the conversation with Pearson. Hell would freeze over before Jason Rogers would agree to return one cent of the funds whose seizure had given respectability to Falcon Capital's debt-recovery efforts and put it well and truly back into the game.

Carl had also had enough of the sanctimoniousness and hypocrisy of this man who had ridden the coat-tails of clients while they flouted the law and casually committed crimes that would put most other people in jail for life.

Pearson, on the other end of the receiver, smashed his office phone into pieces when Carl hung up. Bits flew all over his office including over his office companion.

"Get the fuck out of my office you little prick," he screamed as the junior lawyer flinched, "Give me a fucking moment of peace!!!!" The junior lawyer scurried off.

Sweat poured down Pearson's face. He pulled open his top drawer and, with his hands trembling violently, struggled to open a small envelope containing a plastic wallet. He snorted the cocaine inside the wallet like a man possessed.

As the cocaine made its way to his blood vessels, he felt himself returning to a state of equilibrium, his confidence returning and the sense of hopelessness and impotence that was starting to encroach in his life suddenly felt a little less overwhelming.

"Oh fuck," Pearson said to himself, "thank God for this shit, thank God," and he wiped the sweat away, composed himself and picked up the phone to speak to Kandinskiy, and pass on the bad news that the accounts in Panama were likely gone or in the process of being plundered by creditors who were steadily getting the upper hand.

Whatever happened he had to take the upstarts at Falcon Capital down a peg or two. This shitty little investment bank with its over-paid expats needed to be reminded who was boss. Humiliating the upstart internal legal counsel, Carl Fitzmaurice, was to be priority number one.

CHAPTER 35

DMITRY OVCHINNIKOV HAD NEVER BEEN TO
London. In fact, he'd never been out of Russia. Arranging
for him to obtain a visa to the UK had required significant
greasing of palms in the British embassy in Moscow. Thanks to an
ill-timed documentary on gangsters shown on national Russian TV,
Ovchinnikov had suddenly become a recognisable figure in Moscow,
something he craved and thought good for business but ultimately
made obtaining a visa for anywhere other than North Korea a near
impossibility. But the London assignment Rogers had in mind for his
Russian assassin could not be carried out by just anyone – he trusted
Ovchinnikov and no-one else. So a UK visa needed to be obtained
quickly, whatever the cost.

As Ovchinnikov packed his case he thought to himself he had
absolutely no idea what to expect in England. Rain, cold, yes
certainly, but nothing like a Siberian winter. He packed a few of his
trademark black polo neck sweaters and black jeans, an extra pair of
his knee-length black cowboy boots. Without his trademark Beretta
pistol he would be relying on Roman Lebedev's contacts to equip
him and plan the logistics. It would be a nice change he thought to
have someone else take care of the thinking bit, he just had to pull
the trigger.

"Finally, I get to have some fun without all the work, kill some
pompous British asshole who takes money from Russian oligarchs
and spends it on drugs and whores."

With all his victims, Ovchinnikov invariably found a justification
for their killing – some moral flaw or foible that gave purpose to his
murderous conduct. He'd never killed a foreigner before, but he'd
been sufficiently briefed by Rogers' security apparatus to understand
the rationale for what they were doing and why they were doing it.

It was business but there was another angle as well. Pearson
represented the degenerate Western foreigner leeching off the blood

and money of Russians. He'd ingratiated himself with the fat cats and like a maggot on a piece of excrement sucking the life out of it, he'd enriched himself and at the same time become inextricably entwined in the shitty, pretentious, immoral life these very rich men were leading.

As he sat in the black Mercedes with Roman Lebedev on the way out to Sheremetyevo, they discussed logistics and the first critical moments of the assignment, when Ovchinnikov would be at his most vulnerable – passing through immigration at Heathrow and ensuring that he was not being tailed by British police.

"Dmitry we've handled everything so your entry to the UK should go smoothly, unproblematically," Lebedev told him, expressionless.

"What is critical," he said, his eyes lighting up, "is that you don't attract any attention. You have to act as though you've done this a million times before – try to hide those gold teeth of yours and keep the exposure of your tattoos to an absolute minimum."

Dmitry laughed and replied, "Oh Roman, I know you see me as a bit of an embarrassment – all you Moskvich look at me like I am some hick from Siberia. But you know, underneath this exterior there is someone who is very sensitive to his fellow man. I pick up on everything, every little bird in the tree, every tic in people, every mannerism. I know more about you than you do, I've studied you over the years … that's why one day I will be a great writer. When I've made enough money to live the life I want to live, I'll lock myself away writing stories about the shit I've seen and done, and this trip to London will definitely be part of that story," and he let out a huge, husky laugh.

At Sheremetyevo, Ovchinnikov got a few stares from customs and immigration officials. The immigration officer who checked his passport could barely restrain her excitement once she'd realised who Ovchinnikov was.

"Bitch must have seen the show," Ovchinnikov thought to himself and he shamelessly flirted with her and asked if he could catch up with her on his return to Moscow. She just flashed a wedding ring at him and flashed a big smile, looking at him a few seconds longer than she should have.

"This celebrity stuff is just too fucking easy. I can't wait to get back now …" he said to himself.

Once on the plane, settled into his business class seat, Ovchinnikov was again fawned upon – this time by the Aeroflot hostesses. Champagne was thrown at him as well as red caviar and a hot meal that was the best thing he'd eaten in a long time, not having frequented too many restaurants in Moscow in recent times (aside from when shooting people).

He struck up a conversation with the passenger next to him, a "*chinnovnik*" he presumed, dressed in a shiny grey suit, thick neck. The guy had government apparatchik written all over him, nouveau riche, with new-found power.

"Rosprom, I work with Rosprom," answered his neighbour when asked where he worked. "I used to work in the Ministry of Energy in the Soviet days, rose quite high in the ranks and speak German and English, so have been negotiating gas with these assholes for years.

"Now going to London to see my kids who are in private schools there, they're practically English now, very little trace of the Russian approach to things which is sad," and Ovchinnikov's neighbour reflected for a moment, "But all I can say is thank God they're out and have new passports – just have to work on getting one myself now," and he let out a little chuckle.

Yes, Ovchinnikov thought to himself, the government guys rip the country off and rather than investing back in the home country they offshore money, educate their kids overseas while at the same time telling the rest of Russia to keep their money local.

"Fucking parasites," he thought to himself. But rather than sharing his views with his neighbour and spoiling the atmosphere, he decided to keep silent on this matter and concentrated on the Aeroflot inflight magazine – this one contained a useful section on English customs and etiquette.

"The English are well known for their polite and courteous manners," the article explained. "It can be challenging for Russians sometimes to adapt to English customs and habits. A Russian should never call the waitress 'Girl' as is common in Russian cafes and restaurants. The waitress is likely to take great offence at the use of such terminology. All Russians are advised to simply refer to the waitress (or waiter) as simply 'waiter'."

What a load of rubbish Dmitry thought to himself – what is wrong with these people? They must have been emasculated by years of feminism, a phenomenon he had heard about many years ago and considered, along with homosexuality, a scar on the face of Western culture.

"Fucking decadents. I am sure I will be a force of nature there when I arrive," and he reclined his seat back as far as it would go, much to the irritation of the old Russian lady sitting behind him.

Ovchinnikov breezed through immigration and customs. Roman Lebedev had done his job impeccably. After picking up his bag, Ovchinnikov walked nonchalantly through the arrivals hall.

"Fucking breeze," he thought to himself, if only the whole trip would be this easy.

In arrivals he was to be met by two men holding a card with the name Shevtsov written in capitals. Although Ovchinnikov wasn't a name that inspired suspicion in the UK, both Lebedev and Ovchinnikov had decided against publicising his arrival too much. Ovchinnikov saw the sign held at the other end of the reception hall by a burly blond-haired man, certainly Russian, standing next to a slightly taller, muscular man with a scarred face and tattoos all over his hands.

As he got closer to them, he noticed the older, shorter man was smartly dressed in a black leather jacket, expensive jeans and tailored shirt, slicked back brown hair with smart looking glasses and a Swiss watch that must have set him back several thousand dollars at a very minimum. His name was Viktor and his sidekick was Oleg, clearly the brawn of the combination.

As Oleg drove the men in a black BMW jeep towards West London, Viktor explained every detail of the two-day trip Ovchinnikov was going to have in London. And it wasn't at all the type of trip Ovchinnikov had had in mind. No socialising, meals to be had in his hotel room.

"What the fuck?" Ovchinnikov thought to himself. At one point he stopped Viktor and pointed out that he'd never been to the UK and that he had every intention of seeing the nightspots of London, ramming his penis inside some friendly English girls. "They love Russians Viktor, and I want my piece of English pussy, drink English beer, fight an English football hooligan!"

"Sorry Dmitry," Viktor replied, "the last time Russians came to kill someone locally they caused an incredible scandal dropping polonium all over London, getting photographed all over the place and basically wrecking the ability of just about every Russian gangster to go about his business. This time is going to be different."

"They were fucking amateurs Viktor, and fucking puppets of the President, I know what I am doing," he retorted gruffly.

Viktor just shrugged his shoulders and said "It's all been agreed with Roman – you're to be as low profile as possible – but screw it, we can at least drive you around a bit tomorrow, get your orientation for Tuesday's hit, scope out the restaurant where it's going to happen."

"That's something, I suppose," Dmitry responded, eventually resigned to his fate as hitman, not tourist, on this particular trip.

As they pulled up at his accommodation in Bloomsbury – an unremarkable hotel in central London with very little in the way of security, Dmitry realised this was absolutely perfect for keeping a low profile. No doorman, no camera on the street or in the lobby – the receptionist was a portly, badly dressed Englishman. He showed little interest in Dmitry or his Russian friends – he was glued to the TV, watching what appeared to Dmitry to be a reality TV show with a giant-breasted woman remonstrating with some muscle-bound oaf who, Ovchinnikov could only assume, had probably been trying to screw her best friend.

"Bitch needs a slap," he said to Oleg, who nodded in agreement, but remained silent.

Dmitry took the room key and turned around to Viktor and Oleg. "OK, so the plan is I get room service for dinner, stay in my room and then you pick me up tomorrow. I just hope this hotel has some TV in Russian because it seems I am in for a very boring evening."

"I sincerely doubt it," Viktor responded, unable to suppress a chuckle at the utter naivete of Ovchinnikov.

"Maybe they have a porno in Russian but that will be it!" and he shook Ovchinnikov's hand firmly, bidding him good evening.

CHAPTER 36

"I'M JUST TELLING YOU TO BE CAREFUL, THAT'S all," Kandinskiy told Pearson. "We've heard that someone might be interested in causing you harm. But we're not sure who or why."

"I'll tell you why," Pearson responded, "because I've been doing your dirty work for too fucking long Ari, and it's starting to catch up with me ..." he said a little nervously.

Spencer Pearson's mood and temperament vacillated between bravado and outright fear, with not much between. He'd worked in so many emerging markets, for so many tyrants and wealthy crooks that he often wondered when his luck would run out. But, somehow, he'd always emerged unscathed, making a lot of money for himself and generally helping clients avoid prison and keep their wealth – at least the wealth they'd managed to expatriate to offshore tax havens.

"Why don't you come to New York for a while, relax with Yolanda. I'm sure she'd love to see you. You can work from my offices here. As for me I probably need to lie low as well, I might have to rejoin Avram in Israel for a bit. Even Jewish Russians like me are not safe with the diaspora in New York. The only safe place is Israel."

"Ari, I'd love to do lines of coke with you and Yolanda in those parties you host in New York, Tel Aviv or wherever the fuck you want to host them. But things have got seriously bloody complicated at work and with the family. The wife has accused me of going awol and my kids positively hate me, or rather hate what I've become. They're embarrassed by my job and the press attention hasn't helped.

"The other partners at work, bunch of useless shits, are ignoring all the fucking money I've made them over the years and are now just focused on reputation, repufuckingtation!! Half of them have clients much worse than you (and he stuttered a little after mentioning the word 'you').

"Sorry Ari, I didn't mean that," Pearson stammered.

"You did and I deserve it – no problem. I am who I am. I'm not an angel and nor are you, that's why we've formed such a good partnership all these years. Just take a bit of advice from me Spencer, keep a low profile for a while, keep yourself either in the office or at home, try not to wander about too much.

"If you get nervous at all or have the impression anyone is keeping an eye on you, I will arrange a bodyguard. I know some really good guys in London, all former SAS. They could protect you from Mossad!" and he laughed loudly down the receiver.

For some reason Pearson didn't find his call with Ari Kandinskiy particularly reassuring. Quite the contrary, all his fears regarding the growing number of corpses associated with Kandinskiy's "situation" had him thinking that at some point he may well join them.

But he didn't feel particularly threatened either – so long as he avoided Russia. He knew London well, having moved there from university and spent nearly 30 years plying his trade as a litigation lawyer in a prestigious English law firm, his clients almost without exception rich and famous – a whole assortment of dictators, tyrants and miscreants from Asia, Africa, Europe and of course the UK.

In the process he'd made colleagues in his law firm jealous, insanely jealous, at the life of luxury that he'd been able to lead, courtesy of his proximity to the ultra high net worth individuals he shared his time with. He thought nothing of chartering a client's private jet, if the client was willing, to see the client and perhaps take in a Caribbean island on the way. No expense was spared, his consumption of Krug and fine cigars must have been on par with the richest Russian oligarch.

But in recent years cracks had started to appear. The constant travel and partying had, Pearson felt, started to take their toll on him physically and mentally. His colleagues had noticed, too, but not said anything. They wanted to keep partner profits up and Pearson's enormous earning power was what they wanted to protect at all costs.

Pearson had sworn to himself after his scrape with death in Moscow that his philandering, drug taking, deal making would stop once he'd saved Kandinskiy from this latest imbroglio. But saving him was proving an existential crisis of Russian proportions.

After the call with Kandinskiy, he had the beginnings of second thoughts – maybe this was the time to call it a day right now, before he had his own face deposited into a plate of borsch or his own limbs hacked off.

He stared out of his office window for a few minutes. The thought was dawning on him – a bit like an epiphany – that, after all these years, it was time to bow out, retire from defending uber-rich criminal ratbags and crooked despots.

Perhaps he could even consider taking on boring domestic UK litigation; maybe a fight between a football club and their star protégé or a battle between a hedge fund and its disaffected investors? He anticipated the reaction of his fellow partners – what the fuck did he know about litigating for UK clients? Who could possibly instruct him with all the shit out there in the tabloids about his drug-fuelled parties with clients?

Pearson's wife had reacted positively to his new resolve – they'd even shagged relatively passionately. She could not remember the last time he'd had the energy to have sex with her for longer than 10 minutes.

His kids, Tom and Jessica, both well into their teens, appreciated his efforts to talk to them about school and he'd even ventured on to the topic, completely normal for most parents, of what they may one day do with their lives.

He was astounded to discover that his boy Tom was, and had been for many years, passionate about becoming an artist. His daughter wanted to be an actress – neither career ideal from their father's perspective.

He'd be working forever to support them, but he realised that the little people in the back of the car who drove him to distraction when touring on family holidays had turned into young adults, formed opinions, had desires, become real people.

"Jesus where have I been?" he thought. The last fifteen years felt like a haze, full of crazy temptations that he'd given into without a moment's reflection, now just a jigsaw of random memories that he could not seem to put into any particular order. The hedonism, the excesses of those years had come at the expense of the three people he realised he cared about most in the world. That was all going to change.

◀▶

Next morning, Pearson's alarm rang at 6.30 am. He was overcome with a sense of optimism and confidence, one that was induced by what the day held in store and not, for once, the result of a narcotic giving him a buzz.

Pearson had arranged lunch with the firm's managing partner, Philip Cleveland, to discuss his "change in direction". Cleveland was no shrinking violet – he had terminated any partner unable to pull his weight and was solely focused on making money for the practice: lots of it. As he used to say – what was the point of working every weekend and going through multiple marriages if you couldn't enjoy the finer things in life and have a chance of retiring at 50?

As Pearson made his way to Chelsea underground at 8 am to get the Tube into his office in the City, his mobile flashed with a message from Yolanda – "Hi Spencer, it's Yolanda, I'm drunk, horny and thinking about you right now, when are you coming to see me? Can you call me? Xx"

The message nearly knocked him off his feet. All he could do was hurriedly reply "Miss you too, will be in touch very soon xxx Spencer".

Although he'd resolved to turn his life around and play the role of straight man for as long as humanly possible, part of him wished he was back in New York right then undressing Yolanda and whomever of her friends wanted to be part of the fun, consuming jeroboams of champagne and snorting a table full of coke.

"Fuck it," he muttered to himself under his breath as the train left Chelsea on its way into central London.

As Pearson was travelling eastwards towards the City in the underground, he had a slightly strange and inexplicable sensation that he was being watched. He quickly ascribed this to Kandinskiy's call. "Bastard has made me fucking paranoid," he thought to himself.

He remembered speaking to a client once who'd spent his life avoiding creditors, relying on 24-hour security. The client told him that as a marked man you spend every waking day of your life vacillating between two very different emotions – one of deep paranoia interspersed with moments of blissful ignorance as you forget the impending danger. But ultimately you are always drawn back to paranoia. If your assassin is real, by the time he catches up with you, it's too late.

CHAPTER 37

OVCHINNIKOV HAD WOKEN EARLY AS HE DID MOST mornings, this first morning in London being no exception. He lit up a cigarette, poured himself 100 ml of vodka and switched on the TV. All he saw were fat, cheery faces of TV announcers and weather girls with crooked teeth and frumpy clothes. Switching off the TV in disgust he ventured down to the first floor for breakfast, the cigarette dangling in his mouth.

"Sir, this is a no-smoking hotel," barked a rather buxom waitress in her thick East London accent. Having no idea what the buxom waitress wanted, Ovchinnikov proceeded to pour himself a jug of coffee and single-handedly appropriate the contents of the modest breakfast buffet. But it bugged him that the waitress had been unfriendly, and he had a mind to make an example of her. He'd noticed the other guests had positioned themselves as far away as possible from his table. Not seeing an ashtray he'd used one of the fruit bowls.

"And they call this a four-star hotel," he muttered to himself in Russian.

After 20 minutes effectively demolishing the contents of the breakfast buffet and smoking out the small room where it was served, Ovchinnikov got up to leave. All the other guests appeared to have left almost immediately upon entering the room and seeing him.

The buxom waitress paced up and down outside the breakfast room, seemingly unwilling or unable to do her job properly and take his order.

"Fucking bitch needs a right cross," he thought to himself and he started to clench his right fist to deliver the well-deserved blow on the way back to his room.

At that point Roman Lebedev's words rang in his ears. "No fucking trouble, you do not attract the attention of *anyone* while you travel.

You will enter and leave London as if you'd never been there – any trouble and you'll blow the whole point of your being there which is to get Pearson – and do that in a manner which has the Brits never quite understanding who, how and why – and this is just the way the boss wants it."

So, rather than delivering her a right cross, he smiled politely on his way out of the drab breakfast room and extended his tattooed hand to the waitress with the most sincere "thank you" (in English) that he could muster.

The buxom waitress, Tabitha, who'd been so offended by her guest's appalling manners blushed, her face going a crimson red, and she smiled broadly, showing off a set of crooked and cigarette-stained teeth.

Tabitha had been at the hotel for six months as a waitress and, despite the brutish appearance of this strange guest from Russia, she was inexplicably drawn to him. Ovchinnikov was the personification of the sort of man her father would have forbidden her from seeing.

As Ovchinnikov wandered out into the cold, wet London morning he could smell the rain on the pavements. He noticed people rushing back and forth, in unison studiously ignoring each other. Then he saw Viktor, with Oleg sitting in the black Mercedes.

"*Privet* Viktor," said Ovchinnikov, "what the fuck are you doing here? I thought I had today off?"

"No such luck Dmitry – timing for the hit has been brought forward. It has to be today. Our client is speaking to Kandinskiy tomorrow and he wants to have this past Kandinskiy before that conversation."

Ovchinnikov shrugged his shoulders and took a few deep puffs of his cigarette. He was a little vexed, but work beckoned, and he was too much of a professional to allow pleasure to interfere with making money.

"OK, then let's get to it Viktor. I need to see where the hit is going to take place. I need to know everything about the local area, where the cameras are, secure buildings, police, everything!" he hissed at Viktor.

Viktor stared at Ovchnnikov for a few seconds. He wasn't particularly enjoying the job of managing the grumpy hitman from Siberia. But he would persevere because it would result in a payday that would make him comfortably off for the foreseeable future. So, he gestured to Ovchinnikov to get into the black Mercedes and the men sped off, Oleg driving – towards Clerkenwell.

After a few minutes of silence, Viktor turned to Ovchinnikov and said, "Dmitry our informant has said the target, Spencer Pearson, is having lunch today at a restaurant near the City called the St John."

"There are window tables which would be perfect for a street hit but we can't guarantee he'll be sitting at those. He could be too far away for us to manage that. So you may have to go inside and do the job – we'll need to give you glasses and a hat."

"No fucking question of doing it from the street. I want to see this for myself. I want to see the drama … unfold," and Ovchinnikov gave Viktor an icy smile.

Given the prevalence of security cameras in London and particularly around the City of London, the bustling home of Britain's huge financial sector, Viktor knew it would be impossible to avoid getting picked up onscreen. There would undoubtedly be images of Ovchinnikov walking into the restaurant, as well as the three of them scoping out the restaurant and surrounding streets.

The challenge was to ensure that the authorities would have no idea who Ovchinnikov was, and be unable to connect the dots – this would become just another unexplained assassination of a lawyer who'd worked for problematic clients and overstepped the mark.

Within hours of the assassination, Ovchinnikov would be on a flight to Moscow and safely out of reach of the British authorities. Viktor and Oleg would collect their money and spend the next six months below the radar, doing their very best to avoid the attention of rival criminals, MI5 and anyone who might have a bone to pick with the killers of Pearson.

Over the next hour and a half Viktor drove Ovchinnikov around Clerkenwell in central London, past the St John restaurant, past the Smithfield meat market and down the narrow lanes that led to the nearby Farringdon underground station. They parked in one of the lanes and Vitkor pulled out a small file containing ten or so photographs. The photographs were all of Pearson, in shops, restaurants, walking down the street, all the time oblivious that he was being followed.

"We have been following him for weeks now," Viktor explained to Ovchinnikov. "He's never noticed us despite our being right next to him on many occasions. We've had dinner next to him, we've pushed it right to the limit, but now we think we know everything there is about him.

"We had wanted to do the hit at his place, we have the floor plans, know where he sleeps and where he keeps his cash – we wanted it to look like a robbery but unfortunately we don't have time for that now. It would have been nice to get our hands on some of his money, we heard another gang was planning a hit, they think he has up to ten million pounds stashed. But Roman called and said no time, we must hit now ..."

None of this particularly interested Ovchinnikov. He was simply focused on the imminent destruction of Pearson's existence. Getting his hands on Pearson's material wealth felt like a distraction from the much more significant and important business at hand – cold-blooded murder.

"I don't give a fuck about the money Viktor, I just want to get this done, take my time and enjoy myself *a little*, leave the restaurant and bang an English girl, then I am prepared to leave England, but not before then."

Viktor let out a little sigh. "Crazy Siberian bastard," he muttered under his breath.

CHAPTER 38

SPENCER PEARSON LEFT HIS OFFICE JUST BEFORE midday and almost skipped towards his venue for lunch in Clerkenwell, the trendy St John restaurant, one of his favourites – none of the pseudo-fusion cuisine inflicted on him in nearly every popular restaurant these days. Just good traditional English food albeit in an upmarket, innovative way. The St John was popular with media types, lawyers, bankers and politicians who'd managed to escape Westminster.

Having shaken off the wave of paranoia he'd suffered earlier that morning, Pearson felt an optimism he'd not had in a long while. As he walked to the restaurant, the sun had even started to come out – workers with pints of beer milled around outside the local pubs.

Anxieties about Kandinskiy felt very distant – he was confident that he'd be able to push his problematic Russian client on to one of the firm's younger, hungrier litigation partners.

As Pearson reached the restaurant, he saw Philip Cleveland seated at a corner table by the window, facing out on to Clerkenwell Road, whisky in hand.

"Philip, great to see you," Pearson said warmly, giving the diminutive Cleveland a firm handshake.

"Spencer," Cleveland responded, standing up straight to greet Pearson, "likewise, beautiful day and I love your choice of restaurant. I haven't been here for ages."

Pearson summoned the waiter and, having spotted Cleveland's large glass of whisky, ordered himself one as well. He felt, after everything he had been through, that he deserved this little indulgence.

"You know Spencer," Cleveland began, "there's been a lot of talk internally about your transition to less 'sexy' work – are you sure you want to give all this up?"

"Philip, I've never been more certain of anything in my life," Pearson said, with a sigh. He took a swig of his whisky. "I've well and truly given up on the high life, well ninety per cent of it anyway. My last trip to Moscow got a little hairy."

"Yes, I heard about that. Sounds like you were lucky to get out of that one," Cleveland replied, a little embarrassed that he'd not previously enquired about Pearson's wellbeing.

"That's exactly the point, things got way too close for comfort Philip. I realised that my clients have their limits in terms of being able to protect me. Frankly I don't want to end up in a situation like that again," and he felt a very faint tremor in his left hand, an involuntary reaction that was triggered every time he talked about his last Moscow trip.

Pearson knew though that the whisky would help to soothe his nerves. Within minutes the alcohol passed into his bloodstream and took effect, his equilibrium restored.

"So, OK Spencer, you leave this crazy world you've been living and working in, or rather you *try* to leave it. What if it catches up with you?"

"An occupational hazard I suppose Philip, but one I've lived with for many years now. My presumption is that if it hasn't happened yet then I'm probably in the clear," and Pearson tapped on the wooden table out of superstition.

The two men ordered their meals, Pearson opting for mutton rack with nettle salad, and Cleveland the less ambitious côte de boeuf. They ordered a bottle of Pomerol 1996 at the price of a day's salary for most City workers.

"Fucking brilliant wine," Cleveland muttered after tasting, licking his lips with approval.

Pearson smiled broadly as he took his first swig, the sensuous, elegant wine trickled down his throat and was a source of immediate pleasure to his taste buds. Before he could echo his approval of the Pomerol to Cleveland, Pearson was distracted by a tall, slim man with angular features who entered the restaurant – he had on sunglasses and looked to be wearing a wig.

The man moved effortlessly through the restaurant towards them, very purposefully walking in his cowboy boots, one step at a time, in their direction. Other patrons, too, noticed this strange, menacing figure – he looked completely out of place in the chic, trendy London restaurant.

Pearson felt a surge of dread and adrenalin rush through his body. His brain was working overtime. Every movement of this man seemed to him so slow, yet purposeful. And Pearson felt powerless to react, unable to move – to run. His legs had turned into stone blocks.

In the ten seconds it took to walk to Pearson's table, Ovchinnikov had more or less assessed every patron in the restaurant, their physical capabilities, sense of awareness and the likelihood which of them might pose an obstacle to his murderous enterprise.

Only one man seemed to be aware, and very quickly, that Ovchinnikov was a potential danger. That man appeared to be the bodyguard of a well-dressed fellow with a recognisable face who must have been a celebrity of one type or another.

At the end of his ten-second walk, Ovchinnikov was standing alongside the seated Pearson, Cleveland clasping his glass of the magical Pomerol, both men staring at him in apprehension. Ovchinnikov pulled a large pistol out of his coat pocket.

Before Pearson had time to reflect on his life's successes and failures, that instant "where your life flashes before your eyes", he felt a sharp, overpowering pain in his hand which, when he looked down, had been blown off.

Ovchinnikov, a methodical, fastidious executioner, liked to inflict pain on his victims before they died, it wasn't enough for them to have their existence quashed. He wanted their last moment of life to be their worst, a horrible realisation of impending doom with their own pitiful impotence contrasting with Ovchinnikov's complete omnipotence – his role of destroyer, judge, adjudicator, tyrant, dictator, assassin, all rolled up into one.

Before Pearson could scream, Ovchinnikov had pointed the pistol at his head and pulled the trigger, scattering his brains all over Cleveland's Savile Row suit and depositing a large chunk of his skull on the immaculately presented mutton and beef they'd ordered for lunch.

Blood covered Cleveland's face, so much blood that he looked like a burns victim beyond any hope of survival. All he could do was open his mouth and utter a silent scream.

But as patrons fell to the ground and started running for the exit in a mad dash, Ovchinnikov was just getting started. He was the master of this situation and had executed so many victims that he understood the pathology and psychology of the human instinct to survive.

That drive was absolute – fewer than one in a hundred had any ability to think remotely rationally when faced with mortal danger. Men who considered themselves brave, courageous would discover that they were complete and utter cowards – unable to match the terrible destructive powers of a man like Dmitry Ovchinnikov.

As Pearson's lifeless body lay slumped against the back of his chair, Ovchinnikov aimed his pistol again at the stump where his head had once sat. The next bullet, exploding on impact, took what was left of Pearson's head clean off his shoulders and deposited the chunk of flesh on to a neighbouring table occupied by two media executives who, ironically, had been boisterously discussing advertising strategies for their campaign to sell beachfront property in Cornwall to wealthy Russians wanting to obtain UK residency.

As Ovchinnikov turned, he noticed the celebrity jammed against the ground under the body of his quick-minded bodyguard. In the seconds it took for Dmitry to walk from Pearson's table to that of the celebrity he evaluated the pros and cons of executing the bodyguard.

Any man who was so composed and rational in such a situation would be a good witness in court he thought in second two. Second three he already had his pistol ready and by the fourth second he had deposited one of his three remaining bullets into the face of the bodyguard and by second five he had executed the celebrity for good measure. There seemed little point in having the bodyguard pay the ultimate price for his paymaster without the latter having to share in the misfortune. Equity in life and business was a concept which Ovchinnikov valued highly.

As Ovchinnikov calmly left the restaurant, panic reigned supreme in Clerkenwell High Street – patrons ran out on to the road without any sense of where they were headed. One was thrown under the wheels of a passing taxi and had her legs crushed by the braking wheels.

As Viktor and Igor drove up at high speed to the door of the restaurant, Ovchinnikov jumped into the black Mercedes, barely interested in the madness that he had created.

"What the fuck happened??!!" Viktor screamed at Ovchinnikov, "Six shots, how many fucking people did you kill?" he yelled at Ovchinnikov in Russian.

Ovchinnikov just looked at Viktor, stared at him, with a look of complete and utter loathing. For a moment, Viktor looked like becoming the seventh victim of the day and Viktor knew it.

But Ovchinnikov regained his composure and let out a huge cackling laugh in the back of the Mercedes, a laugh that took him minutes to contain, tears streaming down his cheeks.

"Oh fuck, you make me laugh Viktor … hah hah hah," and he fell into another bout of uncontrollable giggles.

Eventually he composed himself enough to explain the events as they had transpired.

"You see Viktor, I don't just shoot people for money – for me this is …" and he paused for a second, "this is my profession, and every professional should take pride in his work – without it we're fucking nothing, nothing at all, just asshole hitmen!"

Viktor and Oleg kept completely silent as they drove to Ovchinnikov's hotel, dropping him off without the wig, sunglasses and pistol – they would all be meticulously destroyed by Viktor.

"You're on the 7.30 pm flight so you have two hours to get your stuff together, grab a coffee, keep a low fucking profile and then we come for you after we've got rid of this stuff," Viktor said to Ovchinnikov as he jumped out of the car.

"No problem, see you then," and Ovchinnikov let out a little scowl on leaving the car. "Who the fuck do these punks think they are, bossing me around?" he said to himself.

Police cars and ambulances screamed towards Clerkenwell as Ovchinnikov entered the hotel. He didn't even bother turning around. He'd created the carnage and now it didn't interest him. He only had one objective before heading to the airport.

Meanwhile, back at the restaurant – now looking more like a battle zone – blood dripped from the tables and walls. Pearson's soul looked down at his headless corpse sitting upright in its chair at the restaurant. The table and food on it were blood-soaked, a terrible waste of good mutton and wine he couldn't help thinking. Two more bodies were strewn across the floor, along with tables and chairs which had been knocked over as patrons exited in blind panic.

A deep pang of regret came over Pearson. He'd not been able to retrieve his life in time before it had collided in most unfortunate fashion with the assassin from Russia. He certainly didn't feel anger towards his assassin, but he also couldn't help feeling irritation that his body had been left in such an awful state – it would take a funeral company days, even weeks to put him back in a state sufficiently respectable for a service. Or maybe they'd just shut the wooden box and tell his family there was nothing worth looking at. It also did not particularly worry him that his assassin would never be charged with this crime, indeed it would make him a wealthy man. His soul felt a powerful presence dragging it away from the restaurant, feelings of regret, sadness, isolation all slowly drifting away …

Back at the hotel in Bloomsbury, a trickle of sweat started to make its way down the side of Ovchinnikov's face. He felt his penis, engorged with blood, getting harder and harder as he thrust it deep inside the vagina of the buxom receptionist from East London, cupping her large breasts in his huge hands that still contained blotches of blood from Pearson's destroyed head and torso.

It had taken him all of two or three minutes of pidgin English to convince Tabitha, the breakfast-room waitress and part-time receptionist, to come up to his room. Tabitha wasn't in the habit of going to guests' rooms, particularly single male guests from Russia who spoke rudimentary English.

But Tabitha felt completely powerless to refuse Ovchinnikov – she was overwhelmed by his charisma, an animal attraction and slightly hypnotic quality which she had never felt before, at least not for any of the other men she'd met in her 22 years on the planet.

Indeed, despite his age and his menacing appearance, she fell for his tall, angular features. The strange, medieval tattoos he had emblazoned all over his torso only heightened her very irrational, uncontrollable attraction for this strange man from the East.

As Ovchinnikov climaxed and finished fucking Tabitha he let out a deep groan. "You fucking great horny bitch," he exclaimed in Russian and he bit her on the bottom so hard, she screamed in pain. The bite left a large mark over her voluptuous right buttock and blood started to flow freely from the mark.

"Fuck!" she screamed in pain and the powerful orgasm she'd just felt was replaced very quickly by the throbbing, excruciating pain coming from her bloodied backside.

As he lay in bed, breathing heavily, he reached for his cigarettes and lit up. Tabitha, covered in his sweat and semen, dressed hurriedly. She suddenly realised the madness of the past half hour, driven by an uncontrollable, hormone-induced passion, and she wanted to permanently erase it from her memory.

"Bye," she said quietly, and scurried out of the room, down the stairs to reception.

More than a little pleased with himself, Ovchinnikov stretched back in bed and contemplated what had been a busy day.

"What a great city," he thought to himself, "so many people, so much activity, so many quirky, silly traditions and habits."

He could imagine himself settling in very nicely. But this wouldn't be the time for that and he started to get his things ready, packing his clothes into the small black case he had brought with him. Viktor and Oleg would be at the hotel shortly and he'd be back at Heathrow headed for Moscow that evening.

His Russian mobile started ringing. It was Roman Lebedev.

"Dima, you crazy bastard – why did you turn the restaurant into a scene from fucking Scarface?" asked Lebedev, clearly vexed by Ovchinnikov's theatrical execution of Pearson and several other clients of the restaurant, in direct contravention of the agreed plan which was to attract as little attention as possible.

"Roman, Roman," Ovchinnikov responded, himself a little vexed by the question. "As I told your guys Viktor and Oleg, business was taken care of. I don't leave anything to chance. I'm an artist Roman and when I work, I have to be left to make my choices, trust my own instincts, no one else's. Anyway, I'll be back tomorrow morning early. Let's chat about business in the next few days. I want to keep up this momentum. I feel like my finest work is ahead of me."

Lebedev, who realised that the prospect of controlling someone as unpredictable and combustible as Ovchinnikov was a practical impossibility, relaxed a little and moved on to other matters.

"Of course, Dima, I wasn't born yesterday, I get it. Let's speak when you're back. The boss has identified another target, someone threatening the business. We have to move quickly, there are some complications with this one though – it won't be easy."

"Sounds like a challenge Roman, just what I need …" and Ovchinnikov turned off his phone and finished packing his case.

As he walked out of the hotel he blew a kiss to Tabitha, now standing at reception, doing her very best to convey professionalism and respectability. On seeing Ovchinnikov, Tabitha immediately blushed a crimson red, stammered something to the guests she was checking in and then tripped over, in the process bringing down an enormous vase along with its contents of water and flowers, much to the amusement of her colleagues.

The trip to Heathrow seemed to take an eternity for Ovchinnikov, already bored with his handlers. They had little to talk about and he couldn't help but feel a mixture of envy and suspicion towards them. They clearly had made more money than him and while no city in the world could compare with Moscow, he had enjoyed his very brief experience of London. Part of him regretted leaving, he'd enjoyed his first taste of foreign travel and it felt all too brief.

As the black Mercedes arrived in front of the departure hall at Heathrow, Ovchinnikov jumped out and grabbed his bag from the boot. He walked nonchalantly towards departure without even waving goodbye to Viktor and Oleg –they were happy to see the back of him. He headed straight towards the immigration agent in the departure lounge.

The middle-aged border control officer looked Ovchinnikov up and down. Ovchinnikov's paperwork was in order but he'd noticed specks of blood on Ovchinnikov's hands that he'd not managed to clean given his diversion with the buxom receptionist.

"Everything OK sir?" the officer enquired, looking at Ovchinnikov's hand.

Ovchinnikov, pleased with himself that he'd recognised some basic English in the form of "OK", smiled broadly and repeated "OK" to the border officer.

"OK," the officer smiled back. He decided against engaging any further with this mysterious man from Russia. Stopping Ovchinnikov would have meant considerable additional time at work which he didn't have, given that his shift was ending soon, and his wife had arranged take-away curry for the evening with a bottle of his favourite English cider.

"See you," he said to Ovchinnikov, almost willing him towards security and out of his hair.

As Ovchinnikov sat in a dingy bar in Terminal 3, with a beer in one hand and a shot of vodka in the other he saw that the evening news service was dominated by the shooting which he had carried out just a few hours earlier. He noticed a sheet placed over someone lying on the road which aroused his curiosity. "What the fuck," he thought to himself, "I didn't kill anyone in the street."

He could see a large black Bentley next to the body and it occurred to him that in addition to the woman under the black cab, legs crushed under the weight of the braking taxi, another patron must have fled the scene but had the misfortune to choose a two-tonne Bentley as the car to be run over by.

"What an unlucky bastard," Ovchinnikov thought to himself, "some people really are down on their luck," and he took a swig of his beer before finishing off the vodka. Despite being room temperature (a Russian never drank vodka at anything other than near freezing) the vodka was a welcome pleasure as it trickled down his throat – a nice reminder of what awaited him back home in Russia.

CHAPTER 39

CARL HAD BEEN RUNNING ON THE TREADMILL FOR nearly an hour at the gym on the 60th floor of Falcon Capital's office tower at Moscow City. He could see out to the majestic Moscow University, constructed in the early 1950s and overlooking Sparrow Hills in Western Moscow. The building was enormous, vast, reaching up to the sky like a Russian cosmonaut. The spire at the top of the building was painted gold and shone spectacularly in the afternoon light, like a beacon of optimism guiding Russian society through the confusion and contradictions of the modern world. The Moscow University building had become a symbol of past greatness, past educational and scientific successes. Students in modern Russia now were more concerned with finding a fast track to wealth. The old and noble traditions of science and literature had given way to the excesses of a wildly aggressive form of state-inspired capitalism that valued strength and influence above competence, integrity and transparency.

Drenched in sweat, Carl towelled himself down and moved to the barbells standing in the corner of the gym. As he started lifting the barbells, his arms straining under the weight, he saw Jason Rogers out of the corner of his eye, march in – bodyguard and trainer in tow. He nodded quickly at Carl.

Although powerful and physically imposing, Carl thought that Rogers was looking a little less energetic and sprightly than he used to. The shoulders were a little more slumped, the slightly arrogant gait had gone. He had an aura of wealth and power but gave the impression of a man trapped by circumstances. Even his bodyguard, a mountain of a man and one who exuded self-belief and strength, seemed to have become slightly less intimidating.

Jason Rogers was indeed gripped by a realisation that his days in Moscow were likely coming to an end, as had so many foreigners who had come and gone before him. There was a limit to how much money he could make without attracting the attention of powerful locals, driven by jealousy and envy, and who could not tolerate the thought that a foreigner could make himself rich out of resources that rightly belonged to mother Russia.

His coach was barking out orders to Rogers in his primitive English. "Harder!", "longer!", "don't stop!" appeared to be the full extent of his English. As he shrieked the commands at Rogers, occasionally spitting on his powerful client, Carl could not help but be amused by the spectacle of Rogers having to bravely accept the abuse being launched at him.

Rogers, sweating profusely, gestured to his trainer to stop for a minute and he waved Carl to come across.

"Carl, you won't need to worry about that English lawyer who was causing you so many headaches …"

"That sounds promising Roger, why's that?" Carl asked, innocently.

"Because he's had his head blown all over a restaurant in London, clean off his shoulders apparently," and Rogers let out a little smile. He wiped his forehead with his sports towel and jettisoned it at the feet of the brawny trainer.

Carl looked away to avoid Rogers' gaze, not wanting to make eye contact. He had long suspected that Pearson was taking enormous risks and that his luck would eventually run out. But why had it run out now, at this juncture, so soon after he'd threatened the interests of Falcon Capital.

He noticed, too, that Rogers was staring directly at him, breathing slowly and deliberately, his eyes assessing how Carl would react to what was certainly an unexpected event for anyone except of course, Rogers himself. Carl did his very best not to betray his emotions – he suddenly felt his wellbeing depended on it.

"You know Carl," Rogers said, "I've been operating in this world for nearly twenty years. I've faced my share of existential crises, personal and professional. I've learned that either you adapt to the local environment or you leave. There's no convenient half-way house that would allow me to sleep easy at night."

"OK, Jason, I get it. I'm not entirely sure why you're telling me this though," said Carl, feeling uncomfortable that he had suddenly and inexplicably joined the inner circle at Falcon Capital. It might be a slippery slope from there.

Rogers ran his hands through his thick brown hair tinged with spots of grey. "You've shown that you've got it Carl. You've got balls.

We've picked up on this. Most of the expats we hire here are good for two to three years and then they piss off with their money. They learn nothing about the city or the country, they enjoy the perks but ultimately don't have the curiosity or … commitment … to go the extra step."

Rogers gestured to his trainer to resume their session. His little discourse had finished. No need to say anything more to Carl – the latter was now on notice as to how Falcon Capital operated when its back was against the wall.

The ball was now in his court to run – or stay and fight alongside Rogers, Schwartz and the rest of them, in the hope of making more money than he could ever have dreamed possible.

The boisterous, brawny trainer loaded up the weights on the bench press to 100 kilos and barked at Rogers in his accented English, "Give me 10 reps, fast, now!"

Carl grabbed his towel and walked slowly towards the changing rooms. He felt his heart racing a little and assumed it was a combination of the workout and the information Rogers had shared with him. The only reasonable conclusion he could draw, anyone of sound mind could draw, was that Rogers had rubbed out Pearson. If they had rubbed out Pearson, Carl thought to himself, how many other unexplained deaths in the grimy world of Moscow banking could be traced back to Rogers.

"Fuck me," he muttered to himself in the changeroom while he undressed and headed to the showers.

As the warm water gushed over him, he sensed a dull pain he knew was the beginning of a migraine. His head would soon feel like it was stuck in a vice with someone screwing down on it harder and harder. He'd suffered from overpowering migraines ever since he was a child – whenever he was under great stress or a life-changing event intervened to throw off his otherwise unshakeable equilibrium.

The first time he'd experienced one was when his uncle Jimmy had died suddenly at the hands of a robber who had bound and beaten his uncle, aunt and cousins. Uncle Jimmy's efforts to defend his family had cost him his life. Carl had at that time spent two weeks in bed with an unbearable migraine that the doctor put down to stress.

"We're all affected in our own way Mrs Fitzmaurice, this is little Carl's way of reacting …" were the words he would remember, years later, every time he was struck down by this remorseless affliction.

As he returned to his office, Carl reached into a drawer, grabbed three nurofen and hastily took them with a glass of cold water. He could feel the surge of pain coming into every corner of his skull, spreading like a tsunami through his nervous system. He could only hope that the nurofen would work quickly and disconnect this troublesome nervous activity from the rest of his body.

He stared out his office window and spotted a group of migratory birds headed south. They looked so free and happy. What he would do to join them and exit the predicament he'd suddenly found himself in.

CHAPTER 40

THE ENORMOUS, HULKING AEROFLOT 747 CIRCLED over Sheremetyevo for what seemed like an eternity. Out of his window Ovchinnikov could see the vast expanse that was Moscow, grey and forbidding, apartment blocks as far as the eye could see, onion-domed churches, the red brick walls of the Kremlin visible in the distance. What a beautiful sight he thought to himself. Despite considering his trip to London a major success and greatly enjoying his first experiences outside of mother Russia, the sight of Moscow in all its rough splendour filled him with a sense of profound contentment.

He had found Londoners so very different, curious and strange by comparison with his compatriots. He could not help but feel that ultimately they were in general weak and ineffectual. He was perplexed by the preponderance of effeminate men and the number of women who wore suits and walked around, almost pretending to be men. It was as if God had taken normal society and shaken it on its head.

The mores and principles of London were completely alien to Dmitry. Thank God for the civility and purity of Russia, with its pious Orthodox priests, a president who believed in God and where the local men weren't afraid to give their wives a clip over the ear if they misbehaved.

"Dima!" shouted a tall bulky man with blue eyes and blond hair as Ovchinnikov walked through customs in Terminal D of Sheremetyevo.

"Misha!" Ovchinnikov screamed back in return, giving his enormous friend a big bear hug and high five.

The other patrons in arrivals could not help but stare at the celebrity criminal and his man mountain associate.

Mikhail Borisov, "Misha" to his friends, had been summoned to Moscow by Ovchinnikov from the Siberian village where they had grown up together. Misha was a well-known and widely feared member of the community there. He had been a loyal bodyguard to Ovchinnikov and helped carry out some of his more murderous acts while under his employ.

It had become apparent to Ovchinnikov that as he became more prominent in Moscow, he needed to beef up his security – and he needed someone whom he trusted. Misha, with his huge physical strength, talent for street fighting and competence with weapons of any type, whether guns, knives, tables, beer bottles or bricks, was just the person for the job.

"It looks like you really made an impression in London, Dima – the place looked like a fucking war zone. Nice touch to have a few people run over in the street – it was all over the TV!" said Misha, his light blue eyes fixed on Dmitry's, full of anticipation.

"Actually Misha," said Ovchinnikov, sucking deeply on a cigarette, not for a minute impressed by the carnage he had wreaked in such a short time in that giant metropolis, "I can't take any credit, they were completely in the wrong place at the wrong time," and he let out a little chuckle.

"Main thing is," he continued, as they walked towards the parking area, "I got Pearson, and now I can start on the others. This is going to be serious money for us, it will really set us apart from the other bums operating in Moscow."

Misha let out a broad grin. His decision to join Ovchinnikov appeared to be vindicated. He trusted his friend and business partner with his life. He knew that his friend had a cruel, unforgiving side but he had never considered his friend unreasonable or capricious.

As they entered the parking area, a large black Mercedes crawled up towards both men and flashed its lights. The driver jumped out and gestured to both men to jump in. "I hope you don't mind Dima, but I took the liberty of hiring a driver – he's my cousin Slava, you remember him, he did five years in the local prison for rape?"

"Ah yes, I remember Slava. I was hired to kill him by the uncle of the women he raped, never got around to doing the job before I moved here – if we run out of money he might be down on his luck," and Ovchinnikov let out a raspy, guttural laugh.

"Don't worry I'll do it myself Dima," Misha said with an earnest-ness which suddenly had Ovchinnikov thinking maybe they should make a quick buck and dispose of their newfound driver.

As their car sped towards central Moscow, Ovchinnikov noticed a large black Escalade that kept an even distance from the bulletproof black Mercedes they were travelling in. With one eye on his new chauffeur and the other on the black Escalade, he followed its path through the bumper-to-bumper Moscow traffic, the Escalade powering through the mud and slush of the Moscow motorway, careful not to get too close to the Mercedes, but never allowing Ovchinnikov and his men to get out of sight.

In the car behind, he could see two burly men, almost certainly from the "Kavkas" (Caucasus). The smaller of the two men was driving, skilfully negotiating the traffic, effortlessly changing lanes and pushing aside any driver who flinched for a nano-second.

"Misha," Ovchinnikov said, matter of factly, his long angular face looking in the direction of the black Escalade, seemingly transfixed. "The men in the Escalade are following us – they're Chechen," he said, his face immobile. His right eyelid started flickering ever so slightly, a sign of fatigue and stress.

Misha turned around and twisted his enormous neck to get a better view. "Yes, they're Chechen, Dima – why the fuck would they be following us?"

"I wonder if somehow they have figured out who our client is … killing Pearson may have set the cat among the pigeons – the usual gossips and speculators are probably spouting their theories all over Moscow …" and his voice trailed off.

He tapped Slava, himself still oblivious of the wagon of Chechens, on the shoulder and said into his ear – "Slav, when you get to close to Bolshaya Gruzinskaya turn into it – very last minute, put your foot down, don't ask any questions, just do it OK?"

Slava looked at Ovchinnikov out of the corner of his eye and nodded. He knew Ovchinnikov would happily snuff out his existence should he commit an indiscretion or fail to execute one of his orders. Despite having endured one of Siberia's darkest and most unforgiving prisons, Slava feared Ovchinnikov's reputation as a senior member of the criminal order known as "Vory Zakon", or "thieves law" – a kind of guild of Russian criminals who lived and died by a code that was Russia's equivalent of the Cosa Nostra.

As they got close to Bolshaya Gruzinskaya, Slava moved to the right lane of the imposing Tverskaya Street, with its vast pre-revolutionary era apartment blocks and turned the hulking Mercedes violently right, throwing pedestrians to the ground like bowling pins.

The car sped past the Sheraton Hotel, and Ovchinnikov, scouring the road behind him, could not see the black Escalade of the

Chechens. He told Slava to take the next left down Brestkaya Street and within minutes they were flying down the Garden Ring towards southern Moscow, having shrugged off the carload of Chechens armed to the teeth, and hell bent on getting their hands on Ovchinnikov and his crew.

"Pizdetz," Murat screamed as he realised that Ovchinnikov and his men had escaped. He smashed the steering wheel, screamed obscenities in the dialect specific to his village on the outskirts of Grozny and sped towards the next right-hand turn on Vasilevskaya Street, near the upmarket Patriarshiy Ponds area. But as he cruised around the surrounding streets he realised that his prey had managed to escape.

"We lost them," he said simply to Akhmatov who was sitting in the fortified office at his home in western Moscow. Akhmatov hung up his phone, swore and threw a tennis ball at the feet of his dog Ramzan who proceeded to tear it to bits.

"I'll get you eventually Dmitry Ovchinnikov," Akhmatov whispered to himself.

Akhmatov had followed Ovchinnikov's rise in the Moscow underworld with increasing interest. He realised that this bandit from Siberia, with his rough edges, peculiar accent and propensity for violence could at some point prove to be a rival to his interests. Like a forensic scientist Akhmatov amassed as much information as he could regarding Ovchinnikov.

Nor had Ovchinnikov's spectacular assassination of Pearson gone unnoticed by the Russian authorities. For his case officer, Captain Igor Tarasov, at the Ministry of Interior, charged with following Ovchinnikov's every move, keeping an eye on Ovchinnikov had proved a challenge. When the representatives of the Ministry stationed at the Russian embassy in London had traced him to the hotel in Bloomsbury, it became obvious very quickly that the shadowy figures he was associating with were, themselves, former FSB.

But Captain Tarasov had no interest in the shadowy former FSB operatives. The job of monitoring them would have to be performed by colleagues far higher placed than him. The FSB were at the top of the pyramid in Russia, the Ministry of Interior and of Defence would just have to wait their turn.

When Ovchinnikov finally made it to his well guarded residence in northern Moscow the first thing he did was to have Olya Chekunova, his resident *babooshka* – cook/cleaner and overall lady of the house, prepare him a large plate of *"piroshky"* (Russian dumplings), cold meats and vegetables to be downed with a fine bottle of Russian vodka. There was something reassuring about Madame Chekunova's *piroshky* and her domineering, motherly manner.

"You grow skinny Dima!" she rebuked Ovchinnikov, "you clearly did not look after yourself in London. God only knows what you were doing," and she crossed herself several times, as if to cleanse the soul of her employer. She knew that Ovchinnikov was a contract killer, thug and career criminal, but despite all that she saw the good side of the man who could be loyal to a fault, considerate, intelligent and witty when he wanted.

"Olya, the English eat such crappy food and have such strange habits, I felt really quite disoriented there, lost my equilibrium. Thank God for your bossy manner and your magnificent *piroshky*!" and he let out a throaty laugh which brought a smile from her, the lines in her face creasing up and her shoulders shaking as her whole body convulsed with laughter.

Once he'd finished his enormous bowl of *piroshky* and downed half a bottle of vodka from his home region in the Siberian taiga, he picked up his brand-new top-of-the-range mobile phone which had been specially encrypted to permit calls in and out, in relative security. He dialled Roman Lebedev.

"Roman, I'm back, job done," he said simply.

"OK, Dima, let's meet. I'll come with the boss at nine o'clock."

It was already 6.30 pm so Lebedev would have to arrange for whatever appointment was in Jason Rogers' agenda to be summarily cancelled and a driver to be ready for a trip out to Ovchinnikov's safe-house. He realised that he and Rogers had now entered a zone they'd not been in since the 90s – one where the slightest misstep or prevarication in the endlessly changing and incredibly complicated world of business and politics in Moscow could result in enormous financial losses and sudden death.

Roman Lebedev felt a sense of anxiety he'd not felt for a very long time. Now well into his 60s, his enthusiasm for corporate life waning, he'd started consuming a little more Italian red wine at night than he probably should and his old network of contacts in his former employer, the infamous KGB, suddenly seemed less forthcoming with information than they had been previously. That worried him.

Jason Rogers was in a meeting in his office, the biggest in the building, protected by security guards at both entrances, when Lebedev gestured from outside the glass wall that he needed to speak to him. Rogers looked up, nodded and brought his meeting to an abrupt end. Gesturing to Lebedev to enter, he put his reading glasses down in front of the desk and closed his office door.

"Jason, Ovchinnikov is back. We've got to go out to meet him. There are a few things we need to discuss with him – too dangerous over the phone."

Rogers looked at Lebedev for a few moments, his eyes fixed on him, as if he were assessing the state of mind of his most trusted security adviser.

"OK, fine, let's do it. I assume we don't want to come with the cavalry, just a driver?"

"Yes," Lebedev responded, "as few people as possible, any sign that we're being followed and we abort the trip, too risky. The Ministry of Interior may have figured out that Ovchinnikov was behind Pearson's assassination and that is very valuable information. If they could connect us to Ovchinnikov that would put us in a very compromising position."

"You don't say," Rogers responded with a touch of irony, suddenly alarmed at the thought that his association with Ovchinnikov could bring Falcon Capital and his whole career in Russia, crashing down like a felled tree.

Lebedev and Rogers jumped into a large black, bulletproof Maybach that was kept in a basement car park in an adjoining building. They had gone down several flights of stairs and taken a circuitous route through the subterranean series of car parks at Moscow City to ensure that no one was following.

Mobile phones had been left in the office. Lebedev had on him a small Nokia with Ovchinnikov's number that would serve as their only form of communication with the outside world for several hours.

They had minimised the chances of the country's intelligence services tracking their movements but they could never be completely confident that the car itself had not been bugged or that someone in the extensive security apparatus which protected Rogers and senior management hadn't sold information to the FSB or one of their many corporate rivals.

As the long, hulking Maybach sped towards northern Moscow, a police helicopter whizzed past overhead, followed shortly thereafter by a cortege of police vehicles headed east along the Garden Ring, in the opposite direction to Rogers and Lebedev, much to their relief.

As they got closer to Ovchinnikov's residence, Lebedev's Nokia rang and Rogers could hear Ovchinnikov's voice. He and Lebedev spoke briefly, for a few minutes, then hung up.

Lebedev turned to Rogers, "Jason, there's a good chance the Chechens are on to Ovchinnikov. They had to throw them off earlier today – it means that Akhmatov may have figured out what has been going on ..."

Rogers ran his hands through his hair and looked out at the gloomy streets of northern Moscow, the endless expanse of cheap neon lights and massive, uniform apartment blocks. "Roman, what are our options? It seems that half of fucking Russia knows about us and Ovchinnikov now. Do we forget about tonight and move on? We can find another way of paying him – let's stick the money in an offshore account for him ..."

"No Jason," Lebedev responded. "The stakes are too high now. We need a meeting this evening and we need to map out the next forty-eight hours very carefully. Despite his slightly unconventional approach, there is no-one better able than Dmitry to protect us if the situation were to deteriorate further and my best guess is ... that it will."

Lebedev, the old KGB spy, spoke quietly and with purpose. He was in his element, potential saviour of Rogers and Falcon Capital – if he could manage the forces lined up against them. As they reached a long, nondescript road lined by factory buildings covered in graffiti, Lebedev called Ovchinnikov and announced their imminent arrival.

A little further down the road a large metal door creaked as a heavily armed security guard forced it open, waving at them frantically, "*davai, davai*," he screamed in Russian, entreating the driver to speed up. The Maybach glided through the gates and was greeted by a pack of barking rottweilers as well as heavily armed guards.

Ovchinnikov, in combat trousers and a black cashmere polo top, pistol hanging from his jeans, walked into the garage and yelled at his guards to drag the dogs away and give his clients a more respectful welcome.

"Fucking pricks, you've got no fucking respect!" and he slapped a guard across the face, pulling his ear until the guard screamed in pain.

He greeted Rogers and Lebedev warmly, ushering them into a back room which had been fitted out with a pool table, green marble bar and flashing disco light. Ovchinnikov offered both men cigars and poured them two generous glasses of Scotch whisky.

After a few polite exchanges, Ovchinnikov cleared his throat and got down to business. "Mr Rogers," he started, using Lebedev as translator, "the operation against Mr Pearson was successful, we got our target. But …" and he paused for a moment, "the rules of the jungle are in constant flux, we face considerable danger from the *men from the south*," and he looked at Lebedev, who nodded in agreement.

Ovchinnikov was not one to mince his words or to worry about social mores. He considered the Chechens and pretty much anyone from the "Stans" to be an inferior breed, a scourge on Russian society, leeching off the success and relative stability of their northern neighbour.

As Ovchinnikov spoke he surveyed the screens linked to security cameras outside his factory and positioned at roads in the vicinity.

"With that in mind, gentlemen, the nature of our arrangement will have to change, we are going to enter a gang war which I fully intend to win," and he looked at Lebedev to ensure that he was carefully and scrupulously translating every syllable for Rogers, whose blue eyes were fixed on Ovchinnikov while he listened to Lebedev.

"I will need more money and resources to fight these guys – these aren't two-bit thugs that I've protected you against before, but men who are connected at the very highest levels of power."

Ovchinnikov took a long puff from his cigar, filling his mouth and lungs with its rich Cuban smoke. A blood vessel below his left eye twitched but that was the only sign of mortality and fatigue in the Siberian career criminal who was now encountering extreme danger but embraced it willingly, clearly revelling in the challenge.

"This is what you '*inostranitz*' (foreigners) would call a 'game changer'," and he gently placed his glass of whisky on the wooden coffee table as if to steady himself. "No time for fucking around now, we are about to enter a phase of war, gang war, it is going to get extremely dangerous, for all of us."

Rogers did not bat an eyelid as Ovchinnikov spoke. He had been under no illusion as he travelled the grim, grey streets of Moscow out to see him that his fixer of many years would have unwelcome news.

He had perhaps not anticipated the sudden descent of the Kandinskiy file into such a dramatic and dangerous spiral. What had started off as a simple debt recovery had suddenly, turned into a sinking ship dragging him down in its wake, him and Falcon Capital – and there was absolutely nothing he could do about it.

Committing to a gangland war with the Chechens was as good as throwing himself off the nearest building or playing an extended game of Russian roulette.

Rogers took a swig of his whisky, nearly downing the entire contents. The smoky flavoured liquid warmed his throat and steadied his nerves.

"Roman," he said, looking at Lebedev, "arrange for Dmitry to get whatever resources he requires, no expense spared. Let's also reach out to that former KGB guy you introduced me to, the fixer and get him on board as well."

"You mean Yury Smirnov," Lebedev responded. "He's been briefed, and I'll have him co-ordinate with the security services – if anything is to happen to Akhmatov it needs to at least have the support of my old contacts. I can't see the President supporting this but at the very least we need the FSB onside."

Ovchinnikov listened as Rogers and Lebedev spoke in English. He could tell from their body language that they would agree to his terms and provide him with the resources to go at it with the Chechens. He knew deep within his Siberian bones that this could be a step too far, that maybe he had finally bitten off more than he could chew. But his hatred for the Chechens was such that there was no turning back. He'd rather be blown to bits than give an inch.

Ovchinnikov invited Rogers and Lebedev to stay and share the dinner prepared by Madame Chekunova who had entered the room and immediately started fussing over her boss, nagging at him to stop smoking and drinking so much.

"You will go to an early grave if you continue to live your life like this," she chastised him, giving him a little smack on the shoulder. He laughed and gave her an affectionate kiss on her cheek.

"Guys you must stay and enjoy her latest batch of *piroshky*, they're the best she's ever fucking made!"

"Thank you, Dmitry," Lebedev replied, "we'd love to," and he dipped his head in acknowledgement to old lady Chekunova. "But I have to get Jason back to his residence and we're looking at a long trip. We need to get going on various fronts early tomorrow morning, and I need to meet with Smirnov this evening."

"Of course, Roman, you're right," replied Ovchinnikov, "but it's a damn shame when business interferes with a good meal!"

Rogers and Lebedev made their way towards the Maybach which had been moved to the back door of the safe house, ready to whisk them off to west Moscow.

CHAPTER 41

AFTER LEBEDEV DROPPED OFF ROGERS AT HIS palatial and heavily guarded residence in western Moscow, he instructed the driver to take him back to a popular Serbian restaurant for dinner – Boemi, right near the Russian Parliament building on the river. It was there that he had arranged to meet Yury Smirnov, the former KGB agent.

He was greeted warmly by the owner of the restaurant, a tall, thin man with white hair and green eyes. "Roman, so good to see you again. It's been a while. I had wondered if you had forgotten about your Serbian allies," and he laughed warmly.

"Never, Dmitry!" Lebedev responded, "a Russian never forgets his Serbian friends!" and the two men shook hands warmly. The owner, Dmitry Kobzev, who hailed from Belgrade, gestured to Lebedev to follow him to the private VIP room at the back of the restaurant.

The VIP room was reserved for Kobzev's best and most influential clients, and he counted Lebedev among those. He'd had to rely on the support of Lebedev in a battle with a business rival looking to take ownership of the restaurant into which he'd invested years of his life, not to mention his entire savings. The encounter with Lebedev had not turned out particularly well for the business rival who returned to Serbia, never again to set foot in Russia.

As Lebedev sat down in the plush chair next to an ornate dining table with gold trim, Dmitry Kobzev clicked his fingers at the nearest waiter and told him to bring to Lebedev's table a bottle of the restaurant's finest sljivovica, a Serbian plum brandy.

Lebedev checked his phone and took a swig. "Best thing I ever did was to send that Serbian asshole packing back to Belgrade," he thought to himself. He'd ensured himself a lifetime of devoted service and magnificent sljivovica from the grateful Kobzev.

A few minutes later, Smirnov entered, bodyguard in tow, resplendent in a light grey suit with white leather shoes, looking very much the Mr Fixit that he was.

"Roman, *privet*," he said warmly, making himself comfortable on the plush chair facing Lebedev. "Things are getting interesting now with you guys," he opened the conversation, his grey eyes looking curiously at Lebedev, assessing how his old friend and colleague would react.

"Yes, they are unfortunately Yury, a bit too interesting for my liking. I thought this job with Falcon Capital would be easy and boring, perfect at my age, but it has proved far more 'stimulating' than I had anticipated," and he laughed a little ironically. He took another swig of the sljivovica. Perhaps that would improve his mood he thought.

Smirnov unwrapped a pack of cigarettes and lit one with a large silver-plated lighter. Smoke billowed across the room.

"Roman," Smirnov addressed Lebedev quietly, undoing his napkin and looking reflectively at the fire that was burning in the small fireplace in the centre of the room, "there are forces at play here which even you could not imagine. The question with the Governor of Chechnya has become a major issue. The guy is behaving like a complete bandit. We can't underestimate the lengths he will go to Roman," and he took another puff of his cigarette, sending smoke rings floating slowly up towards the chandelier hanging over them.

"I understand he's very focused on Kandinskiy and needs the money to finance some of his more extravagant projects in Chechnya, including equipping his private army. Needless to say, our old colleagues in Lyubyanka (FSB headquarters) are none too pleased by the Governor's 'initiative'."

"That's understood Yury, but we already have a small army protecting Rogers, and it's costing us a fucking fortune. Not to mention, we have to finance Ovchinnikov's operation which needs to be expanded to deal with these guys. We've been dragged into this fucking confrontation and I am a little pissed off with myself that I didn't see it coming," Lebedev said bitterly.

"Roman, don't be so hard on yourself. Modern Russia is a complicated place. Our predecessors had it easy by comparison, a common enemy, lifetime employment provided you could stick to the right path and not get distracted. Things are different now, there are traps everywhere. It's practically impossible to anticipate most of them.

Even Marshal Zhukov would have come unstuck!" and the two men laughed, nodding in agreement.

"What I can offer you Roman," Smirnov continued, "is a measure of protection if things get out of hand with Akhmatov and the Governor, but we'll be taking a risk. This will put us at odds with the Kremlin," he said, taking another long puff of his cigarette.

Yury's got balls, Roman Lebedev thought to himself. Most men in his position would run a mile before risking a fight with the President's ever-expanding circle of interests.

The two men dined late into the evening, reminiscing about their lives as spies during the Cold War, downing glass after glass of sljivovica, laughing boisterously as they recounted some of the more farcical and amusing aspects of their former careers.

For Lebedev it felt like a farewell dinner and Yury Smirnov picked up on Lebedev's nostalgia. But Smirnov believed that Lebedev had one last battle in him – that he still had the tenacity and fight to get the better of Ruslan Akhmatov.

At 1 am both men decided to call it a night and let the staff close up. As they opened the door into the cold night, a blast of wind shook them to their bones. A dog in a neighbouring property started barking and before Lebedev had any time to react or calculate what was happening, Smirnov had fallen to his knees and was gasping for air, his lungs punctured by two bullets fired with impeccable precision. Then a deafening silence reigned.

Smirnov looked plaintively at Lebedev before collapsing to his right side, his legs buckling under him.

The last thing Roman Lebedev ever saw was his assassin walk calmly up to him, pistol held at shoulder level, every step, every movement deliberate and confident, like a master ballet dancer on the stage of the Bolshoi. In the micro-seconds that stood between him and permanent extinction Lebedev felt himself suddenly drawn inextricably and intimately into the life of this man, this man who had come to destroy him. He was completely and utterly at the mercy of this individual – he felt an overpowering impotence, but it didn't bother him.

His liberator had come, there would be no more worldly bothers or concerns, all these would be taken away, forever. The pain that he felt as the bullet entered his carotid artery was ever so short-lived. The second bullet he didn't even see or feel, it was very neatly aimed at his forehead by Rustam Mikhailovich Kabaev, a paramilitary soldier in the Chechen governor's private guard. The bullet ricocheted inside Lebedev's skull and turned whatever was left of his brain into mush. The two former comrades lay silent in the snow next to each other, their bodies completely limp.

His work done, mission accomplished, Kabaev ran off into the Moscow evening, past the enormous Senate building on Moscow River and over the bridge to the palatial hotel on the opposite bank. He calmly walked into reception and took the lift to his room. When he entered, he saw Akhmatov seated at a small table by the hotel window. Both men hugged each other but did not exchange a single word. Akhmatov knew his friends in FSB headquarters at Lyubyanka were listening to him. But Akhmatov's pleasure was undisguisable. He handed Kabaev an open bag with a hundred thousand US dollars stuffed inside. Kabaev smiled and nodded in gratitude. "Allahu Akhbar," he said quietly.

A good night's work Kabaev thought to himself.

For Akhmatov this was a bold move, one which set him inexorably upon a course of confrontation with senior members of the FSB. He touched fists with Kabaev and left the hotel room quickly, accompanied by Murat who had come up to escort his boss to the car waiting in the hotel parking lot. As they jumped into the Cadillac Escalade, the driver started the car with a roar and flew out into Kutuzovsky Prospekt, narrowly missing an old Lada, forcing it on to the footpath – to the consternation of its septuagenarian driver.

Akhmatov lit up a cigarette and drew the smoke deep into his lungs. He sent a short message via an encrypted messaging system to an anonymous contact which just said "Done".

The anonymous contact responded immediately *"Xorosho"* (good). The black Cadillac continued at breakneck speed into the Moscow night.

CHAPTER 42

CARL FELT A WAVE OF EXCITEMENT AS SOON AS HE received the text from Oksana who'd agreed to meet him at his apartment for dinner. "I'm downstairs, can you buzz me up?" was the message. He could not have hit the buzzer fast enough. Within minutes, she stood at his door, all 180 cm of her, in an immaculate black dress that magnificently complemented her svelte figure, with matching high heels and fur coat.

"Jesus," was all Carl could say as she entered his apartment. Oksana laughed, and strode confidently across, placing her Louis Vuitton bag on a coffee table in the centre of the room. She walked up to Carl and gave him a long kiss on the lips.

Carl was just about to pour his beautiful Russian friend a glass of wine when his mobile started ringing. It was Schwartz. "Fucking hell," Carl whispered to himself. He let the phone ring out and gave Oksana the wine. The phone immediately lit up again and a text flashed across his screeen – "Pick up!!!"

"Give me a minute," he said to Oksana. Oksana nodded and affectionately ran her hand through his hair. "Good luck," she said, flashing her perfectly white teeth at him.

"Klaus – what's the matter, it's Sunday night, don't you ever take time off?" Carl remonstrated.

"Shut up Carl, we don't have time for your bullshit. We're in real fooking trouble, real trouble. Roman Lebedev and Yury Smirnov have just been executed outside a restaurant in Moscow. We've just been warned by the most senior levels of the FSB that the Chechens have infiltrated nearly every level of our organisation …" The normally boisterous and aggressive Schwartz was suddenly breathless, struggling for air. The tension was palpable, unbearable.

Schwartz steadied himself and continued. "I understand you have a new lady friend – beware, she's on the list of people I've been handed with connections to Akhmatov. You must find out where she is, and we'll send our guys to take care of her …"

"A bit late for that now Klaus," Carl responded.

"What the fook are you talking about?" Schwartz yelled into the phone.

Carl turned around and looked at Oksana, the mobile phone almost spilling out of his hand. She knew instantly that the phone call had been to warn Carl about her.

"Carl," she said softly.

"Oksana, who the fuck are you?" Carl responded, his pulse racing, suddenly feeling trapped within the confines of his apartment.

But Oksana had no intention of responding to his question and, although her hands were trembling ever so slightly, she calmly grabbed a large knife from her handbag. There was a terrible moment when Oksana and Carl looked at each other – neither wanting to make the next move for fear it would be their last. Oksana moved cautiously forward one step, suddenly fearing that she was incapable of executing the mission which her boss Ruslan Akhmatov had prepared her over many months to carry out.

Carl thought he was yelling at Oksana to stop but his mind was in such a state of confusion that he wasn't sure whether he was yelling or completely silent. He felt a surge of adrenalin charging through his body as his brain programmed the existential risk he was under. He put his hands up, to block the blade which was now within a couple of metres of him. Oksana had, after a moment of doubt, remembered her training and purposefully walked towards Carl making large swooping thrusts with the knife.

As she lunged forward, she let out a primal scream and thrust the knife with all her force in one last crazy swoop in the direction of Carl who had assumed a defensive posture. At the very last moment before the knife made contact with his torso, he grabbed a frying pan from his kitchen bench and swung it at Oksana with all the strength he could muster.

The frying pan connected with her head with such force that she was instantly knocked 180 degrees, smashing against the edge of his dining table. A sickening thud rang out and before her body had fallen to the ground a projectile of blood had doused Carl. Blood continued to pour out of her head as she lay, motionless, on the ground.

Carl's brain was working overtime, he could feel his legs, his hands and just about every muscle in his body shaking uncontrollably – he was having great difficulty processing everything that had happened in the past few minutes. It was as if a century had been compressed into a moment of time. He was frozen in fear and could not bring himself to go near Oksana. He could hear her struggling for air, her eyes were beginning to roll around the back of her head and her hands, which had trembled erratically, ceased moving altogether.

Before Carl could grasp what was happening, he was looking at the ceiling – he was no longer standing. He had no idea why he was on his back and not able to move. He felt a sharp pain in his side and slowly moved his hand to touch the affected spot. He could feel the plastic handle of a knife buried inside him. She had made contact. He could feel something wet which he assumed was blood. It was spilling out of the incision the knife had made in the side of his body. He was going to die, damn it, he was dying …

As he slid out of consciousness the door of his apartment was bashed open with a tremendous thud. Ovchinnikov walked calmly into Carl's apartment and surveyed the bloodshed there. He moved towards Oksana and knelt down next to her corpse. He then walked towards Carl and moved his hands along Carl's arms and torso. He felt the knife protruding from under Carl's left arm and the blood that was pouring freely from the wound. With the skill of a surgeon he pulled the knife out of Carl calmly and professionally. He made a tourniquet which he wrapped around Carl's upper body to stem the bleeding.

Carl's mobile rang – it was Schwartz.

Ovchinnikov picked up the phone with his bloodied hand, "Klaus, it is Dmitry. I am with the South African. He will live," and slammed the phone down.

Ovchinnikov lit a cigarette and made a call, "Misha, get here right away, I'm at the South African's apartment in Patriarshiy Ponds. Bring the Escalade and lots of plastic, we need to take him to the hospital and we will have to dispose of a dead body, the Chechen girlfriend …"

"There in twenty minutes boss," and Misha hung up.

Ovchinnikov sat on the dining room chair, a dead body curled up next to the dining room table, and Carl drifting in and out of consciousness but not in any particular danger of dying.

Carl's blood had dried on Ovchinnikov's hand but before cleaning it he wanted to finish the cigarette he'd started smoking. The dead Chechen worried him. He knew that his cousins from the Caucasus would almost certainly want to extract their revenge for the death of someone who was likely a valuable member of their gang. He gave himself an hour maximum before the Chechens would be at the door of Carl's apartment ready to kill everyone and everything in sight.

Exactly on time, Misha knocked quietly on the door of Carl's apartment and entered with Slava.

"Misha," Ovchinnikov said, "you brought your rapist cousin, I'm sorry the Chechen girl would have been perfect for him but she's a little cold now!" and he chuckled loudly.

Slava ignored Ovchinnikov's slight and helped his burly cousin lift the dead body into a body bag that fitted its dimensions perfectly.

Misha, his huge legs and shoulders on top of Oksana's corpse, carefully compressed the long, thin body into a form that resembled a slightly oversized basketball wrapped in plastic. Bones cracked under the tremendous power applied by Misha. Ovchinnikov and Slava just watched in quiet awe as this bear of a man went to work.

"Fuck me," Ovchinnikov said, his cigarette nearly falling out of his open mouth. "Hey you, the rapist, help your cousin, drag Carl down to the car. We have to get this boy to the hospital!!" Slava nodded obediently, threw Carl over his shoulder and followed Misha to the Escalade.

The powerful engine of the enormous armoured Escalade started up and the car screamed out into Spiridonovskiy Lane heading towards the Garden Ring and then a hospital in southern Moscow where Ovchinnikov knew a very capable surgeon who would do nearly anything for the right fee.

Carl was sprawled across the leather seats of the Escalade. Ovchinnikov could see that blood was continuing to flow from his wound but more slowly. To make sure Carl was not going to remain passed out for too long he gave him a slap across the face, to elicit a reaction.

"He's out cold," Ovchinnikov muttered, "don't fuck around Slava," he bellowed, "get us to the hospital in ten minutes, not a second longer."

"Dmitry," Ovchinnikov said in a booming voice into his mobile, "I have another client for you," and he laughed into the receiver, his fingers cracking with nervous energy. He had dialled Dmitry Lavrov, eminent Moscow surgeon, battle-trained in the Chechen wars and now, the must-have surgeon for every well connected gangster whose protégés had been shot, stabbed or otherwise maimed. He could patch them up as well as anyone in Russia and was trusted never to alert the authorities. For this he was paid handsomely.

"Bring him in Dima, you've caught me at a good time my friend. I can see him right away," Lavrov responded, and without exchanging any pleasantries hung up the phone.

CHAPTER 43

SCHWARTZ TOOK A SWIG OF THE SCOTCH WHISKY from a metallic flask that he kept in the top drawer of his enormous mahogany desk. It was nearly 11 am, and in light of recent events he felt he was entitled to the momentary relief which the smoky Scotch from an obscure island off the west coast of Scotland would bring him.

As he felt the last drip of the whisky he had greedily drunk trickle down his throat like life-saving medication, his private phone rang loudly. The words "unknown number" were emblazoned on his screen. Nothing perturbed Schwartz so much as his phone ringing with an unknown number, and almost without exception he would let the phone ring through. This time he felt an inexplicable urge to pick up.

"Hello."

"Klaus," a deep, male voice responded.

"Yes, who is this?" Schwartz answered.

"A friend Klaus. It is time we spoke. I think we can help each other. I know about your financial problems, your gambling debts. I can erase them with a click of my fingers, because those debts are now mine. But I want something in return ..."

Schwartz put the receiver down momentarily. He rubbed his eyes and look out over the vast expanse of western Moscow with its skyscrapers, parks and Stalinist towers.

"OK, what is it that you want? I'm not the sort of person you want to fuck with."

"I can assure you my friend Klaus, nor am I. I am deadly serious. A car is waiting for you downstairs. A black Mercedes. When you leave your building a driver in a dark suit will be standing in front of the car – he will wave to you and you will follow him and sit in the back seat of the car. There will be two other men in the car with you, *for your protection.* You will travel with them to a location where I will present my proposal to you," and the caller hung up.

In his twenty years in Moscow, Schwartz had never felt so ... afraid. He realised that the caller was in complete control of the situation and, of him. The man had spoken in a calm, self-assured tone. Schwartz understood that he had absolutely no ability to refuse to comply with this man's request.

He grabbed his black leather briefcase, packed his computer, wallet and glasses into it and hurriedly left his office. His secretary Yana waved her hand at him – in vain – to stop him from leaving without an explanation. But he just shook his head as if to tell her not to dare pose the question.

He looks worried, she thought to herself. Her one consolation was that she would not have to deal with his irascibility for a few hours.

As Schwartz entered the lift quickly, he spotted his reflection in the enormous reflective glass of the lift, and he dared not look up. He suddenly felt weak and vulnerable. But the desire to look at himself was too strong and he stared at the forlorn figure facing him.

He understood that unlike his usual elegant self he looked scruffy – his hair was messy and his eyes looked tired, red, his face puffier, more pock marked than usual. His legs looked short and fat, his belly bigger and more burdensome than ever.

The lift accelerated down with a thrust that felt more powerful than normal and nearly knocked him off his feet. As he exited the building, he avoided eye contact with colleagues and the beautiful women at reception whom he usually fawned upon.

In the corner of the car park he saw a muscular, bearded man standing next to a black Mercedes. The man looked at him intently and waved at Schwartz. As Schwartz approached, he saw two other heavy-set men in suits inside the car.

The heavy metallic door was opened for him and he jumped in. As he seated himself, he could see that the men in the car were not Russians, but most likely from the Caucasus.

"Chechens," he immediately understood. His mind started racing. Almost certainly the same men who had assassinated Roman Lebedev the evening before, and the hapless CFO for Kandinskiy's corporate empire whose gruesome murder was still being talked about in Moscow business circles.

A feeling of dread came over Schwartz. His courage and resilience immediately left him and he felt weak, pathetically weak. The giant

4x4 Mercedes left the car park of Moscow City and at breakneck speed flew north along the embankment, past the British embassy and in the direction of Luzhniki stadium. A kilometre before arriving at the vast grounds of Luzhniki, the Mercedes came to a sudden halt in front of an enormous boat moored on the river. A huge sign hanging from the boat advertised the Georgian restaurant that lay inside the boat. Schwartz was ushered out of the car by the muscular guard and towards a metal footbridge leading on to the boat.

Once inside the restaurant Schwartz was overpowered by the strong smell of onions, mutton and shisha pipe. He could see guests, most of them heavily guarded, corpulent businessmen, eating huge platters of Georgian cuisine, smoking, skolling vodka. Buxom waitresses squeezed into impossibly short skirts were fawned over by their patrons who groped them inappropriately without apparent consequences.

A door to a private room was opened and another guard, with a small neat beard, thin and short but with eyes that Schwartz knew he would never forget, gestured to him to enter.

With every fibre of his body Schwartz wanted to leave, but he felt completely powerless. As he entered, he could see a well-dressed man of medium height, clean-shaven with small black glasses seated at a large wooden dining table. On the table were bottles of water and a small golden pistol, ostentatiously placed on top of a black briefcase.

The man looked at him and smiled. It was Ruslan Akhmatov. He gestured to Schwartz to sit down.

"Klaus, it has been a while. So much has happened since we last caught up. I feel like we have almost become strangers which is ... regrettable."

He lingered over the word "regrettable" for a second or two. He snapped his fingers and asked a short, stocky waiter to bring them coffee and shisha. Schwartz squirmed uncomfortably in his chair. He could feel his heart pounding and he felt his brow was dripping in sweat. He knew that Akhmatov could easily finish him off there and then and no-one would bat an eyelid.

As if reading Schwartz's mind, Akhmatov patted the golden pistol with his right hand and smiled.

"You know that I toyed with the idea of killing you today Klaus. You and Jason Rogers have, how do I say, '*unnecessarily complicated* ' things for me in recent weeks on this Kandinskiy matter. But then I was overcome by a sense of ... *mercy* – there is no other way to describe it. This 'mercy' is an emotion which I so rarely feel. For me it is synonymous with weakness. However, you have been such a good client over the years at my clubs that I have taken pity on you. I have even bought up your gambling debts so they are not your concern, any longer."

Schwartz squirmed in his chair. He had dealt with so many Russian businessmen and crooks in his time that he knew Akhmatov would want something in return and that it would be impossible for him to refuse.

"What is it that you want Ruslan?" Schwartz said firmly, regaining some of his composure.

"Klaus, I want you to deliver me Jason Rogers, because I want to kill him. Let me put that a little differently. I need to kill him. With him in the picture I stand to lose far more in the debt collection process from Kandinskiy's assets than I intended to. The 'Governor', my boss, has also made it very clear that such an outcome is completely unacceptable. I must make a return which is a … reasonable recognition of all the effort that we have put in."

Akhmatov paused for a moment and took a sip of the black coffee in front of him. He pushed back into his leather chair and looked Schwartz squarely in the eyes. He started slowly tapping on the table, as if to speed up Schwartz's response.

Schwartz hesitated for a few seconds and then reached forward in his chair, leaning almost on top of Akhmatov.

"What is in it for me Ruslan?" he said aggressively, momentarily regaining his old bravado.

"Your life for one thing, Klaus," Akhmatov smiled, sitting back further in his chair to avoid the discomfort of having Schwartz pressed against him.

"Secondly, I can make this financially rewarding for you, enough to start a new life a long way from this country. And I strongly urge you," he said, staring at Schwartz and cracking his long thin fingers, "to leave this place behind you. You foreigners had your time here, made your money, had your fun, now you must move on. *You are no longer welcome …*" he hissed.

Schwartz had long wondered when the day would come that he would be told to go, to leave, to pack up. But the finality of Akhmatov's words shook him and he felt his palms go sweaty – a pall of death hung over this restaurant by the river, and the sooner he was out of it the better.

"OK, Ruslan, you've got a deal," Schwartz practically whispered, unable to look Akhmatov in the eye. Both men shook hands.

As he stood up to leave, Schwartz had the distinct impression that he had made a deal with the devil. He looked briefly at the patrons who sat there gorging themselves, speaking loudly with each other and yelling into their mobile phones.

He realised that he no longer belonged in this new Russia dominated by the new, bourgeois arriviste class with its proximity to the Kremlin and disavowal of anything that was connected to the mega businesses set up by the oligarchs in the 90s. Like Romans at an orgy they were feasting themselves on the remains of the oligarch class – and their appetite appeared to know no limits.

CHAPTER 44

A S THE WATER OF HIS SWIMMING POOL SKIPPED and jumped in his wake, Jason Rogers swam lap after lap, clearing his mind of just about every thought connected to Falcon Capital and his own precarious hold over it. His doctor, a serious man with small eyes and a narrow forehead, had advised him to exercise to overcome the mind-numbing insomnia that had made nights impossible and his days ineffective.

The doctor's words were still ringing in his ears.

"Mr Rogers, I see many men like you, successful, hard working. They die young because they are unable to find their life balance, their "*radnost* " (happiness). You are a good client, I don't want to lose you," and he laughed, showing a set of immaculate white teeth – too white, Rogers thought, to be real.

After one hour of swimming, with his muscles tired and sore, his mind relatively peaceful thanks to the release of endorphins into his body, Jason Rogers mounted the steps of the pool and reached for his phone. Fuck, he had three missed calls from Schwartz.

"What on earth does he want now?" Rogers thought to himself, a little irritated.

He towelled himself down and left the pool area, heading to the enormous office he had specially designed and built on the top floor of his house. It contained state-of-the-art high tech equipment and was graced with minimalist furniture and contemporary artworks that cost as much as an average apartment in a chic suburb of Moscow. The temperature in his office was kept at a cool 18 degrees and he had extra oxygen pumped into it through a small vent next to his desk. He felt the cool oxygenated air reach his lungs as he opened his laptop to call Schwartz.

The video display on his computer showed the contact details for Klaus. He clicked on them and the screen lit up.

"Jason," Schwartz responded, holding his mobile up to get a better view of the video screen.

"Can you see me?" Schwartz asked, a little off guard.

"I can Klaus, now a good time?"

Schwartz was seated in front of an oak table in his dining room at his sprawling residence in western Moscow. Light filtered in through the windows and ever so slightly obscured Schwartz's face which, Rogers observed, had a slightly worried look to it.

"Thanks for calling me back, Jason," Schwartz started, nervously. He shifted in his leather chair and placed his hands out in front of him.

"I may have a new investor for us Jason. An old friend from Austria has found a Middle Eastern contact who could be interested in dropping us a *lifeline* …" and he smiled awkwardly at the camera.

"Terms Klaus?" Rogers responded abruptly.

"An interest rate of 15 per cent which is of course a little on the high side Jason, but it's new capital, it gives us a shot at continuing the business long enough to get out of this damn rut," Schwartz shot back, his voice a little insistent.

Schwartz could feel his hands shaking ever so slightly. He had never lied to Rogers, not even come anywhere close. But once he had introduced the improbable Middle Eastern investor, he knew there was no going back.

"He is in town in two days' time Jason. He is, I understand, *very discreet* and will meet at a location he chooses and notifies us of half an hour before the meeting."

"This seems a little strange to me Klaus. Do you trust these guys?" Rogers asked. After years of experience in emerging markets and in Russia, Rogers had a spectacular capacity for sniffing out trouble. He scratched his head nervously and reclined in his office chair, surveying the screens on his desk, all with data on every major international market. Numbers and charts jumped on and off the screen like a video game from the 1980s.

"I don't know how to answer that Jason. What choice do we have? We're finished if we can't find the additional funding," Schwartz responded, unconvincingly. His mouth and tongue felt dry and he could feel spittle forming on the corners of his mouth.

Rogers tapped his right finger slowly on the desk in front of him. He couldn't quite figure out what was wrong with the arrangement that Schwartz was proposing but it felt off. He would have expected

Schwartz to have unloaded a barrage of abuse at anyone who came up with a deal as seemingly flawed and dodgy as this one.

"OK, let's do it," Rogers said and hung up the phone.

Schwartz sighed with relief and grabbed himself a large glass of red wine from the bottle of Pomerol he'd brought with him to the dining room. In recent weeks he'd stopped his training routine. He could feel his weight spiralling out of control, only one old suit now fitted him, from a period when he'd worked in the United States and put on 15 kilos. He hated himself. The only thing that brought him momentary relief was the smell, taste and after-effects of red wine, whisky and just about any other alcoholic drink he could get his hands on.

As Schwartz was getting drunk, at the other end of Moscow, Jason Rogers was ruminating about his old friend and colleague. After years of never questioning Schwartz's loyalty, he was overcome with the feeling that he had to tread warily. He needed someone to keep an eye on Schwartz, and get to the bottom of the Middle Eastern investor. It couldn't be anyone in the firm's security apparatus now that Lebedev was liquidated. They were too junior and potentially under Schwartz's influence.

He scrolled through the contacts on his phone and found the number for Dmitry Ovchinnikov.

"Dmitry, it's Jason Rogers," he said in his limited Russian.

"Jason, *privet*, what do you want?" Ovchinnikov responded with surprise. Rogers, who had always relied on Roman Lebedev for his security matters, had never called him directly.

"The enemies are at the gate Dmitry," Rogers said quietly but firmly, switching to English.

"I don't understand Jason, my English is not very good." Dmitry was straining to follow the vagaries of Rogers' Texan accent.

"Don't worry Dmitry, I'll brief you, let's meet this evening."

"*Davai*, see you tonight at your house – that OK?" Dmitry queried.

"Done – 10 o'clock," Rogers responded abruptly, and hung up.

Dmitry picked up his leather jacket and went to the small office at his fortified property to pick up Misha.

"Misha let's go and pick up the South African from the hospital and take him to the safe house. We also have to go and see Jason Rogers."

Misha nodded quietly, signalled to his cousin Slava to get the car ready and went to the drawer where Ovchinnikov kept his arsenal of guns and grabbed his favourite Winchester rifle. There was something so reassuring about it, the weight, the feel and the power of this instrument of destruction.

Ovchinnikov grabbed his Beretta handgun, and the three men jumped into the black Escalade and sped off towards the small clinic in southern Moscow – in the process dispersing a pack of wild dogs which had been sleeping in front of the large metal gate at the front of Ovchinnikov's residence. One of the dogs was too late to escape the wheels of the giant 4x4 and had its hind legs crushed, yelping in pain as the car sped off.

CHAPTER 45

CARL HAD LAIN MOTIONLESS FOR WHAT SEEMED TO be an eternity on a hospital bed in a dimly lit basement room. In fact, it had been 24 hours since he'd been whisked into Dmitry Lavrov's medical practice in southern Moscow and sewed back together under general anaesthetic.

He had woken up two hours after the operation with his hand attached to a drip. A fan on the ceiling circled slowly and rather pointlessly. The only furniture in the room was a 1980s television set on a small bench in the corner of the room and an old, worn leather chair next to the bench. A very spartan environment with a musty, damp smell – Carl quickly realised that he had absolutely no idea where he was.

Memories of the attack by Oksana flashed across his mind like individual pieces of a jigsaw puzzle that he was trying unsuccessfully to put together. What was clear in his mind was that he had survived an experience of terrible violence, one that had threatened his very existence. Despite the pain that was beginning to surge through his body from the very long wound in his abdomen he had an overwhelming sense, of euphoria, of being reborn, of surviving and being given a second life.

He looked at the images that flickered across the TV screen. Russian state media for sure. Endless footage of the Russian President in various macho poses, very staged and all rather comical. Despite the pain from his abdomen he quickly fell back into a deep sleep.

After what felt like an eternity, he heard a gruff voice scream "Wake up Carl," as Ovchinnikov yelled at him gruffly, shaking him violently. Carl grabbed Ovchinnikov's right arm to hold down in a defensive posture and quickly regained consciousness, the fear and adrenalin that he had experienced the day before returning to his system.

"Oh shit it's you," he said when he opened his eyes and saw Ovchinnikov's chiselled face opposite his.

"Yes, it's me Carl, now we leave, *vremenya nyeto*!" (we have no time!). We need to get you to a safe place before our Chechen cousins figure out where you are ..."

Misha threw Carl, still immobile from the effects of the anaesthetic, over his shoulder and quickly left the doctor's offices via the back door. He placed Carl gently over a mattress in the boot of the Escalade while Ovchinnikov paid off Lavrov with a pile of immaculately sorted hundred dollar notes.

"*Spacibo* Dima, always a pleasure," said Lavrov and the two men shook hands briefly before Ovchinnikov made for the car, which was now in the street, ready to head off.

Slava floored the Escalade the second Ovchinnikov was inside and it sped off in a storm of dust away from southern Moscow. Traffic was light and they left the city behind them in a little under half an hour.

Carl had by this stage started to wake but said nothing. He was completely at the mercy of the men who were protecting him.

They drove for what seemed like an eternity on a dirt road past kilometre after kilometre of dense birch forest. The trees were packed together so tightly that the car seemed clouded in darkness. Eventually the forest gave way to open country, and Carl could see in the distance an old, dilapidated-looking dacha up on a hill, and a narrow, tree-lined track leading up to it.

"Careful Slava, I haven't been here for a while," Ovchinnikov said anxiously, gesturing to Slava to stop the Escalade. After surveying the dacha for a few minutes, the Escalade's engine idling, Ovchinnikov nodded to Slava and the car progressed up the laneway to the garage adjoining the small building.

Ovchinnikov and Misha went into the old dacha first and came out a few minutes later. The little building looked like it could be blown over by a strong wind. Strips of wood hung off it and the windows were covered in small cracks. Misha helped Carl up the small wooden steps and on to an old sofa that sat in the middle of a tiny living room next to an even smaller kitchen.

Carl felt as though he had travelled back in time to an old Cold War spy film. Ovchinnikov switched on the TV and adjusted the antenna. An old Russian movie, full of patriotic-looking characters, was showing on the state channel Russia One. Grainy images flickered across the screen.

Ovchinnikov whispered something to Slava and Misha and turned to Carl.

"OK, Carl, I leave you with Slava now. Misha and I need to head back to Moscow – you will be safe here. We will come back for you in a few days," he said half in Russian and half in English.

He placed a gun on the table and loaded it with bullets. "This is for you Carl. Slava has a Winchester for protection and his pistol. I hope you don't need this, but in crazy times like these better you have something," and he smiled broadly at Carl.

Carl didn't say anything in particular other than to nod silently that he understood what Ovchinnikov had said. A few days in the little dacha didn't appeal to him at all and he wasn't sure he completely trusted Slava, Misha's rapist cousin. He sensed that Slava was a mixture of idiot and opportunist – but for the time being he had no ability to object. He had to go along with Ovchinnikov's plans.

As Ovchinnikov and Misha left the vast bushland south of Moscow, home to numerous small, decaying villages with rickety, uncomfortable dachas similar to the one in which Carl and Slava were now staying, Ovchinnikov started to ruminate on what the next few days held for them. He knew that to protect his client against the single-mindedness and brutality of an adversary such as Ruslan Akhmatov would likely come at a terrible price.

After an hour of driving at breakneck speed Misha and Ovchinnikov arrived at the gates of Rogers' huge residence in western Moscow just before the designated meeting time of 10 pm. They were greeted by guards who checked the undercarriage of the rumbling Escalade with mirrors for explosive devices. As they were waved through the huge metal gate at the entrance all the men could see was a sea of flashing lights, 4x4s and Russian "*spetsnaz*" (paramilitary).

Preparing for the final assault, Ovchinnikov thought to himself. Rogers must know his days in Russia were coming to an end, the only reason to hire so many guards. Whatever was going to happen in the next 24 hours would seal his fate and that of his business.

Misha waited in the car while Ovchinnikov entered through the metal door, escorted by one of the paramilitary types. "*Priyama*" (straight ahead) the man indicated towards a room with a door slightly ajar.

There, in front of his computer, sat Rogers, looking blankly at the screen. His eyes brightened a little when he saw Ovchinnikov.

"Dmitry, *privet* (hello)," he said warmly, shaking Ovchinnikov's hand firmly, gesturing to take a seat at the table next to his desk. "Whisky, vodka, beer?" he offered.

"Vodka, Jason," nodded Ovchinnikov. Rogers went to a small fridge next to his desk and pulled out a bottle of icy Beluga vodka.

He poured himself and Ovchinnikov a shot of the white, alcoholic liquid. Rogers and Ovchinnikov touched glasses and silently skolled the vodka.

"Better now," Rogers smiled, pouring Ovchinnikov and himself another glass.

"Jason, what is troubling you? What do you need?" asked Ovchinnikov.

"I need you, Dmitry, to perform one final service," Rogers said, pausing momentarily.

"I need you to kill Klaus."

Ovchinnikov sat back in his chair and downed the second vodka.

"OK, Jason. But do you mind me asking one question – why?"

Rogers's eyes narrowed and focused upon Ovchinnikov's.

"I have information that he is planning to set me up for, let's say … an accident … in the next twenty-four hours," and Rogers, in a reflective mood, sat back in his chair and stared at the shotglass on the table. He filled it with more vodka and filled Ovchinnikov's glass.

"Who has told you this?"

"A source in the Kremlin – Igor Melnikov, Minister for Armaments," replied Rogers.

CHAPTER 46

IGOR MELNIKOV HAD, OVER A SERIES OF WEEKS, VERY carefully managed the various warring factions battling for the spoils of Ari Kandinskiy's empire – like the master conductor of a symphony orchestra. He had seen the parties engage in a violent struggle for dominance and it was now his job to bring the performance to a close and ensure that of the proceeds to be handed out to creditors and stakeholders, his own interests were allotted the lion's share.

Ensuring that the President and Prime Minister would be appreciative of his efforts was to preserve his role as a Minister and as a man on the rise in Russian politics.

As he sat in his office on the 25th floor of the immense building on the Naberezhnaya (Moscow river bank), he looked out over Gorky Park on the other side of the river. Enormous cruise boats glided past on the twisty Moscow river, tourists and Moscovites relaxing on the terraces of the luxury boats with champagne, blini, caviar. He had a feeling of deep satisfaction. Everything in his universe appeared to be in the right place – events were progressing according to the right plan, observing all the protocols which he himself so diligently observed.

He picked up the phone and dialled his assistant.

"Yes Igor Simonovich, how can I help?" responded his personal assistant, Maria Chekova, a thin, serious girl whose sense of dress and overall presentation made her look a little like a North Korean television broadcaster. It was this look which had fascinated Melnikov when he first interviewed her for the job. He rejected the candidates who arrived, one after another, with botox lips, Chanel handbags and inflatable breasts. What struck him about Mademoiselle Chekova was her restraint, the modesty of her appearance, everything that contrasted so strongly with modern Russia and was reminiscent of women in Soviet Russia, when he was growing up as a boy.

"I need you to get the Prime Minister's office on the phone. I need to speak to him."

"Certainly sir, I will do so at once, please hold on, connecting you now ..."

After a few minutes of being on hold, listening to an instrumental version of an old Stevie Wonder classic, Melnikov was answered by a gruff voice on the other end of the line.

"*Schto* (what)? Igor, *schto ty hochish* (what do you want)?" asked the voice on the other end of the phone in a tone bordering on rude.

"*Uvazhiemih gospodin* (honourable sir) Prime Minister, I have some good news," Igor tried to remain calm and positive, despite the unfriendly tone of his interlocutor.

"Yes, go on," the Prime Minister responded, his interest piqued.

"It's best that I tell you in person. I am coming to the Kremlin this afternoon so will make an appointment with your assistant. Needless to say, the property which you wanted in Monaco should not be a problem, as well as a handsome payment," said Melnikov, somewhat triumphantly, banging the table for extra effect at the end of his sentence.

"*Prekrasniy* Igor, *prekrasniy* (excellent), this will make my wife very, very happy. You are proving your worth my friend," and the line went dead.

That wave of deep personal satisfaction which he had felt only moments before came back again. But, even though a man on the rise, he knew he could not rest on his laurels. He had to keep up the momentum and deliver this final chapter of the saga.

"Maria, one last thing," he said over the phone, "please connect me to the manager of Falcon Capital, Jason Rogers. I have some information I need to pass on to him."

"Of course sir, we have his details on our system," Maria responded as efficiently as ever.

By the time Melnikov spoke to Rogers it was nearly midday on Monday. Rogers had just ended a three-hour meeting with his most senior executives that had hit them like a bombshell. He was being forced out of Russia and later that week he would step onto his private jet, likely never to return.

"You've got to be kidding Jason," protested a British senior executive, Andrew Mills, head of European operations. "If you go this place is finished. Klaus what about you? What do you have to say about this?"

Schwartz looked grimly at the men assembled and shrugged his shoulders. "Andrew, I can understand you're pissed, but we're in a very, very complicated situation at the moment. If we don't have emergency funding in place before week's end this business is gone, no matter where Jason is." He folded his hands and placed them on the meeting room table as if to bring the discussion to an end.

After Rogers stood to leave the meeting, he paused to walk around the room and shake everyone's hand. No one uttered a word. When he got to Schwartz, he noticed that his old friend shook his hand firmly but avoided any eye contact. Schwartz looked diminished, shorter and more hunched than he had ever seen him. What a curious situation we are in, Rogers thought to himself. It would be the last time he would lay eyes on his old friend and colleague.

Rogers looked at his phone as he left the meeting, and saw it was Melnikov's office calling. He slipped quietly into another room and asked his bodyguard to stop anyone from entering.

"Jason, do you have a minute?"

"Yes Igor, I do. I've told the board I'm leaving this week," replied Rogers, curtly.

"Good, next step is you take care of Schwartz, and I will have my people take Akhmatov into temporary custody until you leave the country. You will be paid into your Bahamas account once you are on the plane out of Sheremetyevo ..." Melnikov paused briefly, as if to catch his breath.

"This is being reported to the *very highest levels* of power in this country Jason, so you understand that there can't be any fuck-ups or deviations from the plan – otherwise the whole thing gets taken out of my hands and the President himself will dictate what happens, a very bad situation for both of us, I am sure I do not have to explain."

"You don't, Igor, you most certainly don't," Rogers replied.

CHAPTER 47

MURAT SLOWED THE CAR TO A CRAWL AS HIS phone indicated he had nearly arrived at the location where the South African and his minder were believed to be in hiding.

He received a call from Ruslan Akhmatov.

"Ruslan, I can't see the place yet, but I have left the forest, there is a long field and yes, now I see it, a dacha at the end of a path. This must be the place, there is a light on. I park here and walk. Give me half an hour and I will call you back – that should be enough time."

Murat, who was alone, parked the car by the side of the road and jumped out. He went to the boot and pulled a pistol, grenade and hunting knife out of a small black bag hidden under the spare wheel. He checked the chamber of the pistol to ensure it was fully loaded. The knife glistened in the morning light, its jagged edges designed to cause maximum damage to flesh. He walked slowly and deliberately towards the dilapidated dacha.

Carl was seated at the small kitchen table slowly sipping borsch when a terrible explosion ripped through the entrance of the dacha. The door was ripped off its hinges and flew against the window of the living room.

The deep boom produced by the grenade was a noise that Carl had never come close to hearing in his life. It burst his eardrums and the shock wave produced by the grenade had him crashing to the floor covered in bits of wood, debris and the remainders of the soup. His minder Slava lay on the floor of the little dacha, next to the sofa, completely immobile.

Carl started to crawl, slowly, towards the back door of the dacha. An instinctive urge pushed him, despite the pain, through the smoke and debris, to move away from the explosion. As he pushed open the back door and started to crawl down the steps towards the garden he saw two black boots in front of him. He raised his face to see who they belonged to. It was the last thing Carl would ever see – the soulless eyes of Murat as he prepared to kill him.

Murat had no qualms about executing Carl. The young South African had found himself on the wrong side of Chechen justice. Murat killed him quickly and efficiently, a knife across the throat and in the back of the neck, just like killing a goat in his home village.

Carl writhed on the ground for a few moments, he covered his neck with his hands and he could feel the river of warm blood flowing freely over his hands and down his arms, dripping onto the ground. His last thought was that this was not how he was meant to die, outside a shitty dacha at the hands of a Chechen assassin.

Murat, his hands covered in Carl's blood, entered the small dacha slowly and quietly to determine who had survived the blast. He found the body of Slava, motionless in the living room. He lifted the young Siberian's head to ensure that he was dead. The eyes of Slava had rolled around the back of his head and his tongue was hanging out of his mouth. He had been most likely killed by the impact of the grenade.

"Ruslan, they're both dead, it was quick," Murat said matter of factly to Akhmatov who was getting a back massage from a portly Russian masseuse in her 50s.

"Good work my friend," Akhmatov said as the masseuse ground her elbows deep into his lower back. "Next is Rogers, we'll discuss tonight if I survive this massage," and Akhmatov hung up.

As the masseuse dislodged knots which had formed in the muscles in his back over recent weeks Akhmatov had a sudden and very pleasurable feeling of lightness and inner peace he'd not experienced in a very long time.

With his top commander, Murat, dispatching his adversaries and their support staff into oblivion he started to think that the end of the Kandinskiy saga was in sight, that he would be in a great position to pay his boss the dividend he had been expecting for so very long now, and earn himself a nice fat fee in the process.

"Yulia," he said to the wide-hipped masseuse.

"Yes Ruslan, what is it?"

"How long have you been giving me massages?"

"Five years, Ruslan," Yulia said, without any emotion, not the least bit interested by the question.

"Have I changed in that time, Yulia? Fatter, thinner, more tense, more relaxed?"

"Why do you ask Ruslan?" and she ground her elbows deeper, unleashing a wave of dull pain that quickly took his breath away.

"Just curious Yulia, don't worry," Akhmatov replied sheepishly.

Before Murat drove off, he doused the bodies of Slava and Carl in petrol and for good measure the interior of the house. He threw a match at the body of Carl and watched it light up in flames. The flames quickly spread up the back stairs of the dacha like an angel of death making its way calmly into the house. Within minutes the house was a ball of fire.

Murat drove off, pleased with his efficiency. The more frequently he killed, the more he craved the adrenalin rush and the feeling of omnipotence it aroused in him. He could decide whether someone lived or died. If the latter, there were few people who could execute the task with as much brutality, efficiency and loving attention to detail as Murat.

CHAPTER 48

OVCHINNIKOV SPENT THE BETTER PART OF THE morning preparing the logistics for the assassination of Schwartz. He had recently flown to Moscow two of his former associates from Siberia, Roman Primakov and Sergey Pivovar, petty gangsters with a penchant for brutality, whom he could trust implicitly.

Once they had settled in to Ovchinnikov's fortified residence on the outskirts of Moscow, Ovchinnikov called a meeting to discuss how they would arrange the assassination and minimise their chances of being connected with the killing – not easy in a city crawling with security, police and FSB. Ovchinnikov was under no illusions that this may be one assignment too many and that the authorities could use this murder as leverage over his whole operation.

Ovchinnikov noticed that Misha was fretting nervously. "What's up Misha?" he enquired.

"I haven't heard from Slava this morning Dima, which is very strange, he was meant to call me at 7 o'clock – that's two hours ago now."

Ovchinnikov inhaled deeply on a cigarette and stubbed it out in his ashtray. "You better go there now Misha," and he threw Misha the keys to the Escalade.

"Roman and Sergey, you stay here, I need you to follow Schwartz. Misha you head out to the dacha. If something has happened to Slava and the South African then this changes things ..." Ovchinnikov's voice trailed off.

Misha had a sick feeling in the pit of his stomach as he left the main highway and hit the dirt track leading to Ovchinnikov's dacha. Every few minutes he hit redial on his mobile to try to get through to Slava but each time he was greeted with a robotic voicemail message.

He punched the steering wheel with all his might. "*Pizdetz*!!" he screamed in Russian. The Escalade flew down the track at breakneck speed, kicking up a cloud of dust that blanketed the road behind. The enormous 4x4 bounced through the potholes and otherwise made easy work of the dirt track.

As he got within a few kilometres of the dacha he could see in the distance a thick plume of black smoke rising high into the blue sky. The smoke signalled death, and Misha knew it. He slowed the Escalade to a crawl and as he left the road and drove on to the narrow path towards the dacha he could see the fire which had destroyed the dacha was nearly out – all that remained were embers and the footings of the house.

He jumped out of the 4x4 and walked slowly towards the burning remains of the dacha. He could see two charred corpses, both in foetal positions, the flesh and clothes burned off them – all that was left were blackened skeletons, the skulls perilously close to completely snapping off.

Misha grabbed his sleeve and wiped away the sweat that had formed on his forehead. He had seen a lot in his short life of 36 years but never anything as macabre as what he was now witnessing. There was a whiff of petrol in the air.

He picked up his mobile and called Ovchinnikov.

"Dima, it's not good. They're dead," he said, his voice breaking. "They're fucking dead. Who did this? I need to know, was it the Chechens…?"

The grief and the rage welled within in him, he struggled to contain himself.

Before Misha could continue, Ovchinnikov cut him off.

"Mish, Mish, calm, listen to me. I know who did this and I will fix this, but I need you to pull yourself together. This is the time we act like professionals and not bums. Trust me, I will fix this Mish!" Ovchinnikov yelled down the phone.

Misha listened without saying anything. He stared at the charred remains of his cousin and wondered how he would break the news to his aunt.

"*Bozha moy*" ("my God") he muttered to himself as he jumped back into the 4x4 and revved up the engine. He headed back to Moscow. He could still see the trail of black smoke in his rearview mirror from several kilometres away. But as the smoke grew more and more distant, he regained his composure and started to think about the revenge he was going to wreak upon Akhmatov and his gang.

CHAPTER 49

" DIMA, WE ARE BEHIND SCHWARTZ'S CAR NOW. HE IS on the ring road, headed towards Barrikadnaya," Sergey Pivovar announced to Ovchinnikov who was still coming to terms with the phone call he had just received from Misha.

"We can kill him pretty much any time from now Dim, just let us know," Pivovar continued.

Ovchinnikov had no doubt that Pivovar and Primakov, despite this being their first trip to Moscow, could have handled the assassination of Schwartz with consummate ease. Schwartz's bodyguard, who doubled as his driver, posed no risk and would certainly not, given his grievance with Schwartz regarding the previous year's modest, and still unpaid, bonus, risk life and limb to protect his boss from what was likely to be a violent and bloody end.

"Just wait a little Sergey," Ovchinnikov replied, "keep following Schwartz. I want to know where the little traitor ends up," and he hung up the phone.

Schwartz's black Mercedes continued for a few more kilometres and then stopped outside a Georgian restaurant in Malaya Nikits-kaya, notorious for its history of shootouts and disputes between rival gangsters. Schwartz got out of the car and walked towards the entrance of the restaurant, gesturing to his bodyguard to stay in the car.

"I'm not going anywhere, you old fuck," the bodyguard said to himself, nodding affirmatively to Schwartz.

Just after Schwartz entered, a fleet of black Humvees roared into view, followed by an enormous black steel-reinforced Maybach.

"Must be a real Moscow big wig," Pivovar said to Primakov. Half a dozen paramilitary types jumped out of the Humvees and made a circle around a slim, well dressed man in his mid to late 40s. The man walked briskly towards the front door of the restaurant, heavily armed guards on either side of him.

"Dima, its Sergey here, a guy with *Omon* (Russian paramilitary) and very heavy artillery showed up. I got a photo, want me to send it to you? Maybe you know him?" Pivovar asked Ovchinnikov.

"*Davai*, send it through right away," Ovchinnikov replied instantly.

When the photo came through Ovchinnikov realised instantly who it was – none other than Ruslan Akhmatov. The pieces of this puzzle are starting to fall in place, he thought to himself.

He vigorously patted the head of his loyal Staffordshire. "You're a good boy Zakhar, I might need you today my friend."

Zakhar wagged his tail vigorously, his tongue dribbling spittle all over Ovchinnikov's leather boots.

"Misha, where are you?" Ovchinnikov said over his mobile phone.

"On the MKAD (ring road around Moscow) Dima, at your place in twenty minutes," responded Misha.

"Don't worry about coming here Misha. Akhmatov is meeting Schwartz at a restaurant in Malaya Nikitskaya. This is our moment to strike, we won't get another one like this."

Misha gripped the wheel of the Escalade hard and steered it across three lanes of speeding traffic into an overpass and headed in the direction of the restaurant. Drivers in old Soviet Ladas were no match for the giant American 4x4 and they could only gesticulate in anger as the Escalade sped off.

Ovchinnikov went to the basement room where he kept his arsenal of weapons, followed by Zakhar who could sense that something was afoot. His tail wagged and he yelped with excitement. Ovchinnikov pushed the enormous dog out of the way, pulled a key from a small box and unlocked the huge steel locker in the corner of the room. He surveyed the neatly displayed Glock pistols, Winchester rifles and a huge, gleaming rocket launcher. There were boxes of ammunition and a dozen rockets, enough ammunition and firepower to wreak havoc and disrupt the jolly get-together at the restaurant in central Moscow.

He loaded the entire contents of the armoury into two large black bags and, threw them into the back of a black Dodge pick-up truck. The hyperactive Zakhar jumped around wildly, as if pleading with his owner to take him on this next adventure.

"Jump in boy," Ovchinnikov said matter of factly and Zakhar installed himself in the passenger seat, tongue wagging uncontrollably.

The huge Dodge pick-up grumbled its way out of the garage and cruised into the street outside, scattering the stray dogs that were lying on the road, basking in the sunshine.

Zakhar barked wildly at them before Ovchinnikov yelled at him to stop. "Misha, I'm on my way, let's meet at the corner of Novy Arbat and Povarskaya, a few hundred metres away and then drive together. I'm going to have Sergey and Roman create a little disturbance to get Akhmatov out of the restaurant, then we take care of them. Now we switch to walkie talkies, no more mobiles ..."

"OK, Dima, I'll be there in fifteen minutes," Misha replied.

As Ovchinnikov headed towards the meeting point, he knew that this could very well be his troupe's final mission.

He drew deeply on his cigarette and ran his fingers across Zakhar's back. The Dodge glided along Moscow's Garden Ring past Barrikadnaya metro and headed left down Novy Arbat, the immense thoroughfare connecting west and east Moscow, dotted with huge, rectangular Soviet era apartment buildings.

As he turned right from Novy Arbat into Povarskaya Street, past the little Orthodox church on the corner, he saw Misha parked to the side of the road, engine running. As he drew level with the Escalade, he signalled to Misha to follow.

"Sergey! We're there in two minutes. We are going to storm the restaurant from the Povarskaya entrance," he yelled into the walkie talkie.

"They will probably take Akhmatov out the back via the Malaya Nikitskaya exit. You have to be ready for them – get as close as possible so there are no mistakes."

"Dima, we're ready, got it," Pivovar responded, an unmistakable hint of tension in his voice. Sergey Pivovar knew that he could very well be living the final minutes of his life and – if the plan did not work – the last feeling he would experience would be that of his face hitting the tarmac of the Moscow "Kaltso" ("Garden Ring road").

CHAPTER 50

SCHWARTZ THOUGHT THE RESTAURANT SEEMED peculiarly quiet for a Friday lunch time. He could hear a pin drop as he sat on the opposite side of the table while Akhmatov studied the menu for what seemed like an eternity.

"More fucking Georgian food," he thought to himself, "I'm no chance of losing any weight in these sorts of places." His trousers felt a few sizes too small and he could feel his blood pressure rising at the thought of what was going to transpire in the next 48 hours.

He would leave Russia a free man, with financial means sufficient to retire, but it would come at a terrible cost, the life of the man he had considered a confidant and friend for the previous 20 years.

"Why are you fidgeting so much, Klaus? You should be happy. You're getting everything you want.

"OK, your freedom is coming at a price but by the weekend when you are sitting in your villa in Spain with fifteen million dollars in your bank account, no debts, you will not worry about this ..." Akhmatov told him, a broad smile over his face.

"Ruslan, I just want to get this over. I am starting to feel every one of my sixty-four years. I don't feel ... *invincible* ... any more," Schwartz responded.

"Then we get to business now Klaus – call Rogers, tell him to come here. He can drive from Moscow City. It's no more than ten minutes. My team can easily off him – and his bodyguard. Once this is taken care of, you get fifteen million dollars and I get the difference. *No stress, simple, you can kill him yourself if you want ...*" said Akhmatov, patting the gold pistol as he placed it on the table.

Schwartz reeled back, horrified. "Forget it, Ruslan, I'll leave that to your men," he responded tersely.

Schwartz was overcome by a feeling of revulsion that he was sitting discussing the imminent death of Rogers with a man whom he still knew very little about, yet who exercised such tremendous control over his present and future.

Akhmatov was acutely aware of the effect he had on Schwartz, but this was of absolutely no concern for him. None of the assurances he was providing to Schwartz would ever eventuate. He would leave Rogers's men to exact their own revenge.

As a waiter came to take their order, there was a tremendous bang from the street. It shook the windows in the restaurant and stunned an already nervous Schwartz. "Christ what was that?" he yelled in panic.

Akhmatov gestured to the bodyguards sitting at the adjoining table to go outside and take another look. But before they could move, a second loud explosion rocked the restaurant and knocked Schwartz and Akhmatov off their chairs. Particles of glass, wood, and ceramic flew through the air at what seemed to Schwartz to be an impossible speed, filling his eyes and momentarily blinding him.

The explosion was followed by a burst of gunfire from what Schwartz assumed must be high-powered rifles, outside the restaurant. He completely froze, prostrate under the dining table he'd been sitting at only moments before. He soon realised he was alone as he quickly surveyed the room. Akhmatov had been ushered out by his bodyguards and most probably driven off.

Schwartz was stuck there at the complete mercy of whoever was carrying out this violent siege. He waited for what seemed like an eternity under the wooden table.

Then he heard the deliberate footsteps of a man walking over broken glass. Schwartz could see two large cowboy boots crunching glass noisily underfoot until they came to a halt. The man then continued his march towards him. The urge to see who was coming was too strong and Schwartz, as if drawn by the prospect of his own death, peered up from under the table.

There stood Dmitry Ovchinnikov, his left arm covered in blood but otherwise fully composed. He raised his pistol to Schwartz's head and fired. To all intents and purposes Schwartz was dead before his fat body thudded to the floor.

For good measure Ovchinnikov walked up to Schwartz and fired four more bullets into what remained of his victim's head. He looked around the restaurant and saw a waiter cowering in the corner of the room.

He shook his head at the waiter to indicate he was in no imminent danger. He would not kill a working man.

Dmitry nonchalantly strode out of the restaurant and into his Dodge truck. He patted Zakhar who had finished gorging himself on the legs of one of the Chechen guards and was now obediently sitting in the passenger seat of his car, his maw drenched in blood.

Dmitry sped off, followed by Misha in the Escalade, past the bodies of dead Chechen bodyguards, of Akhmatov and the two operatives Sergey Pivovar and Roman Primakov. By the time the police paramilitary response unit arrived, Ovchinnikov and Misha were far away and safe – their assassination of Schwartz successful.

CHAPTER 51

A S JASON ROGERS BOARDED THE PRIVATE PLANE at Sheremetyevo at 4.30 pm on his last day in Russia, bound for London, he received a call from a highly agitated Igor Melnikov. Indeed, Melnikov was incandescent. Spluttering obscenities he struggled to compose himself, eventually yelling "Do you know what your guys have fucking well done Jason?"

"No idea what you are talking about," Rogers replied defensively, worried that his departure from Russia could be compromised by what Melnikov was about to tell him.

All Rogers could hear for a few seconds was deep breathing on the other end of the line.

"They have wiped out Akhmatov and his entire crew, Jason." Melnikov could barely force the words out of his mouth.

"This was not part of the plan, I have no idea what to say to the boss about this," he continued, a little pathetically.

It would be a lie to say that Jason Rogers was displeased by the news that Ovchinnikov had wasted Akhmatov and his goons and upset the finely tuned plans of the Russian *siloviki* to gorge themselves on what was left of Ari Kandinskiy's business empire.

Ovchinnikov had almost certainly complicated the delicate relationship between the President and his most troublesome regional governor.

"Igor, I'm leaving Russia in approximately five minutes. I'm never coming back. After this phone call you will never see me again nor hear from me. I wish you all the very best. If for any reason you come after me there is a man from deepest, darkest Siberia who will come after you, that much I can guarantee ..."

Rogers hung up the phone and looked out his window as the plane glided off the runway and into the air. In the distance he could see his old office building – from where he used to look out at the vast expanse of Moscow. It looked small and inconsequential, and seemed so irrelevant to his new life.

The stewardess offered him a copy of the *Financial Times* and a cold bottle of beer. He enjoyed every drop of the freezing beer and flicked through the newspaper – nothing seemed terribly interesting, so he just looked out the window at the expanse of Russian forest below.

It struck him, albeit very briefly, that he did not feel even the slightest hint of nostalgia for his old life in Russia. There was nothing tugging at his emotional heartstrings, just a profound desire to leave …

"*Dosvedanya* Russia," he said quietly to himself.

THE END